ELEMENTARY™

THE GHOST LINE

ADAM CHRISTOPHER

BASED ON THE CBS TELEVISION SERIES
CREATED BY ROBERT DOHERTY

TITAN BOOKS

ELEMENTARY: THE GHOST LINE
Print edition ISBN: 9781781169841
E-book edition ISBN: 9781781169858

Published by Titan Books
A division of Titan Publishing Group Ltd
144 Southwark St, London SE1 0UP

First edition: February 2015
10 9 8 7 6 5 4 3 2

A CIP catalogue record for this title is available from the British Library.

Printed and bound by CPI Group (UK) Ltd, Croydon, CR0 4YY

TITANBOOKS.COM

For Sandra, always.

"Excellent!" I cried.
"Elementary," said he.

I

SOME VELVET MORNING

The man turned into West 49th Street from 8th Avenue and paused at the corner to swap the heavy plastic grocery bag from one hand to the other. It was early—*damn early*, he thought—the sky still a deep, cool velvet blue, the dawn just bruising the eastern horizon through the narrow corridor of tall Manhattan buildings behind him. He was bundled up against the chill, his coat old and worn but comfortable, a long-favored scarf wrapped around the lower half of his face. Shaking the circulation back into the hand that had been carrying the groceries all the way from the Duane Reade on the corner of Broadway and West 57th, the man continued on his way toward his apartment in a less fashionable backwater of Hell's Kitchen.

He was tired from a string of night shifts. He could have taken a cab. Hell, he could have taken the subway. No. Not the subway. He'd had enough of that place for a lifetime. It wasn't the dirt and the rats and the rush—hey, New York was New York—and it wasn't like he was claustrophobic either. Not an option, job like his. No, it was just the growing sense that he spent far too much time with the city over his head, rather than the sky. The last six months especially. They'd been a killer.

9

But it was nearly over. He savored the crisp air and the clear sky above. Only another block and he'd be home.

He walked for a minute or so, the thin plastic of his grocery bag crinkling with every step. Then he slowed, eventually coming to a halt. He looked over one shoulder, slowly, then turned and looked over the other. His eyes scanned the shadows, places where the dawn light had yet to reach.

Then he shook his head and resumed his journey, slightly faster now.

It was getting ridiculous.

Soon, it would be over. Soon he'd be able to stop worrying that he'd be found out—that *they'd* be found out. Just a few more days and they could have all the open sky they wanted. He'd loved New York City since the day he arrived from Northern Ireland as a teenager with his parents and kid sister. But… maybe the Caribbean would be better. With change came opportunity. Once this whole thing was over, and he and his sister were out of harm's way, they could get to know one another again. He hadn't seen her for half her life but he had her back now, even if it was in bad circumstances. Six months of fear. Six months of looking over his shoulder.

The man frowned to himself as he mounted the steps leading to his building, a modest brownstone in a street that had yet to feel the steady creep of gentrification in Hell's Kitchen. It suited him. He could hardly afford the rent as it was, and the less he had to do with hipsters and their artisanal marmalade, the better. But the apartment had been a real find. Just right for the job. Perfect, in fact.

Key in the lock, another pause, another check over the shoulder. He opened the door and stepped into his building, then selected another key and opened his own door, the first-floor apartment. He wondered what the houses were like down in the Caribbean, and whether there'd be a job for a guy like him.

He closed the door with a kick, the deadbolt engaging with a heavy clunk. He grabbed the chain hanging from the door frame and slid it into the door, before reaching down to push a sliding bolt home. The chain and bolt were new additions—he'd added the same to the back door as soon as he'd moved in. These last six months, he'd felt like he needed the extra security.

He left the lights off; there was enough dawn glow leaking in through the blinds on the front bay window to navigate as he shuffled into the open-plan kitchen/dining room. He dragged the grocery bag up onto the counter, and began unwinding his scarf.

There was a click like a light switch. The man turned around, confused for a moment, and then he saw he was not alone.

There was someone sitting in the armchair, under the window.

The man's heart thundered in his chest, a colossal bass-drum *thud* that made him stagger against the counter.

It was too late. They'd found out.

"What do you want?" His voice was a harsh whisper. The neighbors upstairs would still be asleep. He didn't want any trouble, not when it was so close to being all over. Maybe there was a chance he could talk his way out of it, convince his visitor that the plan was still on track.

The intruder stood and walked forward, his bulky frame nothing but an empty shape backlit by the pale gray wash of dawn behind. He stopped and lifted his hand; the gun held in it caught the faintest glimmer of morning sun.

The man clutched his chest. It felt like his heart was going to explode, the sickening thump against his ribcage matched only by the pounding of panic in his head. He was going to die of a damn heart attack before the intruder had time to shoot him.

Because that's what he was there for. The gun in his hand

was no ordinary pistol. It was large, rectangular, all angles and edges, with a long magazine and barrel that seemed too small for the body of the piece. The man had seen guns like that plenty in the last six months.

He raised his hands, like he was apologizing, like he was trying to calm the situation. And then his hands came together like he was begging, like he was praying.

Which is exactly what he was doing.

He opened his mouth to speak, but it was too late.

The Uzi barked in the dark apartment, the muzzle flashes as shocking as the sound. The man shook as the bullets tore into his chest, and he careened backward, his wheeling left arm swiping the bag of groceries from the counter and bringing it down with him. White cardboard pill boxes spilled across the floor.

The man stared at the ceiling, blood bubbling from his mouth as his life drained away. The intruder stepped over to him, and in his dying moments the man blinked as he recognized his killer. *Ah,* he thought. *So they got to you too?*

Then he saw nothing but shining stars and big open sky, and he coughed up another mouthful of blood, and surrendered to the darkness.

2

AN EXPERIMENT IN FORENSIC ACOUSTICS

Joan Watson breathed deeply and watched the patterns of morning light dapple the backs of her eyelids. The warm sun on her face felt glorious. It was going to be a beautiful day.

There was something about New York. Something indefinable, something magical, a spark to be forever chased but never captured. And New York, on a spring weekend? Her favorite time of year, in her favorite place on Earth. The city suddenly felt alive, electric, as it defrosted from its snow-bound winter slumber, the days longer and warmer.

And, more important, she had absolutely no plans. As she stretched out in bed, kicking at the hot water bottle at her feet, she considered what to do with two wonderfully free days. Some reading. Some shopping. Maybe she could even take a trip up to visit the Cloisters in Fort Tryon Park, in Upper Manhattan. It would be the perfect day for it—

With a soft *whump*, Watson's head hit the mattress as the pillows beneath it were suddenly pulled away. Spitting out a mouthful of hair, she pushed herself up onto an elbow just in time to see the red and green plaid-covered back of her housemate disappearing through the door and down the stairs, her pillows tucked under one arm. A moment later there was a thud, heavy enough to rattle Watson's bed, and the sound of something archaic and mechanical—something with *chains*—being wound up.

So much for sleeping in.

"*Sherlock!*"

There was no response, just a short pause in the cranking before it began again.

Watson sighed, slipped from her bed—her warm, comfortable, lazy weekend bed—grabbed her robe from the back of the door, and ventured downstairs.

Watson padded toward the living room, then immediately pulled herself back, flat against the wall. The barrel of a gun was pointing right at the doorway.

The cranking sound had stopped, replaced now by the whirring of something much smaller. An electric motor, perhaps.

She pushed a strand of hair behind her ear and risked a peek around the door frame. Her eyes widened at the scene before her, and, keeping close to the wall—out of harm's way—she slipped into the room.

Holmes had dragged the large red-topped table into the front room, and was bent over what Watson could only describe as a *contraption*. The object—the machine—comprised a wheel attached to a standing frame made of heavy, dark metal. At the compass points of the wheel were four revolvers, held in place by metal straps that stretched over the handles and screwed into the wheel. Watson risked a closer look, and saw that the handles of the revolvers had been partially dismantled, with a cradle of wires disappearing into each. The device was bizarre and looked exceedingly dangerous, the way the revolvers pointed in four directions at once—the gun pointing at the door was upside down, while its opposite number, right side up, was pointed at a target on the other side of the room.

Holmes was adjusting something on the machine with a screwdriver, but Watson's attention was drawn to the target. She recognized the big black metal frame as a piece of bondage equipment Holmes usually kept out of sight in the hall cupboard. Hanging from the chained cuffs by its feet was the freshly butchered carcass of—

"*Sus scrofa domesticus*," said Holmes, not looking up from his work.

Watson shook her head in disbelief.

"I know what a pig is, Sherlock. What I don't know is why you have one hanging in our living room."

She turned back to the table and waved at the gun machine.

"And what is this thing? Where did you get those guns? Have you been working all night again?"

Holmes stood back from the table, his arms straight by his sides as he rocked on his heels, a tight smile on his face. Watson knew that look. It meant trouble.

"Sleep is an inconvenience, Watson," Holmes said. He gestured at the machine before him. "*This* is an experiment. I would hope your scientific curiosity is piqued, but perhaps it requires a little more effort on my part for my own natural enthusiasm to rub off on you." Then he frowned, like a child told he couldn't go out to play.

Watson rubbed her face. It was too early for this.

"Okay, fine, an experiment. And I'll just assume that those guns are licensed and that you're going to tell me why you want to shoot them at a pig." She glanced at the clock on the wall. It was a little before seven. "But some of us actually enjoy a little sleep now and again. I'm going to make some tea."

She turned toward the kitchen, then stopped when she saw a collection of cushions—and the pillows from her bed—lined up on the floor, next to what looked like a camera tripod with a large customized clamp screwed into the top.

Holmes darted around the table and reached down, picking up a worn cushion in green velvet. Watson recognized it from one of the armchairs.

"Consider this an experiment in forensic acoustics," he said. He looked back at the table and waved his hand. "And yes, you may regard the guns to be licensed and perfectly legal if it were to put your mind at rest."

Watson opened her mouth to speak, but Holmes continued.

"They are *not*, of course, but let us continue this fiction for the time being in order to proceed."

Watson sighed. Holmes raised an eyebrow. "Well," he said, his voice small. "You're in a fine mood this morning." He tossed the green cushion back on the floor.

Watson looked at Holmes, the contraption on the table, and the pig hanging from the frame. She tightened the tie of her robe around her waist, sighed, and walked into the kitchen.

Holmes followed her, standing in the doorway as she filled the tea kettle and lit the gas stove. As she took two mugs from the cupboard, she pointed one of them back in the direction of the "experiment."

"So that was you, moving that pig around earlier?"

"Chekhov did take a little manhandling, yes."

Watson watched the kettle, then turned back around.

"Chekhov?"

Holmes grinned. "Well, he's not quite hanging on the wall, I'll grant you, and while I am loathe to anthropomorphize, it made it seem more…"—he waved his hand, his gaze darting around the kitchen momentarily—"authentic." He clasped his hands behind his back and rocked on his heels again.

Authentic. Fine. Kettle boiled and tea brewing, Watson stepped back into the front room, Holmes on her heels. She knew she was going to regret the next question, but she also knew she really had no choice but to ask it anyway.

"So what's the experiment?"

"Ah!" said Holmes, his eyes lighting up like a pinball machine. "I am investigating the sound-baffling properties of household soft furnishings."

He ducked around Watson and began arranging the pillows and cushions on the floor into some kind of order. He lifted the green velvet cushion and squeezed it like a piece of fruit. Then he moved to the clamp on the camera tripod and positioned the cushion between its teeth, screwing the knob at the clamp's base to secure it. He stood back and gave the cushion a satisfied pat before picking up the tripod and walking it back to the gun machine. With some adjustments to the height of the tripod, he aligned the cushion with the barrel of the first revolver, pushing it close so the soft fabric was squeezed against the weapon.

Realizing what Holmes planned to do, Watson crouched down and picked up one of her own pillows from the arrangement on the floor. She held it up to Holmes's face. "Please don't tell me you're going to use my pillows as a silencer? These are real goose down."

Holmes picked up a control from the table in one hand, his phone in the other. The control had a button on the top, with a cable leading out from the base to the gun machine. In his other hand, he began tapping something on his phone with his thumb. He glanced up for a second, then returned his attention to his phone.

"Very well," he said. "I'll spare them the first round and continue instead with some synthetics."

He nodded to himself, then held up his phone. "Sound meter. Contrary to popular belief, the silencer on a gun doesn't really silence it. More accurately, it is a *suppressor*, reducing both the volume of the report and the muzzle flash. But, unlike what is presented to us in the cinema or on the television, the resulting sound is hardly equivalent to a kitten jumping into a pile of fresh laundry."

Watson nodded. "I know. A suppressed gun is still loud. Hasn't this been studied already? Couldn't you just read about it? You know, quietly? On your own? Without waking me or the neighbors?"

"Come now, Watson. What's happened to your scientific curiosity? As you know, primary sources are the only ones to be trusted. And in this case, the primary source is *me*."

Of course, thought Watson.

Holmes pointed theatrically to the cushion pressed against the muzzle of the revolver. "And in countless works of crime fiction," he said, "guns are shown to be silenced by firing through a cushion or pillow. A bigger load of pig's trotters I have hardly heard of."

Watson shook her head. "Please don't tell me you're actually going to fire a gun in here. What did we say about conducting ballistics experiments in the brownstone? The whole street will call the police when they hear it."

Sherlock rolled his lips and sniffed. "Not if this works they won't," he said with a wicked grin. He ducked down behind the machine—right in the path of the upside-down gun—and squinted, apparently making sure the machine, cushion, and pig were in perfect alignment. "Besides, I can hardly use the stereo to mask the report of the firearm this time, can I?"

Watson braced herself. She stepped back toward the kitchen and jammed her fingers in her ears. She wanted to tell Holmes to put on some hearing protection, and then wondered how to explain her eccentric roommate to the police who were bound to come bursting in shortly, but it was too late. She watched as Holmes stood as far back from the table as the cord on the firing control would allow, and held his phone up in the air.

Watson closed her eyes.

Three seconds passed.

Five seconds.

She opened one eye, then the other. Then her hands dropped from the side of her head.

Sherlock stood facing her, the fire control dangling from his hand while he operated his phone with the other, clearly reading a message.

"What is it?" Watson asked.

Sherlock held the phone up. Watson moved closer and peered at the screen. It was a text, giving an address— *Somewhere in Hell's Kitchen*, Watson thought—and below a message that could only have come from Captain Gregson.

YOU'RE GOING TO LOVE THIS ONE

Holmes put the firing control back on the table, and glanced ruefully at the pig carcass hanging from the bondage cuffs.

"Another time, me old porker." He glanced at Watson. "You'd better put something less diaphanous on. It might be cold outside."

Watson sighed, and headed for the stairs, the brewing tea in the kitchen abandoned.

So much for a quiet weekend.

3

THE HELL'S KITCHEN MYSTERY

Watson had been right about the location of the murder, although it wasn't quite what she'd expected. She and Holmes had made their way to Hell's Kitchen, but not the edgy, cool side of the district. The victim's apartment was in a brownstone on a quiet street that wasn't exactly seedy, more… sedately rundown. The building itself was similar to the one Watson shared with Holmes in Brooklyn, but here, yellow police tape flickered around the stoop while four cruisers sat in the street outside, a handful of uniforms loitering.

The building was now a crime scene.

As they approached, Watson saw a young woman talking to one of the officers, who was busy taking notes. She was wrapped in a silver thermal blanket, and as Watson and Holmes headed up the short flight of stairs to the building's porch, Watson glanced over and made eye contact from under the brim of her trilby. The woman's face was red, her eyes wide. Watson had seen that look before. She could offer nothing but a tight-lipped expression of sympathy. Being caught up in a crime, even peripherally, could exact a terrible toll.

Ahead of Watson, Holmes had paused in the doorway to

give the frame a cursory examination. As Watson got closer, she saw that none of his deductive powers were yet required—the door itself hung half off its hinges, crumpled into a splintered V near the handle. A large chunk of the door frame had been ripped from the wall at a corresponding position. The hallmarks of a police ram.

Captain Gregson stepped out from the first doorway in the hall, turning up the collar of his dark trench coat as he did so. He nodded a greeting to the two consultants. Holmes had his fists clenched, arms straight by his side as he buzzed with impatience.

"Well?" he said, more brusquely than the Captain deserved, thought Watson. But Gregson was as used to Holmes's manner as she was, and he just nodded into the apartment behind him, stuffing his hands into the pockets of his coat. Like the front door, the apartment door had also been forced open by the NYPD.

"Nice to see you too," he said, before turning on a warm smile for Watson. "Sorry to drag you out on a weekend, but..." He extracted a hand and gestured to the doorway. "Well, take a look."

Holmes vanished through the door without a further word. Watson gave Gregson an apologetic shrug and followed her partner.

The apartment was small: narrower than Watson expected, given the exterior proportions of the brownstone. She put the glitch in her observation down to a distinct lack of caffeine, and focused on surveying the crime scene.

The front room was typical of a brownstone, with a high ceiling and a bay window looking out to the street. Interior walls had been knocked through, connecting the front room to a small kitchen/dining room at the back. The decor and fittings were dated, the wallpaper faded, and certainly none of it was period. But the place looked lived in, with a couple of bookshelves stocked with well-thumbed paperbacks and collected editions of *Reader's Digest* magazine bound in faux leather. There was an armchair backed up to the bay window, a couch against the wall opposite the door, and an old fourteen-inch TV in the corner. The floorboards were bare and in need of some restorative elbow grease, but were mostly covered by a thick brown rug, on which lay the victim.

He lay square in the middle of the rug, face-up, his eyes open and jaw slack, head toward the kitchen, feet toward the window. He was dressed for cold weather, in a heavy coat and scarf *in situ*. The coat was open, and the shirt and jacket beneath were a torn and tangled mess stained deep red by the man's blood.

Detective Bell stepped around the kitchen counter.

"Morning, campers," he said, rolling back a couple of pages in his notebook. Watson nodded in response to his sardonic greeting while Holmes, ignoring the body, moved to the chair in the bay window and peered at the floor. Bell and Watson watched Holmes for a few seconds, but with no sign of the consultant paying them any attention, Bell licked a thumb and began to read from his notes.

"Victim is one Liam Macnamara, forty-five. Native of Belfast, Northern Ireland; moved to the States with his folks in the early eighties. Lived alone, worked for the MTA as a subway train driver. The upstairs neighbor phoned it in—you probably saw her outside—but we have 911 calls from half the block. This murder was hardly quiet."

Watson crouched by the body and pushed up the brim of her hat.

"Any family?"

"The neighbor thinks he might have a sister. We're trying to trace her."

Watson positioned her boots carefully so as not to disturb the scene. "There's an awful lot of blood here. It looks like he was almost cut in half at the chest. Multiple gunshot wounds... high caliber or high velocity rounds?"

Bell nodded. "Got it in one. Nine millimeter Parabellum, and plenty of them. Forensics have pulled out ten slugs already."

Watson looked up at the detective with a frown. "From the body?"

"From the wall," said Holmes. He stood up and pointed through to the kitchen. Following his finger, Watson saw that the back wall was pockmarked with holes. "I daresay some will even have penetrated the wall completely and ended their journey in the yard outside."

"Seems a little excessive," said Watson.

"And accidental," said Holmes. "With a muzzle velocity of approximately three hundred and fifty meters a second, and a fire rate of anything up to seventeen *hundred* rounds a minute, an Uzi—even a small one—is both formidable and problematic if you've never used one before."

Captain Gregson reappeared at the apartment door. "There's not many who would carry a weapon like that around the city," he said, exchanging a look with Bell.

"This some kind of gang war?" asked Bell.

Gregson sighed. "That's all we need." He turned to Holmes. "You think this is a hit?"

Holmes shook his head and placed his hands into the pockets of his pea coat, his elbows sticking out like handles.

"I realize it is a little early on a Saturday morning for some of us, but that is precisely the *opposite* of what I said."

Gregson held up his hands in gesture of supplication that Watson knew was not altogether serious. "Sorry," he said. "Keep going."

Holmes gave a curt nod. "We can discount a number of options already—as you say, Captain, the Uzi is an uncommon weapon. Expensive, difficult to get hold of, legally or otherwise. This was no mere robbery or home invasion by a common gun-toting thug. *But*, while this murder was almost certainly an execution, it was not a 'hit.'" He paused, his eyes moving from one person to the next as though expecting questions or objections. When none came he continued.

"Any self-respecting professional crime organization would send its very best to eliminate a target," he said, his tone close to exasperation, as if his theory was patently obvious. "The object of the exercise would be one of efficiency and discretion. Straight in, straight out. Job done, and nobody is any the wiser. In the case of our late train driver, while he was indeed taken out for some as yet unknown misdemeanor, his murder was not performed by a professional. Our killer almost certainly didn't know how to handle the Uzi with which he was provided. In fact, I wouldn't be surprised if his masters didn't even *know* he had taken the gun. And once they find out what he's done, I suspect they may carry out an execution of their own."

Bell blew out his cheeks and closed his notebook. He looked at his superior. "Seems plausible, Captain."

"Okay," said Gregson, turning back to Holmes. "So somebody puts a hit on a subway driver and hands an Uzi to someone who doesn't know how to use one. And when the moment comes, he surprises our vic and gets trigger happy, squeezing off half the clip before he even knows it."

"A useful scenario, Captain," said Holmes. "At least until we have more data."

Watson sidled over to the door and glanced back down the hallway.

"So where did the killer go?" she asked. "The front door was smashed by the police."

"Right," said Gregson. "We have uniforms canvassing the area, but the building was secured. From the *inside*. We can assume the killer was already here waiting, but the neighbor upstairs thinks she heard Macnamara coming in alone at around five. A few minutes later came the gunfire, but that was it. The neighbor locked herself in her apartment, but didn't hear anything else. The first responders had to bust the deadbolt on the building's front door to get in, and the door to this apartment didn't just have a deadbolt, it had a sliding bolt and chain as well, both of which were in place. The back door is the same, and still locked, chain and all, and the windows all have internal locks with a key still in each. As far as we can tell, the place is sealed, from the *inside*."

Holmes bounced on the balls of his feet. "So not just a locked-room mystery, but one involving a locked *house*."

Watson rubbed her temples as she tried to process the information. She knew that the cases she and Holmes were invited to consult on were the more difficult ones that came across Gregson's desk—that was the whole point of their consulting, after all—but she had to admit that his text this morning had been right on the money. Already she could see the spark in Holmes's eye. Ten minutes at the crime scene and he was running scenarios through his mind.

"Okay," said Watson. "So, like I said, where did the killer go?"

Holmes shook his head. "Where he went is less important than where he came from." He stepped sideways and pointed to the floor in front of the armchair. Watson moved to take a closer look.

The rug by the chair was tracked with dirt: light brown, almost sandy. Faint, but noticeable. Watson looked down at her own feet, but the rug on which she stood looked clean. The dirt seemed to be deposited only in front of the armchair.

Holmes crouched down and indicated the deposit with an open palm.

"The killer got here early. He sat in the chair and waited for the victim to return home from Duane Reade—going by the grocery bag on the kitchen floor. We already know our killer was not a trained assassin, and it seems he was not particularly adept at waiting either. While he sat, he *fidgeted*, depositing dirt from his shoes or clothing. Given that the soil is limited to this area, I infer that it was not on his shoes, otherwise it would be tracked all over the place. Perhaps from his knees or trouser cuffs, only dispersed as he crossed and uncrossed his legs."

Holmes stood and waved at the floor. "Watson, if you would be so kind."

Watson stared at her friend, then turned to the two detectives. Both Bell and Gregson were looking at her, their expressions blank. Bell raised an eyebrow. Watson turned back to Holmes.

"I'm not sure what you're—"

"Oh, come now, Watson," said Holmes with a grin. "No need for false modesty. I must admit I have been positively beside myself to see you put this particular aspect of your education to practical use."

With that he returned his hands to the pockets of his coat and took one theatrical step back.

Watson shook her head. "I'm sorry, Sherlock. I really don't know what you're talking about."

Holmes pursed his lips and glanced sideways at the two detectives standing nearby. Gregson still had his hands in his pockets, while Bell had his pen poised over his notebook. Behind them, various uniforms entered and left the apartment as they continued their work as best they could with four people standing in the way.

Holmes sighed, and ducked back down to the floor. He pulled on a pair of blue latex gloves from his pocket and pressed one finger into the residue on the rug. Then he stood and offered the finger to Watson.

"If you would be so kind," he said.

She looked at his finger for a moment, bemused, then

folded her arms as she finally realized what Holmes was talking about.

"Wait, you want me to *taste* it?" One eyebrow inched upward.

Holmes nodded. "I have noted the declining levels of my soil samples back at the brownstone. I assume that you have been studying them in your own time and comparing your findings with my monograph on the subject."

Watson shook her head. She'd lost Holmes's trail of thought. Again.

"Soil samples?"

"Yes," said Holmes. "The ones I keep in the spice rack in the kitchen."

Watson blinked. "I thought those were *spices*!"

Holmes opened and closed his mouth a couple of times. "Ah," he said.

Watson waved frantically at her friend, her shoulders rising. "You put soil samples in spice jars and put the jars in the spice rack?"

"Well, those jars are a convenient size. I noted the Nazca Desert sample was particularly low last time I looked."

Watson wracked her brains. Nazca Desert? She wasn't great with spices, despite her best efforts… but then she remembered one jar in particular she'd been using a lot recently. It was filled with a light brown powder and labeled as—

"I thought that was nutmeg! I've been using it in pasta sauce!"

Holmes chuckled to himself and ran his tongue over his front teeth as he looked, almost wistfully, into the middle distance.

"Hmm. I thought I detected a hint of the Andes in your otherwise excellent lasagna." He gave a small bow to his friend, then raised his finger. "My apologies, Watson. Now *this*, if I'm not mistaken, is actually not far off the composition of that Peruvian sample we've been so inadvertently chug-a-lugging."

Holmes's lips pulled back like he was about to brush his teeth and he rubbed his gloved finger into his gums with gusto, like an addict taking cocaine. Watson frowned and looked at Bell and Gregson, who seemed bored and amused in equal measure. Par for the course when dealing with Sherlock Holmes.

Holmes worked his tongue around his mouth, nodding to himself. "Southern Colombia. Possibly northern Ecuador. Very distinctive tang."

Bell sighed. "Okaaaaay," he said. He cast a sideways glance at his superior, then began making notes. He gestured toward the body with his pen. "So our victim, a middle-aged motorman with no priors is taken out—*executed*—by an amateur with dirt from South America on his pants, who managed to escape from a locked building."

"Precisely that, Detective," said Holmes. As he spoke, a faint whistling sound seemed to sweep through the room, traveling from one wall around to the next. It was quiet, and with everyone crowding into the small apartment, easy to miss. Watson cocked her head and listened. She saw that Bell had heard it too.

"What was that?" she asked.

Bell shrugged. "Plumbing? Sounds like air in the heating."

Gregson nodded. "This is an old building. Can't have been renovated anytime in the last thirty or forty years."

"Yes," said Holmes, shuffling back to the bay window. He reached behind him and laid a hand on the radiator behind the armchair. "But the radiators are cold."

"The heating might be on in the apartments upstairs," suggested Watson. Holmes nodded in a non-committal way, then stepped over the legs of the body and went into the open-plan kitchen. Watson followed.

Spilled across the floor were flat white boxes, all identical, each about the size and shape of a pack of cards. Those that lay face-up all had the same label.

"Beta-carotene?"

Holmes nodded. "Seems our motorman was stocking up."

Bell joined them at the counter. "No sign of any other vitamins or supplements." He grinned. "Maybe he was trying to improve his night vision and didn't like carrots."

Watson frowned. "That's a myth from the Second World War, a way of encouraging the British to grow carrots in their gardens."

"Yes," said Holmes. "Beta-carotene may prevent the progression of macular degeneration when given in combination with certain other dietary supplements, but no, it won't make you see in the dark."

The whistling sound rang out again. Holmes glanced at the ceiling; then he went to the kitchen sink and turned on the faucet. Water flowed immediately. He experimented with turning each of the faucets, but the stream was strong and uninterrupted, steam pluming from the sink as the hot water came out nearly instantly.

"No air in the pipes, either," said Holmes. Then he paused, turned in a circle as he took in the kitchen's contents, and reached for the wooden bread bin that sat on the counter, beneath the overhanging cupboards. He flicked the roller lid, which shot open with a clatter.

From across the counter, Bell whistled.

Inside the bread bin was no bread. Instead, there were three large stacks of money; old bills with crinkled edges, bound together with thick rubber bands. Watson had no idea how much was in there, but the uppermost bills were one-hundred-dollar notes. There must have been thousands—*tens of thousands*—of dollars tucked away.

Holmes put his hands back in his pockets, and turned to the others. Watson saw the sparkle in his eyes.

"I suppose it beats hiding it under the mattress, so long as you don't have a house guest who wants to make toast."

He pointed to the bin. "The corner of a note was sticking out the bottom."

At that moment, a uniformed officer emerged from the small hallway that led off the kitchen and into the rest of the apartment. He nodded at Captain Gregson, and handed him a glossy brochure. Gregson looked down at it, gave an appreciative frown, and held it out to Watson.

"South America, you say?"

It was a pamphlet from the American Museum of Natural History. Watson felt Holmes peering over her shoulder as she read the cover.

"It's for an exhibition of pre-Colombian gold."

She opened the brochure. Paper-clipped inside was a rectangular yellow card.

"And a ticket to the gala launch of the exhibition," said Holmes. "Which is tonight." He looked at the others. "It seems there is more to the late lamented Mr. Macnamara than meets the eye."

4

THE SECRET OF THE BROWNSTONE

"So what does an Irish-born New York City subway driver have to do with the American Museum of Natural History?"

They were standing on the stoop of Macnamara's brownstone. Holmes was gazing ahead, hands in pockets with his arms sticking out, apparently unaware that he was blocking most of the doorway. A uniformed officer jogged up the steps to the door, then paused, glancing first at Holmes and then at Watson. Watson gave a tight, apologetic smile, and pulled herself close to the doorjamb to let the officer pass.

Watson sighed. "I said—"

"I heard what you said." Holmes cocked his head, still looking at the building opposite. Watson followed his eyeline, but the other side of the street was just more brownstones. Glancing left and right, she could see that most of the block was more or less of the same architecture and period, and more or less in the same, unrestored condition. But Holmes had clearly seen something interesting. Watson scanned the row of houses across from them, trying to see what her partner saw.

Holmes rolled a hand in the air as he spoke. "I know

verbalizing the thought process is a highly useful tool to help initiate the cascade of deductive reasoning, but in this particular case the question you asked was so obvious I assumed it to be entirely rhetorical, and therefore did not require an answer." He tore his gaze from the house across the street and looked at Watson. "That there *is* a connection is clear, but we must be sure we are lining the correct pieces. Maybe Mr. Macnamara had an armchair interest in social anthropology or ichthyology or maybe he just liked looking at stuffed elephants. The possibilities are innumerable."

Watson blinked at her partner. "Okay, so you're in one of those moods." She looked away, shaking her head. "Maybe we could work out a schedule. You know, you could give me advance notice or something and I'll know when I can talk to you and when I can't." She wasn't entirely joking, either. Having lived with Holmes for nearly three years now, she knew his moods—and their swings—very well. He could alternate from manic and effusive to withdrawn and self-conscious, his changes sometimes lasting hours, sometimes days. She wasn't quite sure what phase he was in today— smug and self-satisfied, with just a *soupçon* of arrogance, it seemed. But an active case would be enough, usually, to snap him out of it. And all she could do was help, as best she could.

"That sounds like an admirable arrangement," said Holmes. Then he trotted down the stairs, past a uniformed cop standing sentry on the sidewalk, and without pause walked straight across the street. Watson folded her arms and watched him for a moment as he stopped in front of the stoop of the house opposite and looked up at the building, returning her focus to the case at hand.

He was right. There was a connection—possibly many. They just had to find out which one would lead to a murderer. Which meant...

Watson followed Holmes across the street. He was still

apparently admiring the decidedly average brownstone across from Macnamara's.

"It's not the museum at all, is it?" she asked. Holmes turned to face her, one eyebrow raised. "And yes," said Watson, "that question *is* rhetorical. But his connection isn't with the museum. He had lots of books in his apartment, but nothing that suggested he had an interest in the natural sciences. It was all *Reader's Digest* condensed books and Stephen King paperbacks."

Holmes's mouth curled up in a smile to match his eyebrow. "Well observed, Watson."

"Which means," she continued, "his connection is not with the museum but with the gold exhibition."

"Precisely that. But why would a man with not the slightest interest in the contents of one of the country's foremost scientific institutes have tickets to a champagne-fuelled gala opening?"

Watson paused, thought.

"Because," she said, "he's not going for the exhibition. He's going for some other reason."

Holmes replaced his hands in the pockets of his pea coat and gave a curt nod. "Our late Mr. Macnamara had at least fifty thousand dollars stuffed into his bread bin. More than he could possibly have saved even in twenty years of driving subway trains."

Watson took a short, shallow breath, her eyes widening as she joined the dots in her mind. "It's drug money. The museum exhibition is of artifacts from Colombia..."

Holmes nodded again. "The world's leading producer of...?"

"Cocaine," said Watson. She folded her arms. "So Macnamara was a drug runner?"

Holmes turned back to the brownstone. "I will admit that was my first assumption, but unless they've extended the 'A' line all the way to Bogotá, that seems unlikely." He craned his neck to look up at the building. Watson moved next to him and looked up too, but couldn't see anything that was so interesting. She waved at the brownstone.

"Why are you staring at this building?"

Holmes spun on his heel and pointed to Macnamara's house. The street had seen little traffic while they had been there, and across from where they stood four squad cars were still parked against the curb. The brownstone's front door was open as the police worked inside. The uniform remaining on duty on the sidewalk had his arms folded and was watching them from under the peak of his cap, his eyes narrowed.

Holmes waved his hand at the building, quickly, like he was irritated with a particularly difficult puzzle. Which, as Watson well knew, was precisely the problem.

"What's wrong with Macnamara's brownstone?" he asked.

Watson pursed her lips and looked back at the building. From the outside, it was a fairly large row house—on the first floor there were three tall, narrow windows, the stoop and front door on the far left side. There were two floors above, each four windows across. Below the bottom row of windows, the brownstone's construction changed to large, pale blocks, the windows of the street-level apartment—the ones directly below Macnamara's—much smaller than those above. Black iron railings ran from the edge of the stoop across the front of the building, enclosing the street-level apartment, with a short flight of stairs heading down from the sidewalk. Much like every other brownstone in the block.

Watson tilted her head as she regarded the building. Then she shook her head, realizing what it was she had felt inside. "His apartment was too small," she said, turning to face Holmes. "Even with the original single house divided into apartments, the dimensions inside don't match the outside."

"Correct," said Holmes with a smile. He pointed to the far right-hand side of the building. "See anything else?"

Watson sighed. Now that her partner had pointed it out, it was obvious.

The last window on the right, on each floor, was identical in size and shape to its brethren. But instead of blinds or curtains, they were blacked out, from the inside.

"There's another room next to Macnamara's place," said Watson.

"More than that," said Holmes. "A whole, what, *quarter* of the building's exterior width is missing on the *interior*."

"So who lives in the downstairs apartment?"

Holmes turned to Watson. His eyebrow crept up again.

"Nobody does," he said. "Because there isn't one. There's no gate, either."

Watson turned back to the building. Holmes was right. The iron railing that separated the sidewalk from the short drop down into the street-level apartment was the same as all the rest on the block. Only the railing was continuous. There were steps behind the rail, but no opening to access them.

Now that Watson could see the irregularities, it was obvious. *But unless it was pointed out,* she thought, *nobody would pay the slightest bit of attention.* There was something familiar about the apparent oddness of the building, something rolling around in the back of her mind—

She clicked her fingers and turned to her partner.

"That sound inside. It was like water, in pipes." Watson grinned as she looked back at the building. "The brownstone doesn't have a room missing on each floor. There's a pumping station next door."

Holmes nodded. "It's a neat trick," he said. "A large but essential municipal facility like a water-pumping station plonked in the middle of a residential street would be an eyesore by any stretch of the imagination."

"Unless you disguise it as a house," said Watson. "I've seen these before. Just about every city in the country has them."

She frowned. "So Macnamara's building has a pumping station next to it. How does that help us?"

"Really, Watson, weekends are no good for you, are they? Too much lying idle, watching bad television, reading thrilling genre novels like our late Mr. Macnamara."

"Excuse me?"

Holmes pulled closer to Watson, lowering his voice. He was clearly enjoying this more than he should have been. "Macnamara's killer somehow got into an apartment that was locked from the inside. Doors, windows, the works. Ergo—"

Watson's lips parted and she let out a short breath. "He came in through the pumping station?"

Holmes grinned, and nodded tightly, bouncing on his heels.

"Let's take a little look, shall we?"

5

A SURPRISE ENTRY

Holmes led Watson back across the street. Nodding a greeting to the uniform by the stoop, Holmes then walked along the chest-high black iron rail and glanced over it. There were steps on the other side, leading to a door set into the foundation of the stairs. Up close, Watson could see that the small windows of what was supposed to be the street-level apartment were not only blacked out but also barred with iron as thick as the sidewalk railing. The door in the stoop was not the average apartment door—heavy with cobwebs, it was metal and black, and was secured by a thick metal bar running across the middle held in place by a padlock as big as a fist.

Watson ran her fingers over the railing. There was no gate and no apparent way to get to the door without clambering over the railing. Given the decorative triangular caps that topped each railing, this wasn't an athletic feat Watson felt like attempting.

"How do we get down there?"

Holmes took a step back and looked left and right along the rail. Then he pointed down at the siding the rail was set into. The iron poles were all cemented in, except for a row of four that stretched across the top of the steps. Watson trailed her fingers up the rail until she met the crossbars, and she could see that there was a section of railing separate to the others.

The pair exchanged a look, then Holmes turned and called out to the uniform nearby.

"Excuse me, officer, could we beg your indulgence for a moment?"

The cop frowned at Holmes, thick eyebrows knotted over a granite nose, but was clearly unmoved. Holmes sighed. "Your name, if you'd be so kind?"

The cop kept the frown. "Emerson."

Holmes gave a theatrical bow. "Officer Emerson, please come this way. We require your assistance."

Emerson sidled over to them. Holmes gestured to him to grip the rail crossbars on one side. Watson stepped back to give Holmes room as he grabbed the rail on the other.

Holmes and the officer looked at each other. Watson watched as one of Holmes's eyebrows went up.

"Yes?" he asked.

Emerson, still gripping the rail with both hands, glanced first at Holmes, then at Watson. "You need me to get Captain Gregson for you? Shouldn't he—"

"And lift!" Holmes, ignoring the question, heaved on his side of the rail. Emerson had no choice but to help, and together the pair slid the section of railing clear. Holmes dusted his hands and stood back, admiring his handiwork. He nodded to the cop.

"Thank you."

Emerson frowned. "I'm going to get the Captain."

"Do as you will, officer, we shall not impede your duties any further," said Holmes with a broad smile. Emerson kept the frown on his face, then turned and disappeared up the stoop. When he was gone, Holmes sniffed. "Shame. For a moment there the NYPD was mere putty in my hands."

Watson shook her head, then led the way down the steps. She stopped at the big metal door, and gave the padlock an experimental tug, which hardly even moved it. Then she ran her fingers along the metal bar securing the door.

"Well," she said, "he couldn't have got in through here. Even if he vaulted the rail, this doesn't look like it's been opened in a while."

"You guys need a hand down there?"

Watson looked up. Standing on the stoop above them, peering down, was Captain Gregson. Emerson was standing by his shoulder.

"Busted," she said under her breath. Holmes's mouth twitched in response.

"I think we can manage, thank you, Captain," he said, squinting up into the bright sky. "You may continue with your crime-scene investigation."

Gregson gave an exaggerated frown. "Well, thank you for granting us permission." Then he nodded at Watson, pointing down to the street-level apartment with his notebook. "There's no apartment down there. Seems that part of the building belongs to a utility company."

Holmes was bent down, his nose nearly pressed to the padlock on the black metal door. "Rest assured we will call for assistance should it become necessary."

Gregson and Watson shared a look. She shrugged, a gesture that not only said she had no control over what Holmes was planning, but that she renounced all responsibility. It made her uncomfortable, but there was nothing else she could do.

Fortunately, Watson knew that Gregson was just as aware of Holmes's methods as she was—the Captain rubbed his chin, then nodded and disappeared over the edge of the stoop, the uniform trailing behind him.

Watson waved at the door. "We need permission to get in there."

Holmes sniffed and stood tall, tilting his head as he regarded the padlock.

"Mr. Macnamara's killer didn't get permission." He glanced sideways at Watson. "I think one minute?"

Watson shook her head, but she stepped forward anyway and looked down at the lock. From her satchel she extracted a roll of suede fabric. Kneeling in front of the door, she opened the roll and selected a lock pick. She looked back at Holmes over her shoulder.

"Forty seconds flat," she said.

Holmes smiled, gesturing at the heavy padlock.

Watson got to work.

The pumping station was dark, the air musty. As soon as the door had been cracked, a low hum of machinery became audible. Watson brushed cobwebs from her shoulder; she and Holmes had had to heave at the door once she'd picked the stiff lock.

"Forty flat, told you," said Watson as she peered into the gloom, the only light coming in through the door behind them.

"Thirty-eight and a half, if you insist on keeping a tally," said Holmes. He frowned and turned back to the door, feeling along the wall beside it. "Aha," he said.

There was a crunch as he threw an old-fashioned lever switch to the upright position. Fluorescent tubes flickered around the walls, and soon the dank gloom was replaced with a harsh white light that made Watson squint.

They had been right—where the street-level apartment would have been was a water-pumping station. They were in a large rectangular room stretching the full depth of the brownstone, the walls cream-painted cinder blocks. The space was dominated by four large pipes, painted in blue enamel, each of which curved up out of the grilled center of the floor, then continued at a right angle to connect with a fat perpendicular blue pipe. Where the pipes became horizontal, each had a valve with a wheel big enough to steer a city bus.

The fat perpendicular pipes were topped, just above head height, with a black cylinder, looking something like, Watson thought, the engine that would hang under the wings of a large passenger jet, only a fraction of the size. The cylinders each had a gray metal box attached to their side, from which two flexible gray plastic tubes emerged, snaking down to the floor and disappearing into another metal box.

The floor of the chamber was concrete, save for the central grilled area beneath the main pumps, and a series of rectangular manhole covers spaced around the room at regular intervals. Along two of the walls were tall gray cabinets, most with warning signs plastered over them—"high voltage," "no access," emergency phone numbers—their doors secured with more padlocks. The remaining wall space on all sides was covered with smaller control panels consisting of levers and large buttons, set among a maze of smaller pipework and wheeled valves.

"Fascinating, isn't it?" Holmes walked around the main pumps. He nodded at the black cylinders. "Vertical turbine pumps." Then he leaned over and looked down through the grilled floor. Watson looked too—the fat blue pipes continued down, vanishing into darkness. "It's effectively a supercharger," said Holmes. He pulled his hands from his pockets and waved them in the air like he was gathering a bale of wool. "The normal water pressure in Manhattan is typically able to reach the sixth floor—any higher and a basement pump pushes the water up into a tank on the roof, where gravity can take over." Then he stood back, nodding appreciatively as he surveyed the machinery. "But the odd booster here and there around the city where pressure is lower never hurts."

Watson looked around the walls. "And the cinder blocks help insulate the sound from the house."

As she spoke, the air was filled with the sound of rushing water and the loud whirr as the four turbines came to life. It wasn't loud, exactly, but Watson wasn't sure she would want to live next door to the place. As she and Holmes waited, the rushing sound faded, and then the turbines clicked off.

Holmes caught her eye and nodded. "I suppose you get used to it."

As the steady background hum of the station returned, Watson looked up. The ceiling consisted of flat white panels, suspended beneath which were more pipework and the fluorescent lighting. She frowned. "I thought a whole quarter of the house was part of the station?"

"Ventilation probably," said Holmes, pointing to the far wall. Watson turned and saw more large blue pipes running from the floor to the ceiling.

"So what are we doing here?" asked Watson. "We've already established the killer didn't come in or out through the station's main door. It was locked from the outside, and we could hardly open it with the two of us anyway."

"He didn't use that door, no," said Holmes. He walked around the pumps, then stood with his heels together and pointed at a spot between his splayed feet. "He came through here."

He was standing on one of the rectangular manhole covers. It was at least a meter on its long side, its surface studded with non-slip corrugations.

Holmes dropped down onto his haunches and, balancing on his toes, looked more closely at the plate under his feet. Then he crabbed along the floor to the next cover, then the next. He stopped and pointed.

"This one," he said. "Like the main door, most of these covers haven't been lifted recently, perhaps in years. Except this one."

Watson took a closer look. Holmes was right. The plate appeared to be securely in place, but around one of the short edges the concrete of the floor was scraped, the fresh marks lighter than the surroundings. The cover had been moved.

Holmes stood, and marched over to the corner of the room where a stepladder rested. He picked something else up, then returned to the manhole.

"Gulley key," he said, holding the object up. It was a silver crowbar, with a curved hook at one end and a triangular handle at the other. As Watson stood back, he stood above the metal plate, feet spread, and inserted the key into the slot. He heaved on the bar. The manhole cover lifted free from the floor, then Holmes adjusted his footing and, grabbing the key's handle with both hands, used it to slide the cover partially clear of the manhole.

The two consultants crouched side by side, peering into the dark hole that had been revealed. There were square rungs set into one side of the manhole, but Watson could only see down a few meters. How far the ladder went, she couldn't tell.

She looked at Holmes. Something wasn't adding up.

"The killer came up from the *sewer*?"

Holmes grinned, then gestured to the portal. "We have our observation. Now we have our deduction."

Watson shook her head. "But wouldn't he have left a trail of dirt? Far bigger than the traces you found in the apartment, I mean?"

"Not necessarily," said Holmes. "It hasn't rained for a few days, and the service tunnels beneath the streets would be mostly clean and dry."

"But how did he get into the apartment upstairs?"

Holmes looked up at the ceiling. "If the brownstone was originally a single dwelling, this may well have been the cellar or basement. There must be a service hatch or similar, leading into Macnamara's apartment."

The two split up, walking in opposite directions around the pumping station, scanning the ceiling above them for the access point.

Watson spotted it. "Here," she called out. Holmes appeared at her side and she pointed up.

The hatch was rectangular and painted to match the ceiling but with a thick frame that made it obvious. It clearly opened upward, and there was a hinged metal flap with a loop, where another of the ubiquitous heavy padlocks should have been, but wasn't.

"Excellent," said Holmes. He ducked back to the corner of the station and picked up the stepladder, then set it up under the hatch. He turned to Watson and grinned. "I'll hold it steady."

With a sigh, Watson shifted her satchel around her shoulders so it was in the small of her back, and grabbed the ladder. At the top, she gave the hatch an experimental push. It didn't move. She looked back down at Holmes.

"A little more effort, if you please," he said.

Watson frowned and returned her attention to the hatch. She pushed again, but whatever was resisting her efforts was almost elastic—the more she pushed, the more it seemed to resist.

And then the resistance was suddenly gone. She pushed the hatch up, and a moment later it left her hands completely. Watson wobbled at the top of the ladder, one hand flailing for the edge of the opening above her. Then her hand was grabbed by another, from above; looking up in surprise, a long shadow moved into her view.

"Ms. Watson?"

She blinked, recognizing the voice instantly. The shadow that was Captain Gregson crouched down and helped her up out of the hatch. She stepped off the top of the ladder, letting herself be lifted slightly, and found herself in the middle of Macnamara's living room. The heavy elastic something that had prevented the hatch from opening was the rug, now peeled back from the floor, the edge held in Officer Emerson's large fists. Watson turned and saw Bell behind her, holding the hatch back with both hands. There were a few other officers in the room, as well as the last few members of the CSU team. Everyone was looking at her.

Holmes's head appeared through the hatch. He looked up at the Captain, and at Bell.

"Well," he said, "I think we've solved one particular mystery, anyway."

Then, with a nod, his head disappeared back down through the hatch.

6

PARTIES TO PLAN, ERRANDS TO RUN

Watson skipped down the stairs, phone pressed to her ear as she finalized plans for that evening. A little infiltration of the museum gala, a little discreet questioning of guests. It occurred to her that she'd never really gone undercover during her time with Holmes. But the new thought just made her nervous, so she tried to push it to the back of her mind.

"Okay, see you at seven. Bye." She thumbed the phone off and curled around the stair bannister and into the brownstone's front room. She stood in the doorway for a moment and watched as Holmes's fingers flew across his computer keyboard, his whole body hunched over the desk. From the hallway, she could see that he was browsing an Internet forum of some sort, the main page black and covered with tiny text in an eye-watering teal green. His face was twisted into a rictus snarl as he focused all his attention on the heated discussion he was clearly in the middle of. Chekhov still hung on the wall next to the fireplace, covered by a hastily arranged tablecloth that did little to disguise the distinctly... *porky* smell in the room.

Watson thought about waiting for the right moment to cut

in, but quickly realized that, actually, the right moment would never come. She moved to the desk and waved her phone at Holmes, in case that would get his attention.

It didn't.

"That was—"

"Captain Gregson," said Holmes. Still staring at the screen, he held one finger up in the air toward Watson while he continued to type single-handedly. Watson raised an eyebrow.

"Yes," she said. "He's picking me up at seven to go to the museum gala. But he also wanted me to double check that you're sure you don't want to go with me instead."

Holmes snickered but he kept his nose an inch away from his screen. "Captain Gregson is a mighty intellect among the detective class," he said, now typing again with both hands. "He'll be a more than adequate assistance at the exhibition's grand gala opening, and I dare say his well-calibrated features will look rather more at home in black tie than my own. Rest assured, you will make the most elegant undercover couple." He stopped typing and turned to face Watson. He swayed slightly on his chair, as though he were a little drunk, but Watson recognized the body language—the *haptic communication* as Holmes himself would have described it. He was up to something.

Watson lifted one arm to her hip. "'Well-calibrated'?"

Holmes pursed his lips. "Perhaps reminiscent of an older Jason Priestley."

"Jason Priestley?"

"But older," said Holmes. "Much, *much* older."

Watson sighed and let her arm drop. "Okay," she said. This was turning into one of *those* conversations.

"And besides," Holmes continued, confirming Watson's earlier unspoken suspicion, "I have my own little covert investigation to organize."

Watson frowned. "Gregson also said he smoothed things

over with New York City Water Board. Apparently they weren't too impressed with us entering one of their pumping stations without proper permission."

"Ha!" said Holmes, turning back to the screen and resuming his online discussion. "Liam Macnamara's killer likewise entered the station without permission. Perhaps, once he is apprehended, the Water Board can send a stern reprimand to him at Sing Sing."

"But shouldn't the NYPD be working with the Water Board anyway to check out that tunnel?"

"No need," said Holmes. "I have that matter in hand even as we speak. Well, even as you speak *at* me while I try to further our investigation."

Watson ignored the jibe, and pointed her phone at the computer. Holmes hadn't stopped typing even as he spoke to her. "So what are you doing? Reaching out to Everyone again?"

At this, Holmes stopped work, withdrawing his hands from the keyboard like he'd been burnt. "In this particular instance, no," he said. Then he pushed his chair out from the desk, and gestured not to the dark website on his primary display, but to the tablet computer sitting on its stand next to it. Watson walked around the desk and lifted the tablet to get a better look.

The device showed a map—it was recognizably Manhattan, but it was old, a scan of an historic document. Watson slid the image around with her fingers, then zoomed in on a spot. There were some streets labeled, but they were sketchy, a ghostly overlay across a series of darker parallel lines that didn't seem to obey the grid system that covered most of the island. Swiping sideways revealed another map, equally old and faded, and there was the echo of a rubber stamp across one corner that said RECEIVED JANUARY 1899. This map was not of the entire island of Manhattan, but just an area encompassing Hell's Kitchen and, to the north,

Lincoln Square. As with the first map, the streets were overlaid with a twisting maze of dark lines.

Holmes craned his neck, trying to see the tablet from his seat. Watson glanced sideways at him.

"These aren't street maps of Manhattan. Or subway maps."

Holmes nodded. "Very astute. The New York City subway system wasn't opened until 1904." He raised himself up a little and reached over to the tablet, swiping sideways to show a third map. This was still a scan, but much newer. There was a large legend in the bottom corner, providing a key for the various bold lines, each labeled with letters and numbers. The date on this map was 1936.

"These are maps of New York City's sewer systems," said Holmes. "Or rather, the sewer and wastewater network as it existed up to the early part of the twentieth century."

Watson went to hand him back the tablet, then she paused, holding it a few inches from his outstretched hand. A sinking feeling was rapidly developing somewhere near her diaphragm.

"Wait—this is your covert investigation? You're going to go looking in the sewers yourself?"

"Your deduction is correct, Watson."

Watson surrendered the tablet. "But these maps are antiques. Don't you have something more recent?"

Holmes shook his head. "'Antique' is one word to describe them," he said. "Another word is 'useless.'" He looked up at his partner. "Since 9/11 it is difficult, if not impossible, to get current maps of the sewer network. It is considered a security risk of the highest magnitude."

"That makes sense, I guess. Could you put in a request through Captain Gregson?"

"I could, but that would involve forms and red tape and official requests in triplicate and would take *weeks*, if not longer. That is time we simply do not have. A man's body is already cooling somewhere in a city morgue. We must act, and act now."

"Okay," said Watson, folding her arms and thinking back to their conversation in the street outside the crime scene, thinking about the myriad connections that she knew existed but which she—or Holmes—had yet to make. She spoke aloud as she ran the facts through her mind again, trying to find the links. What was it Holmes had said about verbalizing the thought process?

"So we know the man who killed Macnamara in his apartment got into and out of the building through the pumping station." She paused, cocking her head. "Macnamara was a subway driver and he happened to live next to a pumping station which provides access to the sewers. But that has to be a coincidence, right?"

Holmes leaned back in his chair, and clasped his hands over his stomach as he gently rocked back on the springs.

"Apparently Macnamara had only moved into that apartment six months ago. And it took a sizeable, if not *unmanageable*, chunk of his income to make the rent."

"So he took the apartment *because* of the pumping station."

"It seems most probable," said Holmes. "Our Mr. Macnamara worked as a subway train driver, an occupation that meant he spent almost his entire working life underground." Holmes unclasped his hands and mimed "underground" with a wave of his fingers that looked like he was trying to hypnotize a cat.

Watson slumped into the armchair nearby and rubbed her face. Holmes turned in his chair. When she dropped her hands onto her lap, he was watching her with an eyebrow raised and one side of his mouth curled up in amusement.

He was enjoying the mystery, she could see. For Holmes, the art of deduction was like a long and complex chess game.

To win—to find not just the clues but to link them all together, thereby solving the mystery and catching the killer—you had to think several moves ahead. Watson suspected—no, *knew*—that this was a natural skill Holmes possessed, a gift he'd been born with, like perfect pitch or an ear for languages.

But she also knew that the art of deduction, while partly an innate, wild talent, was something that could also be taught, learned. It took work, a lot of it, but it was a skill.

And the work, she had to admit, was something she too had grown to love.

And then she had it. She snapped her fingers and shot forward to balance on the edge of the armchair.

"The pills," she said. "He'd bought a bulk supply of beta-carotene."

Holmes poked an index finger at Watson, a clear indication she was on the same track as he was.

"Because," he said, "he thought it would improve his night vision. Mr. Macnamara might have worked underground for his day job, but he'd hardly need the eyesight of a cat to drive a subway train."

"So he was spending time underground—in the *dark*—doing something else." Watson slumped back in the armchair. "But doing what?"

"Perhaps you will find this enlightening." Holmes stood and grabbed the tablet off the desk. He tapped at the screen a couple of times, then walked over to Watson and handed her the device. She cast her eyes over the screen. It was an email.

"From Detective Bell?"

Holmes nodded and waggled his finger at the screen. "Crime-scene photos. Worth a look."

Watson raised an eyebrow, unsure she really wanted to look at the dead body of the poor man again, but she scrolled down regardless. There was a series of photos embedded in Bell's message, showing Macnamara's apartment, the body *in situ*, the scattering of beta-carotene boxes. Watson frowned, and moved to the next image, and the next.

"Okay," she said, "that's weird."

There were a dozen images in total, taken from several different angles. The pictures were dark—Watson immediately recognized them as CSU photos taken under UV light. Large areas of the floor, the walls, even the furniture glowed a bright bluish-white. There was a plastic triangular police marker placed next to each patch.

Watson lowered the tablet and looked at Holmes. "That can't all be blood?"

Holmes rocked on his heels and nodded. "No, it isn't. The CSU team used luminol to try and trace the route Macnamara's killer took into and out of the apartment—confirming, of course, our own discovery of his escape route."

Watson looked back at the photos. Holmes crouched beside her and pointed at the glowing blue patches.

"But their UV camera picked up something else. It was all over the apartment. And," he said, reaching forward to swipe through a few photos, before settling on the final one, "all over Macnamara too."

The last image was a close-up of the deceased's hands, palms-up. They glowed from wrist to fingertip.

Watson looked at Holmes. "UV ink?"

Holmes chewed on his bottom lip. "That's my guess. But he must have had a small accident and broken a pen to spill it everywhere like that. Of course, the problem with UV ink is that without a lamp it's invisible. He might not even have known he'd got it all over his apartment."

Watson handed the tablet back to Holmes. Holmes returned it to his desk and lowered himself back in his chair. "Fluorescing ink being ideal for leaving secret messages in the dark, of course."

Watson ran her hands through her hair as she took the

facts in. Macnamara was into something deep, something connected to both his job and, on the face of it, the other tunnels that crisscrossed below the city streets.

Something deep enough, dangerous enough, that it had cost him his life.

"Okay," she said after a few moments' thought. She gestured back to the tablet resting on the desk. "What exactly do you plan to do while Gregson and I are at the museum, if you can't use those old maps?"

Holmes swiveled his chair back to his main computer. "There I have enlisted the help of an expert. It is vital on occasions such as these that one acknowledges one's own shortcomings, don't you think?" He looked back over his shoulder at Watson. Watson's frown sent him turning back to the computer, which he waved at with a theatrical flourish. "Enter Judge D."

Watson pulled herself out of the armchair and went back to her desk. She leaned across it on her hands and peered at the screen.

She'd been right. Holmes had a chat window open on an Internet forum, his ID showing as **SUMATRAN RAT**. Watson only scanned the last few exchanges, but he seemed to be in the middle of a lengthy debate with just one other user, **JUDGE_D**. According to the status bar at the bottom of the chat frame, there were a lot of other users—perhaps even hundreds—logged in, following the discussion but not, as far as Watson could see, daring to interrupt. She knew the feeling.

"And Judge D is?"

Holmes cracked his knuckles and quickly composed a new reply, then hit enter. Almost at once, the chat indicator showed Judge D composing his response. Holmes leaned back and watched the screen.

"I haven't the foggiest," he said. "But he is one of the most active members on this particular forum. They call themselves 'urban historians,' but more accurately the pastime is described as the art of urban *exploration*, which is—"

"Illegal," said Watson. She folded her arms.

Holmes glanced up at her, his jaw moving silently as he rolled his hands in front of him, his train of thought derailed.

"Well," he said eventually, "I was going to say the fine and illustrious endeavor of exploring abandoned, disused or otherwise secret facilities, but I will admit your description is also accurate." He gave Watson a sheepish look.

Watson glanced at the screen again. Underneath Holmes's username was a forum-join date of April 2005.

"You've been a member quite a while."

"I used to pursue the hobby myself with a group of explorers back in London, a decade ago. In point of fact I learned a great deal that proved extremely useful later in my work with Scotland Yard. But I haven't been particularly active in the community for some time. The thing with addiction is that it tends to narrow one's interests somewhat."

"So how is this Judge D going to help?"

"Maps!" said Holmes. "His team has been exploring the tunnels and waterworks on the west side of Manhattan for months. He says he'll show me a thing or two."

"Did you tell him?"

"About the murder? No. In fact, I will admit I was unsure as to the value of a personal exploration into this city's vast underground wonderland, at least without more information to go on. I logged into the explorer's forum simply to ascertain whether any of its members had seen or heard anything unusual recently. Naturally, once you start making inquiries of that nature on such a forum, other users are drawn like bees to honey."

Watson raised an eyebrow. "Including Judge D?"

"Including Judge D! Engaging chap, must be said. As it happens, he has been planning a little subterranean expedition for this very evening. I've just spent the last hour teasing him with information I have about a secret government facility I once stumbled into under Whitehall in London. A few pages of that and Judge D was more than happy for me to tag along in exchange for a more detailed report about what I found down there."

"And what did you find?"

Holmes grinned. "A gentleman must keep his secrets, Watson."

Watson rolled her eyes. "Sounds more like something you'd troll conspiracy theorists with on swirltheory.com."

Holmes sighed. "'Troll' is such a strong word, Watson. But no, this is genuine personal experience."

"Why doesn't it surprise me that breaking and entering disused government facilities counts as a hobby for you."

"You misunderstand. The Whitehall bunker was far from disused."

At this she just shook her head again, then checked her watch. It was heading on for two in the afternoon.

"Okay, whatever," she said, "I need to run some errands before I get ready for the museum. I'll be a couple of hours."

She scooped her bag from the floor next to the armchair and headed for the hallway.

"Ah, excellent," said Holmes. Watson heard him rifling through some papers and she paused at the porch, one hand on the door handle. Holmes appeared a moment later from the front room, proffering her a folded note. "I have my own list of requirements for this evening's excursion."

Watson took the slip of paper and unfolded it. She looked up at Holmes, who waved his hands dismissively.

"Just some batteries and a few other bits and pieces."

"Including UV marker pens?"

Holmes nodded. "Useful for writing in the dark, remember? I've noted down the address of a stationer's that carries my preferred brand."

Watson examined the note again. She read his directions jotted at the bottom.

"This is halfway across the city," she said, but when she looked up, Holmes had gone.

Watson pocketed the note and pulled on her hat. "And do something about that pig while I'm gone," she called out. "It's starting to smell."

There was no reply save for the sound of Holmes typing furiously.

With a sigh, Watson let herself out.

7

A LITTLE OVERTIME

Marcus Bell stood in the Captain's office, notebook in one hand, cellphone hanging heavy inside his jacket pocket. He was expecting a call—an important one—and pulling overtime at the precinct was cramping his weekend just a little.

It wasn't that he minded, as such. Hell, he'd sworn a duty to serve and protect and the detective's shield clipped to his jacket wasn't just a badge of identification, it was a badge of *honor*. New York City was a big place full of bad things and he was doing his damnedest to make it just that little bit safer.

Police work was a vocation, but one that came at a price. Too many officers—good ones, the *best* ones—burned themselves out as they did their bit fighting for justice. Bell was good, even if he said so himself. Hell, even Sherlock Holmes had said he was "adequate" that one time. High praise indeed. Bell also knew the Captain was even better. The city needed cops like them. The city also needed to make sure cops like them didn't drive themselves into the ground pursuing a case.

"Something on your mind?"

Bell blinked out of his reverie and, out of habit, smoothed

down his tie. Captain Gregson stroked his chin as he looked up at his subordinate from behind his desk.

"Ah, no, sir," said Bell. "Just been doing some long hours, that's all."

The Captain nodded. "You and me both."

Bell rolled his neck and straightened his back. "Just doing the job, sir."

Gregson chuckled, then he tapped himself on the breastbone. "*I'm* on duty. You're not. Unless you're in desperate need of the overtime I suggest you head home."

"What about the Macnamara case?"

"What about it? I've got the Water Board up in arms about unauthorized entry to their pumping station and we're still trying to locate the victim's next of kin to notify them."

Bell pursed his lips. "No luck with the sister, then?"

"Nope. We found some contact details but it looks like they're years out of date." Gregson glanced over the paperwork on his desk. "Go home, Detective," he said, then he looked up. "Or don't you think I can handle a homicide investigation?" The Captain grinned.

Bell smiled and shook his head, and then his phone started buzzing. This was the call.

"Hey, I gotta—"

The Captain waved him off. "Get out of here!"

"Thank you, sir," said Bell. He turned on his heel and left the office, fishing his phone out of his pocket as he closed the door behind him. Glancing at the screen before he hit answer, he saw the number of the caller but, instead of his friend's picture, the familiar green and white elliptical logo of the New York Jets.

Bell grinned to himself. Time to get a little R & R on.

He thumbed the answer button and drew the phone's mouthpiece close to his lips, tucking his head down as if discussing a matter of the highest confidentiality.

"Ah, Mr. Pizzolatto," said Bell, "I think you'll find this is a secure line."

His friend's laugh was deep and loud. "Commissioner Bell, I apologize."

"Yeah right," said Bell, snickering as he walked back to his desk and sank into the chair. Around him was the quiet hush of the Saturday day shift hard at work. "Just let me talk to my BFF the governor and then maybe you can call me that, Sammy."

"Oh, you didn't know?" Sammy's voice was thick with sarcasm. "The governor is coming with us tonight."

"I thought he was a Giants supporter?"

"That's a classic burn, buddy. I think you can kiss the commissioner's job goodbye."

"You might be right."

"You got the tickets?"

Bell patted his chest. Two seats, row eleven at the fifty-yard line of the MetLife stadium. Almost, but not quite, the best seats in the house. Tonight's game was going to be *epic*.

"You can count on it."

Bell looked up as the door to Gregson's office opened. He let his chair swing back to the vertical as the Captain appeared in the doorway. Gregson lifted the coat from the back of his door and nodded at Bell.

Bell raised his phone to his mouth again. "Hey, see you at six, right?"

"On the dot, bro."

"Later."

Bell locked the phone and placed it on his desk, then stood. Gregson stopped by his desk and pointed down to the other end of the precinct. "Out, Detective," he said. "You're not allowed back in here until Monday. I, meanwhile, have got to go pick up a tux."

Bell lifted an eyebrow. "Getting ready for a big night out?"

Gregson shook his head, holding up a hand. "Ms. Watson

and I are going to the museum gala tonight using the tickets we found at Macnamara's apartment. We need to figure out his connection, see if anyone there knows him."

Bell nodded. "Nobody knows he's dead though, right?"

"Not until we can find his sister."

"Surprised Holmes isn't going to the party."

Gregson's smile was tight. "Trust me, this isn't going to be a party. Anyway, he just emailed. He says he's onto another lead and will fill us in as and when."

With that, Bell's phone buzzed on his desk. Sammy must've forgotten something of no doubt vital importance to their night out.

Gregson glanced at the phone, then looked up at Bell with a smile Bell wasn't sure he liked the look of. Then the Captain turned and headed out.

Bell watched his departing back, his hands on his hips, then he scooped the phone up without checking the caller ID.

"Detective Bell at your beck and call," he said into the phone. "What did you forget this time?"

"I can assure you I have an excellent memory," said Sherlock Holmes, "but I am pleased to find one of New York's finest so eager and ready for a new assignment, even outside of your normal shift. Most excellent. I shall have to reassess my opinion of the New York Police Department."

Bell's shoulders dropped. "Sorry, Holmes, I was expecting someone else."

"Ah, well, in that case my opinion remains unchanged."

Bell rubbed his forehead and sat back down. He was on his way home. He had tickets to a football game he'd been looking forward to for days, with an old friend visiting from out of town who he hadn't seen in months. The last thing he wanted right now was to fight his way out of a circular conversation with his department's consulting detective.

"Look, I'm about to head out," said Bell. "The Captain's

the primary on the Macnamara case."

"It is your services I require, Detective Bell," said Holmes. "Come to the brownstone at seven this evening wearing something waterproof."

"Waterproof?" Holmes's unexpected call had set Bell's teeth on edge. This was so not how he was going to spend his Saturday night.

"Holmes, I—"

The phone was dead. Holmes had rung off. Bell pulled the phone from his ear and stared at the screen for a few seconds. The Captain was long gone, and glancing around the precinct, all Bell could see were other detectives buried in their own paperwork, chasing their own cases, their own investigations.

Of course he could ring Holmes back, but he knew it was no good, even if Holmes answered. One thing the consultant was good at was guilt-tripping. Anything less than total commitment to the task at hand was met with withering sarcasm and disappointment that Holmes was not afraid to show. And...

And Bell knew that he really had no choice. If Holmes was onto something, if there was some way that Bell could help solve the murder—maybe even *prevent* others from taking place—then it was his duty to act. His own disappointment aside, he thought again about duty, and about his vocation, and about what he had to do.

With slumped shoulders, Bell flicked through the contacts on his phone until he found Sammy Pizzolatto. Sighing at the logo of the New York Jets, Bell hit call and lifted the phone to his ear.

"Hey, Sammy," he said, wincing in anticipation of the news he had to break. "Listen, something's come up. I've got some work to do tonight.

"Yeah, I know. But trust me, it's pretty important."

8

THE TEAM ASSEMBLES

Bell sniffed and idly lifted the edge of the black cloth between two fingers. Beneath the cloth he saw something metal, silvery. He frowned and lifted the cloth higher.

He, the Captain, and Holmes had been waiting in the front room of the brownstone Holmes and Watson shared, Gregson looking good in his rented tuxedo and Holmes standing across the threshold that separated the room from the hallway and stairs, his back to them ramrod straight, his hands curled into tight fists by his side. Holmes was distracted and silent—*Impatient, just like a kid*, thought Bell—and had so far mainly ignored the two cops. He was already wearing his navy-blue pea coat, ready to head out the door as soon as Watson joined them.

Bell froze as he revealed a silver revolver under the cloth, attached to some kind of wheel. It looked like there was more than one gun, too.

"I'm in the middle of a delicate experiment," said Holmes, his back still to the two detectives. "So if you would be so kind?"

Bell let the cloth drop and glanced at the Captain. Gregson raised an eyebrow, but Bell just shook his head and did his best to look innocent, turning his back to the hidden machine and clasping his hands in front of him.

"Don't ask," said Bell.

"Watson!" Holmes called out, making Bell jump. "Time is of the essence!" He strode over to the foot of the stairs and looked up. "If I knew it would take you this long to get ready, I would have put on a spread for our detective friends. Perhaps some sherry and *amuse-bouches*." He cocked his head, clearly waiting for a response, but when none came he merely huffed and marched back into the front room, resuming his previous position almost exactly.

Gregson checked his watch. "It's only seven fifteen," he said. "The museum gala doesn't start until eight. We've got time, don't worry."

Holmes turned to face him, his expression dark. "None of us have time," he said, "not when there is a killer on the loose."

Bell and the Captain exchanged a look. Gregson turned back to Holmes and sighed. "Okay, point taken."

Holmes faced Bell, looking him up and down. Bell, suddenly self-conscious, adjusted the zip of his New York Jets hoodie. Holmes scrunched his nose.

"I said to wear something waterproof."

Bell glanced down, like he needed the reminder. The sneakers below his black jeans were *not* waterproof, he knew that, but then he didn't really have much else to choose from. He also didn't really want to think about why Holmes had made the request. His Saturday night was just getting worse and worse.

He glanced down at Holmes's feet, and saw he was wearing dark green, knee-high rubber boots with adjustable buckles at the top. The white label on the top front, outlined in red, just said HUNTER.

Bell shrugged. "Yeah, well, you get what you get. Not all of us can be so well prepared."

Holmes nodded, like Bell's statement held some deeply

profound meaning. He lifted a foot, pointing it in the detective's direction.

"Hunter wellington boots. The Queen wears these, you know? I couldn't leave England without stocking up. I have a closetful, if you would care to borrow a pair? You're a ten. I believe I can accommodate that size."

Bell rolled his eyes. "I rest my case," he muttered, then he held out his hands. "I'm good, thanks."

Holmes's eyes flicked down to Bell's inappropriate footwear. "So be it," said Holmes, then he returned his attention to the busy task of waiting. After a few seconds he nodded again, more to himself than anyone in the room. "But don't say I didn't warn you."

A few moments later a door opened somewhere upstairs. Standing next to Bell, Gregson withdrew his hands from his pockets and straightened his jacket and black bowtie. Bell grinned at him, then turned to face Watson as she descended the stairs and entered the front room. His eyes widened.

Watson looked momentarily flustered, then she smiled. She was wearing a striking black strapless dress which stopped just short of her knees, with a plunging neckline and peaked bustier trimmed in white. Around her neck was a simple silver chain with a large mirrored pendant, circular but curved. Completing the outfit were a pair of chunky yellow heels and a black clutch.

Holmes stepped up close to Watson, and clasped his hands behind his back. Bell saw Watson's smile evaporate as Holmes looked her up and down before he stepped back and nodded appreciatively.

"Adequate, Watson," said Holmes.

"Gee, thanks," she said.

Holmes pointed at her shoes. "I see you have been reading those magazines again."

Bell's eyebrow went up and Gregson glanced at him, clearly

bewildered by the turns of Holmes's conversation. Holmes, apparently noticing, turned to face them. He waved one hand in the air as he spoke. "Of the five to ten pairs of shoes every woman must apparently own, one pair at least should be yellow." He paused. "A much maligned color, I agree."

Gregson blew his cheeks out, then stepped forward. He reached out and took Watson's hand in his, bringing it to his lips as he gave her knuckles a gentle kiss.

"Ignore sourpuss here," he said. "I think you look beautiful, Ms. Watson." He stuck out his elbow. Watson smiled and hooked her arm through his.

"Captain," she said, with a bow of the head. "You're not looking so bad yourself." She faced Holmes. "We all good to go?"

"We are indeed," said Holmes. "I suggest we reconvene here at midnight for a debrief." He turned to Gregson and Watson. "If for any reason you cannot make it back in time, send a text. If you are not here and I haven't received a message, I will assume the worst. Don't forget who we are likely to be dealing with." Holmes's expression was tight, the muscles at the back of his jaw hard bundles under his skin. Bell felt his heart rate kick up a notch at the thought of what they might be in for.

"Understood," said Gregson. "We'll be careful." He looked at Watson, who nodded, and the pair turned and headed toward the front door. Bell, hands stuffed in the pockets of his hoodie, followed.

"Are you sure I can't tempt you?"

Bell stopped and turned. Holmes had lifted his foot again, indicating his green wellington boots.

Bell shook his head. "Thanks, but I'll manage somehow. So long as you're not planning on dragging me through the sewers I think I'll be okay."

Holmes smiled and dropped his booted foot. "My dear detective," he said. "I wouldn't dream of it."

9

THE WAITING GAME

Bell and Holmes sat in the dark in Watson's car, parked up on the broad sidewalk underneath the overpass of the Joe DiMaggio Highway at the end of West 59th Street. Ahead of them, as 59th Street cleared the overpass, it turned a sharp ninety degrees to head southwest. Across the corner was the narrow end of the Hudson River Greenway, and the two-story portico façade that marked the entrance to the New York City Department of Sanitation's Hudson River dock. The traffic was light but steady, and since pulling up by one of the four large prefab huts erected under the overpass for construction workers doing some nearby maintenance, just a handful of pedestrians had crisscrossed in front of the dock gates as they walked or jogged along the Greenway.

Bell cracked his window a notch and breathed in the cool evening air. They'd been sitting in the car for a half hour, and Holmes hadn't spoken in nearly all that time. He was half-turned in the driver's seat, his back to Bell, his attention focused on the view out of the rear.

But enough was enough. Bell turned in the passenger seat, trying to get comfortable, trying to see what it was that Holmes was looking for. The car rocked a little on its suspension, eliciting a tut from Holmes, although he didn't move his gaze from the rear view.

"Look," said Bell, "I've been on plenty of stakeouts, but it helps if I know what I'm watching for."

Holmes's eyes flickered left and right as he scanned the street behind them.

"Holmes?"

"We are not watching for anything. We are waiting."

"Waiting for...?"

"A contact. Someone who, I hope, is going to be of great material assistance to this case."

Bell frowned, and turned back around in his seat to face the front. Contact? Nobody had mentioned a contact before. How much was Holmes holding back on the case? What else had he discovered during the day while Bell and Gregson had been at the precinct?

There was something off about Holmes's mood. Okay, sure, so Holmes was obtuse, rude and childish, very often all at once. He was generally infuriating to deal with and occasionally even impossible to talk to. But that was just how it was. Sherlock Holmes was Sherlock Holmes, and after nearly three years working with the consultant, Bell was well used to it. Because he also knew that Sherlock Holmes was a *bona fide* genius, and that here he was, sitting with him in the car, chasing the case. Bell knew that while some at the NYPD viewed the arrangement his precinct had with the consultant with little-disguised contempt, he also knew there were many more detectives in the city who would give their right arm to be in his place. Even if that meant missing the New York Jets.

Bell frowned at the thought, and pushed it out of his mind. He needed to be on top of his own game tonight.

But something was up. Holmes was concealing something,

something he didn't like to show but which Bell knew affected him like it affected every other human being—as much as Holmes tried to demonstrate he wasn't the same as everyone else on the planet.

Sherlock Holmes was anxious. Bell could sense it. Anxiety was all part of the job, but like any good cop, Bell used that feeling, that energy, turning it around and feeding it back into the case at hand. It was the only way you could handle the pressure.

And as much as Holmes liked to portray himself as cool and calm and in control, sometimes he wasn't. Sometimes he tried to hide it. Sometimes he wasn't very good at the deception.

"Look," said Bell, then he stopped, unsure for a moment, not of *what* to say, but *how* to say it. But then he decided to just go for it. Holmes preached rationalism, the scientific method. Bell didn't quite follow some of what Holmes talked about, but he knew he would probably appreciate it if he didn't try to cushion his words.

Holmes spun around in the seat until he was sitting sideways, facing Bell. Bell flinched back in the passenger seat.

"Feeling guilty, are we?" asked Holmes.

Bell blinked. "What?"

"Guilty," said Holmes. "About standing your friend up."

"How did you—?"

"Your friend," Holmes continued. "The one you haven't seen in some weeks. The friend who, with some careful planning, and in your honor, very graciously spent a lot of money on what are quite possibly the second-best tickets in the entire MetLife stadium."

Bell sighed loudly and shook his head. "I'm not guilty, Holmes, I'm *pissed* is what I am." He slapped the top of the car seat in frustration. "I'm missing a game with my boy so we can sit here doing... whatever the hell it is that you won't tell me we're doing."

At this, Holmes merely smiled, then turned again to look out the rear. "I was not criticizing, Detective, merely *observing*," he said. "But guilt is a natural response. I don't expect you to have yet learned the self-control required to recognize and quell such emotions, but I have hope yet. There is no need to apologize."

Bell frowned, his brow furrowing. "*Apologize?* Are you even listening to me?"

Holmes didn't even turn around. Bell sighed again. Of course Holmes had worked it out, but he'd learned from past experience not to bother asking how. He probably just knew the game was on tonight and realized it was no coincidence Bell was wearing a New York Jets hoodie. Hell, maybe Holmes had bugged his phone and had listened to his conversation with Sammy. Nothing would surprise him about the consultant's methods now.

And maybe it wasn't Holmes who was anxious. Maybe—*dammit*—it was Bell.

"Okay, fine," said Bell, making a conscious effort to calm himself. "Maybe you can ease this guilt of mine by telling me what we are actually doing? Who are we waiting for?"

Holmes glanced sideways at him and grinned. "A contact."

Well, that clears that up. Bell ran his tongue around his teeth, refocusing on the case. He decided on a different tack. "So you think the victim was involved in drug-running then?"

Bingo. This got a response: Holmes nodded, and he turned back in the seat to face the front, then reached up and adjusted the rearview mirror.

"How else would you explain the large amount of cash hidden in Macnamara's bread bin, the soil residue from South America tracked into the carpet, the manner of our victim's violent end?"

Bell nodded. "And his invite to an exhibition of Colombian artifacts."

"Quite so."

Bell frowned. "But it's a bit obvious, isn't it?"

Holmes glanced sideways at the detective. "Go on."

"Well," said Bell, getting comfortable in his seat. "We seem to be running on the basis that the exhibition is a front, a way to smuggle drugs into the city from South America, right? Our subway driver had an invite to the gala, so he had something to do with it. Something they paid him a lot of money for."

A smile spread across Holmes's face. "But it doesn't add up, does it?"

Bell leaned forward. "No, it doesn't. Drugs come in and out of the city all the time—you don't need to hide your import business behind a fancy high-profile museum show. And you don't execute someone who's in on the plan and leave all that money behind."

"Indeed not," said Holmes, nodding. "And even if we are half-right, on an operation of this scale, you'd have hired assassins to carry out the disposal cleanly. Trained killers, experts at their craft. The man who shot Liam Macnamara had never fired an Uzi before."

"And he left the money right where it was. He didn't even know it was there." Bell rubbed his chin. "Rival gang taking out the competition?"

"A rival gang who used the same subterranean route Macnamara had been traversing the last six months? Unlikely."

Holmes leaned forward, peering into the rearview, then he turned in the seat to look out the back. "Time to begin," he said.

Bell glanced at Holmes, then followed his pointed finger. Behind them, at the corner of the narrow 12th Avenue that joined West 57th just before the overpass, someone wearing a baseball hat was loitering, hands in their pockets, a slim pack strapped to their back.

"Time for *what* to begin?" asked Bell, but Holmes was already stepping out of the car.

With a sigh, Bell opened his door and followed Holmes back to the intersection.

10

JUDGE_D

Holmes, hands in the pockets of his pea coat, came to a stop at the curb. Bell followed a step behind, casting his gaze around. They were the only pedestrians out but nobody driving by was paying them any heed. Bell chastised himself for being so overly cautious, but then he had no idea what Holmes was up to. It always paid to be prepared.

Holmes's contact was leaning against the ornate green iron streetlamp just down from the corner of 12th Avenue. He was short, slim, and was wearing baggy jeans and a plaid shirt, the color bleached out by the orangey glow of the light above. Bell couldn't see his face, which was hidden in the deep shadow cast by the peak of his baseball cap.

Holmes cocked his head. "Judge D, I presume?"

A flare from the shadow, the smell of tobacco. Holmes's contact took a drag on a cigarette, then rolled around the lamppost, keeping his head down.

Another drag on the cigarette and the baseball cap nodded in Bell's direction.

"Who's he?"

Bell frowned and took a step forward before Holmes

gently grabbed his left arm and pulled him back a little. Judge D jerked back from the lamp as Bell approached, lifting his head as he did so, the streetlight finally catching his face. He was in his late forties, perhaps older, with thin pockmarked cheeks covered in a fuzzy salt-and-pepper stubble. His graying hair escaped in wisps from under the baseball cap. He was rake thin and shorter than either Bell or Holmes, and he looked suddenly afraid, the self-confident pose long gone. Bell stopped where he was and held up his hands.

"Hey, sorry," he said. "No need to be so nervous."

Judge D threw his cigarette to the sidewalk. "No need to be nervous?" He laughed and waved at Holmes. "What the hell, man? You thought you'd bring a *cop* with you?" He shook his head and looked at the sidewalk, one hand creeping up to pull at the brim of his cap. He swore at the ground and scratched at his whiskers.

"How do you know he's with the police?" asked Holmes.

Judge D looked up, his expression drawn, desperate. He gestured at Bell. "Trust me, I can tell. Come on, man. What gives? I'm doing you a favor here, man. I don't just take any tourist on these little walks."

Holmes nodded. "I understand, and believe me when I say I appreciate your kind offer." He turned to Bell. "Detective Bell, this is Victor Judd. Victor Judd, this is Detective Marcus Bell of the New York City Police Department."

Judge D sucked in a breath and interlocked his fingers on top of his baseball cap. "Holy crap, man! You know my real name too? What. The. Hell."

Holmes sighed. "Look, I also know you have a brother called Robert and that you are quite adept at the rhythm guitar, which you play not infrequently in a covers band whose singer is a former flame of yours. But none of those facts are particularly relevant either, are they?"

Bell sighed and held up a hand. "Hold on, Holmes. Are

you going to explain what's going on?" He waved at Victor. "Who is this guy and where is he taking you, exactly?"

"Hey, Axel Foley," said Judge D, "I'm right here, douche."

Bell turned to him, hands on his hips. "Hey, cool it, pal," he said, taking another step toward the other man, who took a step backward himself, nearly tripping on the curb. Holmes quickly stepped between them, holding his hands out. He faced Bell.

"Detective, please, I've gone to a lot of trouble to secure Judge D's assistance."

"Assistance for what? I still don't know what any of this is about. Or what *I'm* doing here."

Holmes gestured to his contact. "Judge D here is an urban explorer, Detective. He is part of a group who have done remarkable work mapping the undercity beneath our feet."

As Holmes spoke, Bell could see the glitter in his eyes, the fire sparking as his plan started to unfold. Bell pursed his lips.

"I'm afraid to ask my next question," he said, glaring at Judge D.

Holmes grinned, nodding. "Judge D has agreed to take us with him on a short tour of the tunnels underneath the streets of Hell's Kitchen and Central Park West, yes. He has been planning this trip for some weeks, and has most graciously invited us to accompany him." Holmes turned back to Judge D and gave him a small bow. "An invitation we are most grateful to accept." Then he turned back to Bell.

"Tunnels, huh?" Bell shook his head. "And by tunnels I suppose you mean *sewers*?"

Holmes lifted one of his feet again. "I did offer to lend you a pair of wellingtons."

Bell glanced down at Judge D's feet. The urban "explorer" was wearing what looked like hiking boots. He looked down at his own sneakers, and sighed.

"The Water Board is already bugging the department

about your little B and E at the pumping station. I suppose it's not worth me asking whether you got a permit this time?"

"Indeed it is not. Judge D and his friends operate outside the law, shall we say."

Judge D slid his thumbs under the straps of his pack and shook his head, backing away slowly. "Yeah, well, I don't think I'm taking you anywhere tonight. Not with him. Sorry." He nodded at Bell, then turned on the toes of his boots and, pulling his cap down, headed to the corner, turning to walk inland down West 57th.

Holmes sighed. "Wait!" he called, moving to follow. Judge D slowed and turned so he was walking backward, but he didn't say anything and his face had vanished into the shadow of his cap once again. Holmes fumbled for something in his coat pocket, and a moment later held something small and black between a thumb and forefinger. Bell moved closer to get a better look, and as Holmes held it up the silver cap on the end of the object caught the streetlight and glinted brightly.

It was a USB stick. Bell raised an eyebrow and looked at Judge D.

The small man stopped and lifted his head, so Bell could see the lower half of his face. His stubbled chin moved around as he chewed on his bottom lip.

"*Whitehall*," Holmes whispered. He waggled the USB stick. "Oh, the things I found in that government bunker."

Bell blinked, fairly sure that Holmes was turning up the campfire creep to get Judge D interested, but he had to admit he was curious himself. Holmes glanced sideways at him, the glint in his eye not entirely from the streetlamp on the corner.

Judge D walked back to the pair, extracted one hand from the strap of his backpack, and reached toward the stick. Holmes didn't move, except to pull the stick slightly farther away. Judge D's eyes moved from Holmes's face to the stick and back.

Bell had no clue what was going on. Whatever Holmes had saved onto the stick—did he mean Whitehall, London? Holmes had mentioned a *government* bunker. Bell really didn't want to ask about that—it seemed to be more than just a little interesting to Judge D. No, more than interesting. *Intoxicating*.

Then Holmes returned his hand and the data stick to his pocket and turned around to face Bell.

"*But*, never mind," he said. He made a show of checking the empty street and started heading back toward the car. "Come along, Detective, I'm sure we can find a better way to spend our Saturday night—"

"Okay, *fine*."

Holmes stopped in his tracks. He glanced sideways at Bell, a small smile playing over his lips. Both men turned. Judge D lifted his baseball cap and ran a hand through his hair. Finally, with a slump of the shoulders, he sighed, then grinned.

"Okay, dude. Let's do it."

He held out his hand, palm up.

Holmes took a pace forward and brought out the USB stick again. He held it along the edges with a finger and thumb, twisting it in the streetlight like it was a rare jewel, then he handed it over. It disappeared into Judge D's pocket. The explorer nodded at Bell.

"But not him. I agreed to take you with me, but I don't want anything to do with the police. I've been planning this trip a long time and I don't need the law knowing where I'll be going."

Bell held up his hands. "Hey, suits me." He checked his watch, a sudden thought occurring to him. If he was lucky, he might just be able to catch the second half. Sammy had only taken the single ticket, insisting that his old friend join him if he got the chance. "If you don't need me then I'll say goodnight."

"We still need you, Detective," said Holmes. He turned back to Judge D and gave the gnarled explorer a nod. "I propose that we go into the tunnels as a pair, while my colleague here waits at the entrance to ensure we are not followed."

Judge D shrugged. "Followed? Whatever." Then he nodded down the street, back toward the underpass. "We go that way, take a right into the Greenway. It's the easiest place to get into the system from here."

Holmes nodded vigorously. "Excellent. Lead the way."

The pair headed off. Bell paused, his fingers trailing around the cool frame of his cellphone as it sat nestled in the pocket of his hoodie.

Then he sighed, shook his head, and followed the other two. It looked like he wasn't going to get out of it that easily.

11

WATSON AND THE CAPTAIN CASE THE GALA

" I don't know about you, but I'm starting to feel a little underdressed."

Watson glanced at Gregson and shook her head. "Don't be silly, you look fine. We'll fit right in."

Gregson chuckled, casting a quick look at Watson's elegant attire. "Easy for you to say."

The gala evening at the American Museum of Natural History was exactly that, but if Watson was honest with herself, she hadn't really been sure what to expect. Sure, she'd been to her fair share of gallery openings and special members' evenings, to venues ranging from microscopic art studios in Brooklyn right up to a champagne reception she'd been dragged along to at the Guggenheim by her surgical consultant back when she'd been a resident. But a grand, invitation-only opening of a museum exhibition was a new one. As their taxi had pulled up outside the museum's grand entrance on Central Park West, Gregson and Watson both peered out of the cab windows to look. Gregson let out a low whistle and turned to Watson, his eyebrows raised.

His reaction was understandable.

The entire front of the museum was lit not by the

regular floodlights that came on every night, illuminating one of Manhattan's landmark buildings, but by two giant projectors set up on either side of the entrance. The museum frontage consisted of four columns, two on each side, with a high arched entrance; onto the columned façade on each side were projected two huge images of what must have been the star attractions from the Colombian exhibition—on the left, a golden mask, roughly circular, the facial features stylized and simple, but none the less impressive; on the right, another artifact in gold, this one the stylized figure of a man with a bird's face, the beak and feathered head vastly exaggerated in scale.

Watson and Gregson exited their cab, Gregson paying the fare. All along the sidewalk, cars far more salubrious than their own transport were pulling up in a steady stream, unloading guests dressed to the nines.

"I told you I'm underdressed," Gregson muttered to Watson as, arms linked, they headed for the steps leading up to the broad sidewalk outside the museum entrance.

"Nonsense," said Watson, but she cast her eyes around their fellow guests. There was a lot of haute couture on show, with jewelry to match.

Gregson adjusted his tie with his free hand. "This is a rented suit. Everyone here is in designer gear."

He had a point. The guests were high-fliers, that much was obvious.

So what was a subway driver doing with a ticket?

Once through the doors, the ushers on duty didn't say a thing as Gregson offered them the pass from Macnamara's apartment, merely offering a polite greeting and directing them through to the security desks. There were four airport-style security scanners set up in a row to screen guests as they came in.

Watson hesitated and looked at Gregson. She had nothing

to hide, but she had a feeling the Captain would be wearing his detective shield somewhere inside his tux, and there was a more than fair chance he was armed as well.

Gregson nodded and touched Watson on the shoulder. "Don't worry," he said. "I got this. Stick close."

He moved to the nearest scanner and beckoned to one of the two security guards on duty; the other was busy monitoring the scanner as an elderly lady—wearing furs complete with intact fox heads—walked through. Gregson drew close to the guard, whispering discreetly to him as he pulled his wallet from inside his jacket. Watson's view was obscured, but the guard nodded his understanding and Gregson returned his ID to his pocket. He turned to Watson and gestured for her to follow. Watson gave the security guard a smile as he sent them both around the side of the scanner.

On the other side, the gala was underway, the huge fossilized forms of the museum's famous *Allosaurus* and *Barosaurus* skeletons overlooking the guests as they sipped champagne and picked *vol-au-vents* from the roving army of servers. As Watson and Gregson took it all in, a young man in a smart black apron materialized in front of them, offering his tray of drinks. Gregson muttered his thanks as he took two glasses of champagne and passed one to Watson.

Watson sipped her drink and surveyed the room, her eyes moving from one immaculate bespoke dinner suit to the next, from one elegant designer evening gown to another. Although she'd meant what she'd said to Gregson outside, she was starting to feel pangs of sartorial jealousy herself. Her own dress hadn't exactly been cheap, but it was nothing compared to what was on display here. Gucci, Tom Ford, Vivienne Westwood. All were represented.

There was nothing about the scene that seemed to fit with the victim, Liam Macnamara. Watson leaned toward Gregson, her eyes still scanning the room.

"Do you think anyone here knew Liam?"

Gregson frowned. "Maybe. It's usually a mistake to judge by appearances..."

Watson nodded, following the Captain's train of thought. "*But*," she said.

"But somehow I don't see our train driver mixing with the rich and anonymous of Central Park West."

"Unless he was using some of the money he was paid?"

"I could think of better things to spend my ill-gotten gains on than a ticket to a fancy party."

Watson frowned and took another sip. "Which means someone here must know him."

"Agreed," said Gregson, "but remember if the vic was caught up in something fishy, then people might not be so keen to advertise that fact."

"Okay, softly, softly."

"Right." Gregson checked his watch. "And we should start to move. There must be two hundred people here and we haven't got all night."

The pair wandered the hall for a while, then came to a large sign pointing the way down a side passage lined with red velvet ropes. The sign was printed with the same golden mask that was projected onto the outside of the building. Guests came and went down the passage, carrying their drinks. Gregson gestured for Watson to go ahead of him.

They walked down the short passage and into a large, long gallery—the exhibition proper. Information panels high on the walls showed maps of the upper half of South America, with various points of interest and archeological sites marked, blocks of text description beside them. But Watson's eye was drawn to the case immediately facing them, one of dozens arranged in the room. This one stood in the center of the gallery, with enough space around it for large crowds of visitors to all get a good look.

It was the golden mask. Seeing it in person took Watson's breath away; up close, the object was stunning. It was the size of a large dinner plate, curved, but only slightly; the surface had a dull sheen that could only be twenty-four carat gold. *It didn't look like a mask you could put over your face,* Watson thought—it was the wrong shape, and if nothing else, it must weigh fifty pounds. She glanced down at the card in the corner of the case and read it aloud to Gregson.

"'Chest-plate in the shape of a mask. Muisca people, AD 600.' Wow."

"Incredible, isn't it?"

Watson and Gregson turned as a woman in a short sea-green dress walked up behind them. The newcomer nodded at the object on display.

"We believe this piece is part of the haul the Spanish conquistadors took from Lake Guatavita, in Northern Colombia in the mid-sixteenth century." The woman stepped up to the glass and folded her arms, staring at the object within. "When the Muisca appointed a new ruler, legend has it that they would coat them in gold dust and send them out into the middle of the lake on a raft loaded with gold and jewels which the leader would throw overboard as an offering to the gods. One account says that when the Spanish tried to drain the lake, they took out nearly forty tons of gold."

Watson turned to Gregson, wide-eyed. "That's amazing. And quite a lot of gold."

The woman turned around, extending her hand toward Watson, the heavy bangles on her arm clanking together. Watson hesitated, thinking that she and the Captain had been made. She forced a smile onto her face and shook the woman's hand.

"Dr. Lisa Harley," said the woman. "I'm the curator of this exhibition."

Watson relaxed. "Joan Watson. This is my... *friend,*

Thomas Gregson." She blinked, her expression tightening, but Dr. Harley didn't seem to notice anything, and certainly couldn't know that Watson had almost introduced Gregson as *Captain*. Beside her, Gregson shook the curator's hand and nodded a greeting.

"It's a pleasure to have you both here," said Dr. Harley. "And on behalf of the American Museum of Natural History and our exhibition sponsors, I'd like to thank you so much for coming. We couldn't have put this exhibition on without the help of generous benefactors such as yourselves."

Benefactors? Watson felt her eyebrows go up. Of course. That explained the high level of wealth on display—and not just in the museum cases. The gala night was a ritzy affair for rich members of the museum. Which, apparently, now included Watson and Gregson. At least, Dr. Harley thought so.

Watson sipped her champagne, burying her nose in her glass as she looked at the display, using the moment to compose her thoughts. Was the curator testing them? Surely not. She might have been responsible for managing the exhibition—and hosting the gala—but she wouldn't have bothered herself too much with the details of individual invites, would she? Besides which, she and the Captain had only managed to get in because the ticket from Macnamara's apartment *wasn't* personalized. Which meant, as far as the curator knew, Watson and Captain Gregson were just two more anonymous supporters.

"We're just glad to help," said Gregson, getting into character as he gestured with his glass to the display case. "The collection is certainly fascinating."

At this, Dr. Harley's eyes lit up. As Watson suspected, she might have been playing the perfect host, but her real interest lay in the archeology on display.

"This exhibition is the best single collection of pre-

Colombian gold outside of South America," the curator explained. "We have four hundred objects from the Museo del Oro in Bogotá, as well as items from the British Museum in London and our own collections. The artifacts span the period 1600 BC to AD 1700, covering the Muisca and Quimbaya, but also the Tairona, Tolima, Calima and Zenú people."

Gregson nodded and glanced sideways at Watson, who moved around to the other side of the case, intrigued by the glittering contents but also wanting to keep an eye on the curator as she spoke. Dr. Harley pointed out various parts of the golden chest-plate in the case, and began describing in great detail how she believed the object had been made. Gregson nodded politely and was doing his best to keep the curator talking as Watson watched.

Then, as Watson moved around to the rear of the case, where another equally large but less intricate chest-plate was on display, she noticed something. Something odd, and, she thought, important.

As Dr. Harley talked without pause, every now and then her eyes would flick up, glancing over to her left, away from Gregson on her right. Watson thought she was probably keeping an eye out for someone—as the official host of the gala, the curator would have to make sure she did the rounds of every guest, personally welcoming them, and, as with Watson and Gregson, talk about the objects in the exhibition with anyone who showed an interest.

But there was something else about the furtive glances. Harley didn't seem nervous exactly, but she was tense. Watson shook her head and sipped her champagne. She was seeing things that weren't there. Not every observation led to a deduction. One of Holmes's key lessons. Dr. Harley was tense because she was responsible for the gala evening. The academic may well have felt uncomfortable dealing with such an important social gathering as this.

And then Watson looked over to where Harley kept glancing, and she saw him.

He was Hispanic, maybe in his thirties, with the heavy muscular frame of an offensive lineman which, squeezed into a tuxedo, made him look like the kind of nightclub bouncer you really didn't want to get on the bad side of. He had a shaved head and a thick black chinstrap beard, and just visible around the collar of his shirt were the curlicues of what looked like an intricate tattoo.

The man was standing at the periphery of the exhibition hall. He wasn't holding a drink, and had no company with him as he gazed out across the crowd, his big hands clasped in front. Occasionally he would glance at Harley; then he glanced at Watson, who quickly lifted her champagne glass again and turned back to the display case.

Dr. Harley had completed her mini lecture as Watson rejoined her and Gregson on the other side of the case.

"That was wonderful and educational, thank you," said Gregson.

Dr. Harley smiled and bowed her head. "My pleasure, Mr. Gregson. Now, if you'll excuse me, I think I'm going to have to circulate. Enjoy your evening." She nodded at Watson, then slipped away across the gallery.

Gregson pulled close to Watson, nudging her with his elbow. Watson looked at him and he nodded over to the other side of the room. The big bald man was still there, his side now turned to them as he watched Dr. Harley move across the room.

Gregson licked his lips. "Is that who she kept on looking at over my shoulder?"

Watson nodded. "She was making eyes at him the whole time. He looks like a bouncer—is he security?"

"The museum has its own guards."

"Maybe he came with the objects on loan, from South America."

Gregson *hrmmed*. As they watched, the big man walked over to a waitress, holding his hand up to stop the woman in her tracks before lifting a glass of champagne from the tray.

"Okay," said Watson, "so not security. He wouldn't be drinking if he was."

Gregson turned on his heel as Watson kept her eye on the big man. A moment later the Captain nudged her again. She turned around, just as Gregson glanced at the ceiling, trying to disguise his interest as he took a sip from his glass.

"Over there," he whispered.

Watson frowned and glanced around, once again using her own glass as a barrier to detection.

There. On the other side of the room. Two more men, both Hispanic like the bald man, both wearing tuxedos that didn't quite fit over their powerful frames. This pair was watching the crowd as well, but were talking to each other.

"And one more," said Gregson. Watson glanced over and saw another man, this one shorter, more athletic than powerful, slowly walking among the guests, scanning the people left and right as he moved.

"They're watching the curator," said Gregson. Dr. Harley was now talking to an elderly couple, flashing her smile but all the while her eyes darting to the left, toward the first man Watson had spotted.

"And she's watching them," said Watson. She sighed, her shoulders slumped. "They *must* be part of a security team."

As if to confirm her suspicion, the smaller man reached Dr. Harley as he crossed the gallery. He briefly interrupted her conversation with the elderly couple, leaning in to whisper in the curator's ear. Dr. Harley nodded and the man moved away, then the curator resumed her discussion with her guests.

"Yeah, I think you're right," said Gregson. "But we should keep Dr. Harley in our sights, just in case. She seems a little *too* anxious, even with the extra security." Gregson checked his watch again. "Come on, we've got work to do. I suggest we split up, take opposite sides of the room. Work the gallery first, then meet back out in the main hall. Okay?"

Watson agreed. Gregson rubbed his chin, slid one hand into his trouser pocket, and with a wink, sauntered off into the crowd.

Watson considered her empty glass. If she was going to do some canvassing of the crowd under the guise of polite society schmoozing, she needed a prop. Switching her empty glass for a full one from a passing server, she took a breath, put on a smile, and headed for a group of guests.

12

SHERLOCK'S ADVENTURES UNDERGROUND

Judge D walked ahead of Sherlock Holmes in the dark tunnel; it was, so far, dry underfoot, and the passageway itself was large, concrete and square—they were clearly in a modern section of the New York City sewer system.

They'd entered at the Hudson River Greenway, near to the Department of Sanitation docks. As Holmes and Bell had kept watch for passersby, Judge D had extracted his own two-part gulley key from his pack, slotting the pieces together and using the tool to lift a large rectangular manhole cover on one side of the roadway. Judge D took a headlamp from his pack and slipped it around his forehead, replacing his baseball cap so its peak rested on the top of the lamp. Holmes fitted his own headlamp, pulled from the pocket of his pea coat.

They had descended the small, awkwardly placed square rungs bolted onto the side of the manhole; after a few meters, the light from above cut out as Bell slid the cover back into place with a funereal *ka-thunk*.

They'd been walking for fifteen minutes. Judge D hadn't spoken since they'd entered the system. The concrete tunnel was straight, the darkness ahead absolute.

"You haven't told me where you plan to go," said Holmes.

His guide trudged onward a few steps ahead, the edges of his plaid shirt waving as he walked, his light bobbing, casting long shadows. Although the passage was dry, the sound of rushing water came from somewhere near, and was getting closer.

Judge D gave a grunt but didn't stop walking.

Holmes rolled his lips. "You're nervous about something."

Judge D huffed and he slowed for a second, before returning to his previous pace. "Yeah, well, why's that, do you think? This trip was not meant to come with a side order of cop. What the hell am I doing here?"

"You're here because you *have* to be," said Holmes, a hint of theatricality creeping into his voice. "The thrill of exploring places abandoned, disused, *restricted*."

Judge D stopped and turned, spotting Holmes with his headlamp. Holmes spread his arms, gesturing to the gray walls around them. "Not just exploring. *Charting*. There is an entire hidden world here, a parallel universe. Millions walk the streets above our heads without ever realizing that a secret city exists beneath their feet. A secret city that only a chosen few, such as yourself, ever see. Your work is important. It's freelance social anthropology and urban history rolled into one. There are *discoveries* to be made."

Holmes dropped his arms and stepped toward his guide, the light from his lamp playing over the man's thin face. Judge D squinted, his face twisted into a frown as he stared at Holmes.

"And *that* is why you are here," said Holmes. "To solve a mystery is the greatest calling. And here we are, quite literally, standing right in the middle of one."

Judge D didn't say anything. Then he sniffed and wiped his nose with a shirt cuff. "No, man, I mean, what the hell am I doing here with you? Jeez, dramatic, much?" The explorer shook his head. "I can't believe I said you could come. You're cramping my style. I've got a serious case of the second thoughts going on here."

Holmes sighed. "Rest assured that Detective Bell will be keeping this little excursion to himself. I brought him because I am myself a consultant to the NYPD. I apologize for withholding that information, but your kind offer came at a most opportune moment for this case."

"Case?"

"A man was murdered in Hell's Kitchen this morning. I am determined to bring his killer to justice."

Judge D's eyes went wide as his frown melted away. "So... I'm helping you solve a murder?"

Holmes gave his guide a curt nod. "You are, and your assistance is most valuable, let me make that quite clear."

"Okay," said Judge D. He grinned. "I can dig that. Cool." Then the smile dropped again and Judge D pointed a finger square at Holmes's chest. "But look, your cop buddy isn't going to bust me as soon as we get back to the surface, right?"

"Victor, you can trust me." Holmes gestured into the darkness in front of them. "Shall we continue?"

Judge D glanced ahead, in the direction of travel, then looked back at Holmes, his thin face split by a lopsided grin.

"So we're solving a murder now, right?"

Holmes nodded. "A murder, yes."

"Cool," Judge D said, like it was nothing at all. He adjusted his cap. "Okay, Mr. Consultant, if you would care to follow me, I'll show you some things that'll make your eyes pop out."

They walked on, Judge D's manner now much more relaxed. As they moved ever deeper into the tunnel he became more talkative, his low voice echoing dully all around them as he gave a potted history of how he got involved with the urban explorers. Every now and again they would pause as he consulted a thick folded map he kept in his back pocket.

Twenty minutes earlier, the clean, dry concrete of the new tunnel had given way to damp, curved brick as they entered an older part of the system. The floor was wet and slimy, and water flowed freely down a channel cut into its center. From the curved ceiling hung long stringy tendrils that Judge D referred to as "snotsicles."

As they walked, Holmes scratched at the wall with his finger, which came away covered in residue that glistened blackly under his lamplight. Periodically, metal pipes emerged from the wall, ran along the tunnel, then disappeared again. There was also the occasional metal plate bolted into the brick. Reinforcement of some kind.

"This must be part of the original sewer tunnel system," he said.

Judge D nodded and came to a halt. "Yeah. This line runs nearly straight through to Central Park, diagonal under Hell's Kitchen then up to Lincoln Square." He took out the map. "Here," he said, holding it out to Holmes.

Holmes took it. The map was laminated to make it waterproof, and folded several times—how much area it covered couldn't be seen, but looking at the cartography and scale, it must have been several square miles. The map was hand drawn but with precision and skill. It was also, unlike the maps available to the general public, accurate and up to date. Holmes brought the map close to his face as he studied it. He nodded with appreciation.

"Your own work?"

Judge D shook his head. "Nah, not just me. There are several groups trying to map the system. We put them all together on the forum to try and get the full picture. Trouble is we don't really know how accurate it is. Mapping underground in the dark is difficult. Even the city planners don't know what the full network looks like."

"Really?"

"Sure, man," said Judge D. "They have teams down here too, part of some big mapping project. We've met them a few times. But the system is a mix of tunnels, pipelines, old, new, you name it. And the old stuff goes back at least a hundred and fifty years, and when you fix the old stuff and you put in the new stuff for so long you lose track of what's actually down here. Some parts of the system are abandoned but some are probably just forgotten. We've found old sections that aren't on *any* official map we've been able to get."

"Secret spaces ripe for discovery," Holmes muttered.

Judge D smiled. "Damn right."

Holmes drew a finger along the map, identifying their entry point near the Hudson River and recalling the twists and turns they'd made. Judge D's finger joined his own, tapping a spot.

"You. Are. Here," he said.

Holmes peered closer. Their tunnel was marked in black, and he could trace its course right up to the northeast where a large white empty space was labeled as Central Park. A little north from their current position, on the edge of the park, was the American Museum of Natural History.

Holmes frowned. Alongside their own tunnel were three other lines, drawn not in black but in dashed red. Holmes tilted his head as he followed them. There was something oddly familiar about one line in particular. As he watched, Judge D drew his finger up the red line, heading north, then came to a stop at an indicator. It was the "A" line subway. The other lines were labeled "B" and "1."

Holmes raised an eyebrow. "You explore the subways too?"

"Not me, but some people do. The sewer and subway systems run pretty close to each other in a lot of places. Think the tunnels are practically parallel. You can feel the trains passing."

"I suppose they would," said Holmes. There were two

other red lines, drawn with dots rather than dashes. "If those are the main lines then these are…?"

Judge D shrugged. "Service tunnels I guess, or maybe disused lines. The subway has old and abandoned tunnels just like the sewer system, although the MTA knows exactly what they have, of course. I don't go near them mostly."

"Too dangerous?"

"You got that right. Running between stations trying not to get hit by a train isn't my idea of fun. Even the old lines are used to move cars around. Exploring the subways takes a special kind of stupid, if you ask me."

Holmes chewed his bottom lip. Then he turned the map in his hands and looked at his guide.

"What's your planned route?" he asked.

Judge D tilted his head and tapped the map again. "I was planning on heading northeast a while. There's a convergence of tunnels somewhere up there. I got a look once but didn't map it properly. About time I fixed that."

Holmes stared at the map, plotting the suggested path along the carefully drawn lines.

Northeast. Now, there was a stroke of luck. If he'd understood the map correctly then northeast would take them almost underneath a very interesting locale indeed.

The American Museum of Natural History.

Holmes nodded. "Lead on."

Judge D took the map back and folded it in half, then into quarters, and held it up in front of him. His headlamp played across the tunnel as he got his bearings, then he nodded. "Just ahead we can fork left, then straight on for about a mile." He looked over his shoulder at his companion. "It gets a bit cramped up there. But it hasn't rained in a few days, so we should be pretty dry."

"Excellent," said Holmes, waving forward with a smile. "Please, after you."

Judge D grinned and headed off down the tunnel. Holmes was close behind, the knowledge that the subway and sewer systems ran close to each other in places playing on his mind.

And, if Judge D's map was accurate, one of the big sewer tunnels and one of the dotted subway services lines ran in parallel, right underneath the museum.

It seemed that motorman Liam Macnamara had indeed been spending a lot of time underground.

And not just on his subway train.

13

THE SOMETHING IN THE TUNNEL

Judge D had been right when he'd said it would get a little cramped. The brick tunnel got progressively lower, narrower, and wetter the farther north they went. They'd made several turns, more left than right, and even one backtrack when they hit a bricked-up archway. At that point, Judge D pulled a marker pen from his backpack and drew a red square on the part of the map to show where it needed correcting.

It was warm in the tunnels, and humid, the brickwork that had earlier just been damp now running with water, the hanging snotsicles of slime now more frequently thick and ropelike, requiring the pair to dodge around them. The stream of water running down the middle of the tunnel had now overflowed, splashing around their feet as they moved on. The system smelled dank and musty, but they seemed to be well clear of actual effluent.

Judge D slowed, his shoulders hunched with tension. He hadn't spoken in a while.

And then he stopped. He looked around, back into the tunnel they had just come down, then ahead into the darkness. *Something* had clearly made him stop, some feature of the endless tunnel that Holmes couldn't pick out. Shaking his head, Judge D yanked the map out of his back pocket, nearly dropping it in the running water at their feet in his haste. He held the map close to his face, scanning it intently.

Holmes looked at the tunnel around him, trying to understand why the man appeared so uneasy. But their surroundings were basically the same as those they'd been trudging through for the last hour, just smaller, older. There were more metal reinforcing plates in the ceiling, as well as the walls. A newer metal pipe, thick and black, sprouted out of the wall on their right at about head height, and sped off into the darkness ahead.

Holmes glanced over Judge D's shoulder at the map.

"How close are we now? To the tunnel conjunction you wanted to look at?"

Judge D nearly jumped out of his skin when Holmes spoke. He continued to study the map, rotating it in his hands.

"Okay, time to go," he said, turning and, head down, marching back down the tunnel in the direction they had just come. "Tour's over. Please return your audio guides to the desk and don't forget to tip."

Holmes watched his retreating back in confusion for a moment, then glanced back up the tunnel. There was nothing ahead but darkness. He turned and splashed after his guide.

"Victor? What's wrong?"

Judge D didn't reply. Holmes picked up the pace, ignoring the hanging tendrils of slime brushing against him, and reached out, grabbing his arm. Judge D stopped and pulled away.

"Hey, what the hell, man?"

Holmes noted the increased respiratory rate and the dampness clinging to Judge D's stubble... dampness that could have been moisture from the tunnel, or a cold sweat brought on by something else entirely.

Something like *fear*.

Holmes stuffed his hands into his pockets and bent down to peer under Judge D's cap. Judge D squinted at Holmes's lamplight and lifted his arm to shield the glare. Holmes reached up and turned his lamp off. Judge D dropped his arm and now it was Holmes's turn to shield his own eyes from the other's light.

"What are you doing, man? We need to get a move on."

"What is it?" asked Holmes, his voice a low whisper. "There's something here, isn't there? That's what you came to look for. You've been in these tunnels before. You reached the convergence. And you saw something, didn't you? What was it? What did you find down here?"

Judge D appeared to hold his breath for a moment, his eyes locked onto Holmes's. Holmes waved his fingers in front of his guide's face, like he was coaxing a particularly stubborn rabbit out from a magician's hat.

Then Judge D sniffed loudly and wiped his nose again with the back of his sleeve.

"Sorry about this, dude, really," he said, then he sighed before jerking into action, sprinting down the tunnel, the light of his lamp bobbing wildly as he ran.

Holmes hissed in annoyance and turned his lamp back on, then ran after his fleeing guide. Judge D was far ahead, but his light was more than adequate to follow. Holmes's footfalls echoed loudly as he splashed through the water, drowning out the sounds of Judge D making his escape.

Then the tunnel ahead went dark. Holmes slowed. Judge D had taken a turn—Holmes recalled the route back to the Hudson River Greenway was off the left fork, so, picking up the pace, he retraced their journey. A moment later he splashed to a halt. In front of him, the tunnel archway was bricked up. He was back at the dead end he and Judge D had hit what felt like hours before.

Holmes spun around, then stood very still, listening. There

was nothing but the babbling of water in the tunnel ahead, and the constant dull background roar of greater volumes of water moving somewhere nearby.

Holmes moved back to the tunnel intersection. He checked his watch. It was just past ten—time enough for some more exploration before he was due to report back to the others at the brownstone. And he'd come this far—he didn't have a map like Judge D, but so long as he counted tunnels and kept track of his progress, he would be able to find his way back, he knew he would. The excursion to the dead end he put down to an error made in haste.

Holmes made his way back to where Judge D had taken flight, water rushing around his ankles, the walls around him covered with more of the metal reinforcing plates. They consisted of three bands, maybe ten centimeters wide and a meter long each. It was hard to tell how old the repairs were— the brick of the tunnel itself was at least a hundred years old, and it was more than likely the metal plates were half that.

Holmes moved forward. The sound of rushing water increased, and quickly too. Then the light of his headlamp vanished as the walls of tunnel suddenly expanded outward. A few more steps, and he was in an atrium, a junction with a high vaulted ceiling and five tunnels leading off before him, spread out like the fingers of a hand. In the far wall, between two of the tunnels, was a deep, arched culvert, from which came the roar of water. The chamber was filled with pipes too, of various size and apparent age, curving out of the walls, a few with wheeled valves.

Holmes moved to each of the tunnel openings in turn. One was bricked up a few meters back from the entrance. The next was blocked by a pile of broken bricks, the roof apparently having collapsed years ago. The other three were passable, at least as far as Holmes could see, but without Judge D's map it was impossible to know if any would lead to his desired destination, and there was the very real danger of getting lost in the tunnels for *hours*.

Northeast was still the right direction. Holmes reached into his pocket for his phone. It was too deep for the GPS to work and he was unlikely to have cellphone signal, but the compass function would still be operational.

In his pocket his fingers brushed against something else besides his phone.

He pulled out the UV marker pen, stared at it for a moment, then quickly reached inside his coat, pulling a flat, rectangular object from the inside pocket. He turned the device over in his hands, found the switch, and turned it on.

One long edge of the object glowed purple-white. Then he reached up to his forehead and turned his headlamp off, plunging himself into a darkness illuminated only by the UV lamp. The damp walls and floor of the chamber glittered like crystal. But there was something else too. Something bright.

Holmes lifted the light up. There, on the metal reinforcing plates next to one of the tunnel entrances, markings fluoresced a brilliant green under the UV, their glow so bright it made spots jump in front of Holmes's eyes.

There was a large arrow, pointing down the tunnel, and a series of numbers and something else in a scrawl that wasn't English, Spanish, or any other language Holmes recognized. He pulled his phone out and took a photo of the writing.

One thing was for certain—the markings were directions. Directions he intended to follow.

14

THE ENIGMATIC DR. HARLEY

Watson sighed and let her attention wander, casting her eyes around the assembled guests. Everyone was back in the museum's entrance hall as the exhibition curator, Dr. Harley, gave her welcome speech from a raised podium set up at the back of the room.

Watson spied Gregson nearby. He was watching the speech, but his somewhat deflated body language suggested his canvassing of the guests had been just as fruitless as hers.

It was frustrating, but what could they do? Watson had been careful with her conversation—as she and the Captain had agreed earlier, if anyone here knew Liam Macnamara, there was a more than fair chance they wanted to keep that fact hidden. Not only that, Watson had kept her own identity vague, but not so much that it would raise suspicion. Thankfully she'd been able to draw on her past life as a surgical registrar and had come up with a fairly solid, and entirely false, line of chitchat based on one of the rather wealthy consultants she'd once known. That, at least, had worked, but it hadn't gotten her any closer to learning anything about the murder victim himself.

Watson frowned. They hadn't been able to talk to

everyone either, but as she had made her rounds, it soon become clear there was no point. As she had suspected, the guests at the gala were a mix of high-flying socialites, businessmen, and lifetime members of the museum. The chance that any of them were friends with a subway worker became increasingly unlikely the more Watson schmoozed, her face aching from smiling, the untouched champagne in her glass getting warmer and flatter as she moved from one group to the next.

Dr. Harley began to wrap up at the podium, thanking a long list of corporate sponsors. She was a good speaker, Watson gave her that.

Watson glanced around. The burly men squeezed into their tuxedos were still spaced around the room, their attention on the speaker along with everyone else. She'd tried to talk to one of them earlier, but he had just shaken his head and said something in Spanish that Watson took to mean that he didn't speak English.

Watson sensed movement beside her, and she turned. Gregson sidled up to her, lowering his voice as he spoke.

"As fun as this party was, I've come up with nothing. Nobody I've spoken to knows our vic."

Watson sighed. "Same here."

"I think it's time to be a little more formal," said Gregson. He glanced back down the hall, toward the main entrance. The uniformed security guards were still at their posts near the security scanners. "If invites for this little shindig were sent out, then there must be a guest list."

"And Liam Macnamara must be on it."

"Right. We get the list, find out who put it together, maybe we get a little closer."

Watson turned back to the podium. "Did you talk to the curator again?"

Gregson shook his head. "No, didn't get a chance. I think

our little history lesson was all we got."

"Okay," said Watson. "You talk to the security staff. I'll see if I can get a word with our host."

Gregson nodded, reaching into his tuxedo to get his detective shield ready. "Good luck." He walked away, toward the security desks. Watson watched him, as around her the crowd erupted in applause. She turned back to the podium, but instead of Dr. Harley there was another speaker, an older man with silver hair and half-moon glasses with a chain loop hanging from the arms.

Watson craned her neck to see over the other guests, but she couldn't see the curator. She sighed inwardly, scanning the room.

There she was.

Leading out from the entrance hall to the rest of the museum were a number of corridors, their archways wide and tall. As the gala was a special evening event the museum proper was closed, the corridors blocked off by red velvet ropes, the galleries beyond dark.

Watson had caught sight of the bright teal of Lisa Harley's dress through a gap in the crowd as the curator headed toward one of the roped-off archways. As Watson moved to get a better view, she saw Dr. Harley sidestep the barrier and head toward the other gallery.

Watson looked over her shoulder. Captain Gregson was in conversation with two of the security guards at the main desk, his back to her.

With the curator clear of the assembled gala guests, this was the perfect opportunity to go and talk to her, in private. She could drop the act and come right out with some direct questions. She felt like she and Gregson had wasted time at the gala, but she had one last chance to gather some information.

Gripping her clutch purse tightly, Watson headed after Harley. At the archway she paused at the velvet rope, checked to make sure nobody was looking, then slipped around the barrier and followed the curator deeper into the museum.

The wide corridor led to the next gallery, full of diorama displays showcasing the mammals of Africa. She skirted a display of stuffed creatures of the Serengeti, craning her neck to see where Dr. Harley had gone. Although the main lights were off, the gallery was fairly well lit, which, Watson thought, made sense, given that the whole place would be patrolled by night guards. She walked on, eying the animals on display, making a conscious effort not to imagine the exhibits coming to life around her.

There were footsteps ahead, walking fast, hard heels clacking on the hard floor. Harley, it had to be. Watson tried to hurry but her own heels weren't made for pursuit. She paused, slipped off her yellow shoes, and padded forward in stockinged feet.

Another passage, another gallery; on the far wall, a plain beige door in the plain beige wall was slowly swinging shut. Watson rushed forward, catching it by the edge before it could lock itself. She stepped through.

Away from the public spaces, the museum was a curious mix of grand nineteenth-century neo-Gothic architecture and modern office furnishings. It was also much darker than in the galleries—*No need for security guards to patrol the back offices,* Watson thought. The hard marble floor had given way to carpet tiles, the softer surface no longer the sounding board that had been so useful in following Dr. Harley.

Watson crept forward, straining her ears to listen for the curator. She couldn't have been that far ahead, but she had one advantage over Watson—she knew the museum inside out, and she knew exactly where she was going. Where that was, Watson had no idea. For all she knew, Harley was just going to grab something from her office. Watson suddenly felt ridiculous, skulking around. She slipped her shoes back on and strode forward, determined to find her quarry.

Watson headed down the corridor, passing wooden doors, some with narrow rectangular windows, some without. Several were much larger than the others, their dark wood and the gilded writing carefully stenciled onto them clear indicators they were original to the museum's construction. As Watson passed a few more, she noticed the writing fit a pattern—a number (perhaps for the room, or a collection?), and a short description. On her left was 766—ZOOLOGY COLLECTION A STORE, then 800—ARTHROPODS, and a room designated 802 with no description. On the right, 808A—THE BAILEY COLLECTION, 3691—NATION, DAL to LEK. Watson frowned, unable to make sense of the numbering system or order. Not that it mattered, because what she *hadn't* found was Lisa Harley. The exhibition curator was gone and Watson was alone, the offices and storerooms silent.

Watson paused, considering. She could spend all night wandering around the museum's private offices, and the longer she did, the more she risked annoying the museum staff when she was inevitably found. More than that, if there was something strange going on, she risked tipping their opponents off.

It was time to head back to the main galleries. Captain Gregson should have gotten the guest list by now. Maybe it would give them a useful lead and their night wouldn't have been a total waste of time. And then, depending on what they found, they could come back to the museum and talk to Dr. Harley a little more officially.

Watson turned, ready to leave.

From the corridor behind her came the sound of shuffling papers and something sliding open—it sounded like drawers, each slide terminating in a quiet *donk* of wood-on-wood.

Beneath the heavy dark door of one of the storerooms ahead on Watson's right, a light moved. Someone was in the storeroom, looking for something with a flashlight.

Lisa Harley, it *had* to be. Watson moved closer, her shoes thankfully quiet on the carpet beneath her feet.

Then the flashlight went out, the sounds ceased. Watson froze, waiting, counting in her head. There was nothing but silence. She moved toward the door, wincing at every sound she made.

Like the others lining the corridor, the door had no window, just more gold lettering revealing that this room was 1024—S. AMERICA STORE B. Watson pressed her ear to the wood. It was shiny and cool against her skin, but she couldn't hear anything from inside.

She grasped the ornate brass knob, turned it slowly, then put her shoulder to the door and gently—very, *very* gently—pushed it open. The door glided on well-oiled hinges without making a sound.

The storeroom was dark; in the weak light she had let in from the corridor, Watson saw that the walls were lined with tall shelves and cupboards with wide, shallow drawers in dark wood—like the door, they looked as if they had been in the museum since its construction. Filling the floor space were modern metal archive shelves, rows and rows of them, holding a variety of objects—books, boxes, folders and files. Some, like a sequence of enormous leather-bound books, were clearly old, while others—such as two transparent plastic crates stacked on top of each other, computer-printed labels stuck on their sides—were very recent additions. Ignoring the shelving, Watson let the door swing closed behind her and walked to the cupboards and drawers along the nearest wall, her eyes adjusting to the gloom. She ran her fingers over the wood—the drawers, shallow and wide, looked like specimen stores. Watson had seen a similar setup in the pathology museum at NYU, recalling the many hours spent browsing the historic collections housed in just such drawers.

She dragged her attention from the stores, and turned, leaning against the cupboards as she surveyed the room. It was huge, the ceiling high, the shelves numerous. In the dark there were plenty of places for someone to...

Hide.

Watson froze. Of course. Dr. Harley had heard her in the corridor outside and was hiding in the storeroom. Watson wondered if she should call out, but quickly decided against it. If it was the curator then there was definitely something strange and secretive going on at the museum. The sooner Watson got back to Gregson and filled him in, the better. She wondered if Holmes and Bell had managed to come up with anything while she and the Captain had been busy at the museum.

Watson glanced around, then cut back to the storeroom doors through the shelves in front of her, taking a diagonal route that was quicker than skirting around the cupboards. As she hurried to the exit, she looked around, suddenly thinking she really, *really* shouldn't be here.

Watson rounded the end of one set of shelves, turning for the door, and brought herself to a fast stop as she nearly walked face-first into a large man in a tuxedo, the white teeth of his snarl bright in the gloom against the empty black of the ski mask he was wearing.

Watson jumped in fright, just managing to stifle a cry of surprise with one hand. She took a reflexive step backward, but the man was fast and he grabbed her by the wrist with one hand.

In the other he held a gun. He lifted it up, thumbed the safety off, and pointed it at her forehead.

15

THE MYSTERY MEN

Holmes walked on through the tunnels, unheeding of the time, lost in the mystery as his innate curiosity took over, driving him onward. The tunnels were mostly dry and quite passable; so far he had not come across any more blockages or bricked-up archways, although he had the secret directions to thank for that. At each intersection or fork he came to, Holmes turned his headlamp off and scanned the walls with his UV light, finding without fail another glowing green arrow, another set of numbered notations. Each time he took a photo, then proceeded in the direction the arrow indicated.

After another half-mile, Holmes slowed. The sound of rushing water had come and gone on his journey, and the water in the tunnels he travelled through was never more than a few inches deep.

But here the acoustics seemed different as another sound echoed down the tunnel, much louder, more complex than the rush of water, yet still distant, separated from his current position by who knew how much Victorian brick. But it was unmistakable, muted as it was. Holmes leaned against the damp wall, placing his hands flat against its slimy surface.

The sound reached a crescendo, vibrating the wall beneath his fingers. Hidden within the roaring was a rhythmic clack, and the squeal of metal on metal.

A subway train. There was a tunnel nearby.

Grinning to himself, Holmes pushed himself off the wall, rubbed the slime from his hands onto his coat, and pressed on.

Soon the tunnel widened and he came to another large chamber. Here was evidence of visits by sewer workers, although nothing recent—old equipment was stacked against a wall, large metal tools now reduced to brown lumps of corrosion by a century of dampness. The chamber's structure was also in a dire state, fragmented bricks scattered across the floor where part of the roof had collapsed, blocking the way forward. Workers had, at some point, tried shoring up the ceiling with timber beams like a mine, only for the tunnel's structure to fail on the other side of the chamber.

The wall on the right was hidden behind a pile of rubble and the rusted tools. On the left, the brickwork was buckled, and halfway along the chamber the wall had fallen in completely, producing a large opening through which poured light and sound.

Holmes ducked back against the wall, dousing his headlamp.

The sounds were not the rush of water, or the roar of a subway train. They were voices and the noise of people shuffling around. Four—no, *five*—heavy men, making no attempt to hide their presence. As they moved around in the neighboring chamber, their shadows were cast long through the opening. The room beyond was lit by low lighting—industrial floodlights on tripods, most likely.

Holmes fell into a crouch and crabbed toward the split in the wall, keeping as close to the brick as possible without making a sound, although over the noise the men were making and the ever-present rush of water, it was unlikely he would be heard. Holmes squinted as he focused on their speech, then, with a frown, he reached for his phone. He had to get a recording.

Because these were no sewer workers. The men in the other room were having a discussion in a language Holmes didn't recognize.

Shielding the phone against his body to prevent any light from the display revealing his presence, Holmes selected the audio recorder, then he sat still, balanced on his haunches, holding the phone out to record the voices.

Their tone was conversational. Over the next minute or so, at least two of the men in the other chamber laughed at something another man said. As the men shuffled around, Holmes watched their shadows as though it were an artistic performance. It was hard to judge, but from the sound of their voices and their movements, and the way their shadows twisted and turned, the men seemed to be big, strong. Then there was a splash of water and one of them spoke loudly, clearly complaining. The response he got sounded apologetic.

Holmes glanced at the brick next to him. The damage to the wall had loosened the mortar farther along from the hole, and faint light shone through the gaps around the bricks closest to Holmes's face. He reached up and gave a brick an experimental push. When it gave, he pushed, and again, and then, ever so gently, managed to twist it in the wall enough that he could put his eye to the gap and see into the other chamber.

The other room was vastly different to the one Holmes was crouched in. It was long and rectangular, with two walls of gray cinder block, interrupted by two passageways leading off in different directions—the tunnel convergence, Holmes realized: Judge D's intended destination.

As Holmes had surmised, there were four industrial work lights arranged around the corners of the room, their yellow boxy forms atop black metal stands, their cables snaking away down the dark passage opposite Holmes's line of sight.

Other than that, the room was empty, save for the five men within it.

They were Hispanic, muscular, the four nearest Holmes filling out black coveralls that, zipped to the neck, looked professional, even paramilitary. The fifth man was built like his friends and had a shaved head and chinstrap beard.

He was wearing a tuxedo.

Holmes ran his eyes over the man. His pant legs were shiny, wet; this was the man who had complained about being splashed, complained about getting his dinner suit dirty in their unusual, rhythmic language.

The five men continued to talk, clearly at ease, unaware they were being spied on. After a few moments they seemed to agree on something, and after some friendly backslapping and chuckles, the four men in black headed in single file through one of the tunnel openings, while the man in the tuxedo turned and headed through the other tunnel behind him. He paused at the exit and called something out over his shoulder, which elicited more laughter from his colleagues, the sound echoing out as the group moved away.

Then the man in the tuxedo disappeared down his own chosen route, and Holmes was alone once more.

Holmes clicked his phone off and returned it to his pocket. He waited a moment, listening for the men as their voices receded, but just then the sound of another subway train rushing past somewhere nearby drowned everything else out. It sounded like the tracks were very close, just down one of the tunnels that led out of the neighboring chamber.

Holmes stood and glanced around. He pulled the UV flashlight out and gave the walls of his own chamber a cursory scan, but there was nothing. No further direction was needed, of course. Because if you had made it this far and reached the breach in the wall, then you would know exactly where you were...

Holmes stepped up to the hole in the wall and glanced around the edge. The industrial lights fizzed in the damp air as the echoing clack of the subway train faded away. He stepped through the opening, casting his gaze around for anything he might have missed. The large space was empty, the lights just the same as any sewer or subway maintenance team would erect to work in the dark.

There were marks on the floor, however—something else had been in the chamber besides the lights. The floor itself was cement, covered with years of grime and brick dust. On one side of the chamber—the dry side—was a series of rectangular indentations in the dirt, with the characteristic arcs of something heavy being dragged as the person carrying it slid it around to get a better grip. The size and shape indicated boxes or crates had been stored here in the not too distant past.

Holmes picked his way across the room, following the flat footprints left on the damp floor by the dress shoes of the man in the tuxedo. The other footprints, leading to the opposite tunnel, were, in contrast, heavily treaded.

The passageway was lined with more cinder blocks and was narrow and dark. Holmes turned his headlamp on and proceeded forward. After a few more meters he came to a dead end, the tunnel sealed by a cinder-block wall.

Holmes looked to the left, then to the right. There, recessed into an alcove was a set of the now familiar square ladder rungs, fixed to the wall. Holmes moved to the bottom of the ladder and looked up, his headlamp shining off the dull black metal underside of a hatch.

It was the only way forward, the route the man in the tuxedo must have taken.

Holmes began to climb.

16

THE MIRANDA COLLECTION

Holmes crouched next to the floor panel; his finger slipped through the inset brass ring on its surface as he let it slide back into place. The panel was tiled in vinyl, as was the rest of the floor of whatever space he now found himself in. He flicked his headlamp on, and looked around.

It was a construction site, a large interior space being stripped and remodeled. Partition walls of bare plasterboard had been erected, and, looking up, Holmes saw a new ceiling framework was being installed, a cradle of metal struts designed to support cables and a ventilation system. Around him were sawhorses, workbenches, toolboxes, a large table saw, a stack of timber, and a pile of orange power cables coiled in the corner. The floor was lightly covered with wood and plaster dust, enough to reveal a multitude of footprints. Holmes examined them, casting his lamplight around, but it was impossible to pick out a single trail.

Creeping forward, ever alert for his quarry, Holmes made his way to the door, itself stoppered open, a thick plastic sheet spread across the threshold, typical of a worksite. Holmes poked his head around the corner, trying to keep to the edges of the sheeting so as not to make a sound.

The corridor beyond was clear. There was more construction here—he was in what looked to be an office building in the process of renovation. Holmes stepped out and picked a direction, keeping himself close to the walls as he silently tracked through the unknown building. Any dusty footprints left by the man in the tuxedo had vanished, and as he made his way through the maze of corridors, Holmes could not see or hear any sign of him.

He came to some stairs leading upward, and took them. The lack of windows on the lower floor indicated that he had come up in the basement of the building. Indeed, the fact that new offices were being installed must have been fortuitous for the man in the tuxedo and his colleagues, the perfect cover allowing them to come and go, entering the water main that ran under the building as they pleased.

The corridors on the next level were wider, the ceilings higher.

Holmes continued his exploration.

Finally he reached a corridor with a different sort of door, large and made of dark-stained oak. It was locked with a deadbolt, which Holmes twisted to unlock. Entry from the other side required a key. If he was going to proceed, there would be no way back.

Holmes slipped open the door and slipped into the next room. As he let the door click shut behind him, he heard the unmistakable sound of a large group of people echoing from somewhere nearby. He looked around, his headlamp reflecting back at him in myriad shafts of light.

With a frown, he stepped forward, stepped closer. The reflecting something in front of him resolved into a cabinet, tall and wide, constructed entirely of glass, with dozens of thick edges and flat surfaces that shone his light back at him in a kaleidoscope of color. Holmes swept the lamp off his head and held it in one hand, angling it sharply so he could look inside the case properly.

There, arranged on a frosted glass shelf inside, were diamonds. Holmes counted twelve, arranged in a single row by size, with the stone on the far left no bigger than a pea, whereas that on the far right was the size of a golf ball.

Holmes spun on his heel, shining his light in every direction. The gallery was long and filled with identical cases, ten in total, arranged in a long staggered V from one end of the room to the other. The next case along appeared to be filled with rubies, the next emeralds, the next sapphires. He stepped over to the case of blue gems, counting the number of sapphires on display. There were some as small as tic-tacs, others the size of a thumbnail. They were cut into lozenges, cushions, drops. There were brilliant cuts and princess cuts and trilliant cuts. The jewels scintillated as Holmes moved his lamplight across them.

He had come to the right place, anyway. He was in the American Museum of Natural History.

As the bustling sounds of the museum gala filtered through from a neighboring gallery, Holmes slowly wandered between the cases of the jewel display, toward a different case that sat at the center of the room.

It was smaller, a perfect cube of glass. Within, it held just a single jewel, balanced on a delicate transparent tripod so it appeared to magically float in the air.

Magical was just the right description too. The jewel was a blue gem the size of a fist. Holmes played his light over it. The gem seemed to glow, absorbing the light and throwing it back across the walls and ceiling of the gallery like a disco ball. His eyes widened in surprise.

He recognized it immediately.

Holmes saw another light in the corner of his vision. He froze, glanced up.

There. In the corner of the room, the winking red light of a motion sensor. He looked around, counting six more arranged to cover the room. The cases would be alarmed too, for vibration and movement, and there was a more than fair chance the star attraction had its own special security and sensors.

Holmes was surprised that such a collection didn't have its own security team on duty, patrolling the room in shifts, 24/7.

"Hey, sir! You're not allowed in here, sir."

Holmes turned. A uniformed security guard, flashlight in one hand, the other resting on the holster on his belt, approached from the other side of the gallery. Behind him a door swung closed.

Holmes smiled and stood tall. He gave the guard a tight nod as the man approached.

"Sorry, I was just looking for the lavatory," he said. Then he patted his stomach. "Too much champagne I'm afraid."

The guard grimaced and shone his flashlight up and down over Holmes, pausing on the green rubber boots, the dirty, slime-streaked pea coat, the headlamp hanging from one hand by its strap.

"Yeah, right," said the guard. "I think you need to come with me."

The man reached forward, at the same time tilting his head as he squeezed the radio clipped to his shoulder. "Control, this is Laukkanen. Look, I've got someone down at the Laverick Gallery. I need to hold him until we can get the police down, and—"

"It's quite all right," said Holmes. "I can find my own way out."

He turned and marched across the gallery, toward a set of double doors with a push bar across them.

"Hey!" The guard rushed after him. He clicked his radio again. "He's heading to the Roosevelt Hall." He looked up, running after Holmes. "Not that door!"

Sounds came from the other side of the door. The murmur

of conversation, punctuated occasionally by laughter. Faint music, something orchestral but thin—a live string quartet. The clink of glassware, the muted footsteps of servers. Ice sloshing in a champagne bucket. Someone dropping a small metal object which rang against the hard floor—a cake fork.

As the security guard laid a heavy hand on Holmes's shoulder, Holmes slammed the horizontal bar to unlock the door. Immediately a shrill alarm rang out, echoing off every hard surface as Holmes stepped into the cavernous Theodore Roosevelt Memorial Hall.

The museum gala was thrown into confusion, half of the guests wandering slowly toward the main exit as the alarm continued to bleat. The remainder seemed frozen in place as they watched Holmes being tackled from behind by Laukkanen, just as two more security guards came running from the museum's entrance.

Holmes relaxed and allowed himself to be held in place. "It's a fair cop," he said with a smile.

Then Laukkanen shoved him in the small of his back, and, gasping, Holmes fell face-first onto the hard floor.

17

SAVED BY THE BELL

The man in the tuxedo and ski mask gestured sideways with the barrel of the gun he had aimed at Watson's forehead. Careful to remain facing her captor, Watson slid sideways in the direction indicated, then, hands raised, she walked ahead of him back toward the door of the storeroom.

He pushed her into the corridor, then through another door nearby. She realized that they were now in an office. The lights were off, but ample illumination from the night-lit city outside came in through the row of windows high in the opposite wall. There were three desks, each covered with books and papers, and three identical computer displays, squeezed awkwardly into the small space. Whoever shared this office had to put up with some pretty cramped conditions.

She turned around to face her captor. He was clearly one of the burly men she and Gregson had seen orbiting the gala. He raised the gun and ducked the barrel, twice. The instruction was clear and Watson obeyed, sitting on the edge of the desk behind her.

Dark eyes still staring at her from behind his mask, the man reached into his tuxedo jacket with his free hand and extracted a phone. It was small, cheap—a burner—and as he thumbed the keypad the buttons and tiny screen lit up in amber. The dark eyes glanced at it momentarily, then he lifted it to his ear.

A pause, a beat, and then:

"*Sí*," he said into the phone, his voice a low bass grumble. Another pause, and then he gave a small shrug, said, "*No sé*," then he listened, nodding to himself. All the while he didn't break eye contact with Watson.

Watson pursed her lips. Her Spanish was pretty rough, just a handful of phrases picked up when she worked in the busy city hospital.

And then he started speaking something else, something that definitely *wasn't* Spanish. Watson listened, a frown growing on her face as she concentrated. But it was unrecognizable, the man's speech rising and falling, multiple soft syllables tripping over his tongue in a constant stream.

Watson thought this was important. It had to be. She'd walked into a dangerous situation, but she held her cool, controlling her breathing, trying to ignore the nauseating way her heart was beating against her breastbone.

Gather data. Be cooperative, but not pliable. Look and listen. There would be something useful to learn here.

Observe.

Watson concentrated, pushing her fear to the back of her mind as she gained focus.

The man spoke quietly, quickly. There was no fear or tension in his voice. His initial confusion—"*No lo sé*" meant, Watson remembered, "I don't know"—had gone, and now it sounded like he had the situation under control and that he was dealing with the problem—her.

Watson had clearly interrupted something, and although she had no doubt the man holding the gun was dangerous, she didn't think he would dare fire it in the museum. She turned her attention to the weapon, absorbing every small detail. It was chunky, compact—an automatic pistol, but without a silencer. Its metal surface glistened in the dim light, but where there would normally be a make and model, perhaps even a serial number, etched onto the side of the barrel, the surface was dull, matte. Any identifying text had been filed off. That was something only criminals did.

The man nodded into the phone, then—

An alarm rang out. Watson started, standing from the desk in surprise as a burst of adrenaline flooded her system. Her eyes wide, she watched the man with the gun as he looked in the direction of the noise, the phone held away from his head, the gun still pointing in her direction.

But... not quite. Distracted by the alarm, his aim had drifted to her left.

The man returned the phone to his ear and raised his voice, shouting into it to be heard over the wailing siren. *Now* he sounded worried. Watson didn't need to understand what he was saying this time. She was pretty sure she got the gist of it— *what the hell is going on* was at the top of her list of guesses.

It was now or never.

Watson ran. She knew she would be no match for the man in a fight—the sheer size difference between them alone was enough—but, pushing off from the desk behind her, she shoved his gun arm out of the way and ran past him, ducking under his other arm and speeding toward the door. As she swung around the door frame the man behind her shouted something, but she couldn't tell if it was directed at her or whoever it was on the other end of the phone.

Watson didn't pause to worry about it. She just ran— straight ahead, then a left, then a right. That was the way back to the gala. To safety.

Wasn't it?

She took the next left, then skidded to a halt. She didn't

recognize this corridor. Was this the right way? The alarm was like a jackhammer, making it hard to clear her thoughts. If the man with the gun was giving chase, there was no way she'd be able to hear him coming over the din. Nor could she hear the gala—which would be evacuating from the main hall by now anyway.

Then the alarm stopped, the sudden silence leaving a ringing in Watson's head. Then the lights came on. She blinked and turned around in confusion.

"Hey!"

There was a man at the other end of the corridor, smaller than her captor and instead of a tuxedo and ski mask he was wearing a uniform not unlike a policeman, complete with peaked cap, radio and utility belt loaded with equipment. He jogged toward her, one arm pumping the air, one hand resting on his holstered gun.

"What are you doing here?" asked the security guard, puffing slightly as he came to a halt. His expression softened as he looked Watson up and down, clearly taking in her evening wear. "Are you okay, ma'am?"

"Everything's fine, Gerald."

Watson turned. Dr. Lisa Harley walked toward them, her footfalls soft on the carpet tiles. Watson stifled a gasp as behind the curator came one of the tuxedoed heavies, although without the ski mask, it was impossible to tell if it was the man who had pulled a gun on her or not.

"Sorry, Dr. Harley," said the guard, nodding a greeting. "Do you need assistance with anything?"

The curator turned on her smile and quickly linked arms with the stunned Watson. "Sorry Gerald, I was just showing my guest around the museum and we got separated. Can you do me a favor and go back to the Theodore Roosevelt Hall and find out what the alarm was about? One of the gala guests probably just wandered off somewhere."

The guard frowned, his eyes flicking between Watson and Dr. Harley. Then he nodded and touched the peak of his cap.

"No problem," he said, then he turned to leave.

"Wait," said Watson, moving to follow the guard. He stopped and turned back, but as Watson drew breath to speak, Harley squeezed Watson's arm, drawing her closer to her side. The curator pursed her lips at the guard. "That'll be all, Gerald," she said, then she leaned in to whisper into Watson's ear.

"If you want to get out of here alive, you'll keep quiet and do exactly what I say."

Watson held her breath as Harley's words sank in. She watched Gerald—her potential savior—vanish around the corner.

With the guard out of sight, Watson yanked herself free from the other woman's grip.

"What the *hell* is going on?" she hissed. She looked at the tuxedoed man standing at the curator's shoulder like a personal bodyguard. "Someone pulled a *gun* on me, took me to—"

"I said keep *quiet*," said the curator, her jaw clenched. She glanced at her burly companion. "I think it's time we got back to the other guests, don't you?"

She turned back around, pulling Watson's arm. Watson let herself be led, glancing over her shoulder as she did so. Harley's compatriot wasn't coming with them. "Staff a little uncooperative?"

Dr. Harley stopped and swung them around. She jerked her chin at the man in the tux.

"What is it?"

The man spoke in the language Watson had heard on the phone, but this time her eyes were on the curator. Dr. Harley frowned and shook her head. Whatever dialect the man was speaking, she didn't understand it.

The man stopped speaking. Then he shook his own head,

perhaps in frustration, then turned and walked back down the other corridor, taking the same path Gerald had moments before. Watson felt Dr. Harley tense beside her.

"What was that about?" she asked, turning to the other woman. "Who are those people? And what have you gotten yourself into?"

Dr. Harley just sighed and then dragged her forward, her grip on Watson's arm painfully strong.

"Hey," said Watson. "They pulled a *gun* on me, okay? Whoever they are they don't seem like your typical annual pass holder. They work for you, don't they?"

Dr. Harley bit her lip, but kept her eyes focused ahead.

"If only," she whispered.

"Talk to me," said Watson.

Dr. Harley jerked Watson's arm. "You're not very good at following instructions, are you?"

Watson jerked back, bringing them to a halt. "I've had my life threatened enough for one night, Dr. Harley." She sighed, softened her voice. "Look, if you're in trouble, maybe I can help you."

The curator stared at her for a moment, then she shook her head and they kept going. Watson didn't resist; new thoughts percolated in her mind.

Whatever was going on, the curator was involved. But— perhaps more important—Watson suspected that it was not a voluntary arrangement. If she could just get *through* to her, she might be the key to unlocking the whole mystery.

The pair rounded a corner, and stopped. Ahead was a set of open double doors, beyond which was the Theodore Roosevelt Memorial Hall.

Just inside the doorway stood Captain Gregson, hands on his hips. He looked around as the two women approached, his expression one of surprise and relief.

"Ms. Watson, where the hell have you been?" He stepped

forward and paused, looking between her and the curator. "Is everything all right?"

"Just fine," said Dr. Harley, her smile tight. She unhooked her arm from Watson's and, head lowered, she made to walk past Gregson.

"Whoa, hold on there," said the Captain, catching the curator by the arm.

"I'm sorry, but if you'll excuse me, I have other guests to attend—"

"Yeah, I'm sure you do," said Gregson. He lifted his other hand, the leather wallet held in it flipped open to show his detective shield. "But I'm starting to think we need to have a little chat, Dr. Harley."

The curator froze, staring at the badge. Then she glanced up, looking not at Gregson, but at Watson, a look in her eyes that Watson recognized all too well.

Fear.

But not fear of Gregson, fear of something else. Fear of what would happen to her—not at the hands of the police. At the hands of the big men at the gala, including the one with the ski mask and gun.

Watson stepped forward and laid a hand on Gregson's elbow. He glanced at her, raising his eyebrow as he lowered his badge.

"It's fine," said Watson. She nodded at Dr. Harley. "Go look after your guests. We'll talk later."

The curator's eyes were wet, and she blinked a couple of times, then she gave a tiny nod and, with a final glance at the Captain, headed into the main hall.

Watson and Gregson watched her for a moment.

"What the hell was that about?" asked Gregson, returning the badge to his jacket pocket.

Watson folded her arms. "It's a long story."

"I've been looking for you all over. You've been gone

nearly an hour. What the hell happened?"

Watson outlined the story to Gregson: how she had followed Dr. Harley and heard *someone* searching the storeroom, only to be held at gunpoint, and how the curator had reappeared after the alarm had been shut off.

Gregson blew out his cheeks and put his hands on his hips. "You've had quite a night."

"Tell me about it," said Watson. Now she was back with the Captain and in a public space, she felt lightheaded. She wobbled slightly on her feet, then she closed her eyes and rolled her neck.

"You okay?"

She opened her eyes. Gregson was peering at her, his face a mask of concern.

She smiled. "I'll be fine."

Gregson frowned but gave a small nod. He cast his gaze around the hall, which was now half-empty.

"So, any idea what she was looking for in the storeroom?" he asked.

"*If* it was her," said Watson. Gregson looked at her with a quizzical expression. She shook her head. "She's a senior curator. Surely she can look in any storeroom she likes, and she doesn't need to do it when she's supposed to be hosting a gala."

"The guy who pulled the gun then?"

Watson chewed her lip and shrugged. "Maybe."

"Okay," said Gregson. "I can have this place crawling with police and Feds. The inter-agency taskforce needs to be called in on this one. If we've found a drug-smuggling ring we're going to need some back-up." He pulled his phone from his jacket and squinted at the screen as he brought up the appropriate contact.

"Wait," said Watson, laying her hand on his.

Gregson looked up from the phone. "What is it?"

"Softly, softly, isn't that what you said?"

The Captain sighed. "I think it's time we went in on this one, don't you?"

Watson rubbed her forehead and closed her eyes. "The curator. Lisa Harley. I think she's in trouble. She's working with those men, but did you see her reaction when she saw you were a cop? She wasn't afraid of you, she was afraid of *them*. Of what they would do to her if they think she's talked to the police."

"So she's being forced to cooperate?"

"Yes," said Watson. "She's a respected academic in a prestigious job. Why else would she get caught up in something like this?"

Gregson shook his head slowly, but lowered his phone. "Whatever 'this' is." He sighed. "Okay. So, I'm all ears. What do you want to do?"

"Talk to her. Get her trust."

"Softly, softly."

Watson nodded. "If she's in some kind of danger then we have a duty to keep her out of harm's way."

"Agreed."

Watson paused, her thoughts finally catching up with her, her curiosity turning to another topic. "So what was the alarm, anyway?"

Gregson chuckled. He lifted a finger, curled it toward his face.

"Follow me."

18

THE OLD CASE

The night was crisp and cool and the steps and broad sidewalk outside of the American Museum of Natural History's Central Park West entrance were crowded with gala guests, milling around after their expulsion thanks to the alarm.

Captain Gregson led Watson down the stairs, across the sidewalk, then down to the second set of stairs leading to the street itself. There, near the top, two uniformed security guards were standing over Sherlock Holmes. The consulting detective sat on the steps, elbows on his knees, resting his chin on his fists.

Watson felt her eyebrows knit together in confusion.

"Sherlock?"

Holmes turned as they approached, then leapt to his feet.

"Watson! You will have quite literally no inkling as to what I have discovered—"

Immediately one of the security guards put his hand on Holmes's shoulder. Holmes turned on him.

"Unhand me at once, sir," he said, and then he sniffed. "And try breath mints. They'll work wonders for your halitosis."

As she got closer, Watson drew her hand to her nose.

"That smell is *you*, Sherlock."

Holmes glanced at her, then the Captain. Gregson nodded, his face screwed into a grimace.

Holmes flapped his arms against his sides. "Yes, well. Spores, molds, fungus. A little damp, maybe. Perhaps a touch of excrement, hard to tell. But that was to be expected. I have, after all, been walking through the bowels of the city for most of the evening."

He rounded on the guard again. The guard frowned and turned to the Captain.

Gregson nodded. "I can vouch for him," he said, fishing his badge out again. He gestured to the two guards and took them to one side for a private conversation. Holmes watched them, and nodded to himself, clearly pleased at something. Then he moved closer to Watson, who took a sidestep away but dropped her hand. If she just breathed through her mouth...

"So what happened?" she asked. "We were supposed to meet back at the brownstone." She looked around. "Where's Marcus?"

Holmes held up a hand. Watson sighed. Clearly, he wanted to tell the story *his* way.

"I had the most *extra*-ordinary journey through the wastewater systems, starting at the Hudson River Greenway and leading to..."

He turned and gestured to the impressive, historic façade of the museum.

Watson frowned. "The sewers led you here?"

Holmes nodded. "As I suspected they would. Judge D led me part of the way, but then I had some additional help. *Directions*, written on various pieces of metalwork in the tunnels. All pointing the way."

"You're telling me the sewer opens up inside the museum?"

"Not quite," said Holmes. "There is a water main running directly under the building"—he gestured back toward the museum, miming the watercourse with hands held in parallel—"with inspection access in the basement, for when workers from the Water Board need to get in. Not an uncommon feature in a lot of large city buildings, of which Manhattan has more than its fair share."

"So you came up into the basement?"

Holmes nodded. "I stumbled across some other subterranean travelers. One of whom was wearing a tuxedo. I followed him." He spread his arms, a grin plastered onto his face. "And here I am!"

"Setting the alarm off in the process?"

Holmes dropped his arms, his expression now tight-lipped. "Must you constantly focus on the negative, Watson?"

Watson shook her head, but she felt herself smile. Holmes's exuberance meant one thing.

The game was afoot.

"Was the man in the tuxedo kinda… big?"

Holmes bounced on his heels. "Six foot five inches and no wider than a beer truck."

"Right," said Watson, nodding. "There were more of those men at the gala." She related her own evening's experience. When she had finished, Holmes's expression was dark. He looked into her eyes, and he nodded, rolling his lips.

"Excellent work, Watson. You kept your calm and you gathered vital information."

Watson smiled, but it felt weak. Forced. Relating the story for a second time had taken it out of her a little. She had had enough for one night.

Holmes cocked his head. "I would ask if you were all right, but I know you better than most."

At this, Watson felt her smile grow wider.

"Thanks," she said. Then she nodded at Captain Gregson, still in a huddle with the two security guards. "They look like they're taking some convincing."

Holmes turned to them, sliding his hands into the pockets of his pea coat. "Unsurprising, considering I was caught red-handed standing right by the Blue Carbuncle."

"The Blue Carbuncle?" Watson frowned. "Wait a minute. You've mentioned that before, ages ago. You said you'd worked a case on it?"

"Indeed. The Blue Carbuncle is a gemstone, one that used to belong to the Earls of Morcar, passed down the female side from countess to countess. Fascinating history. In the late 1880s it was stolen and later found in the crop of a Christmas goose."

Watson raised an eyebrow. "A... goose?"

"A *Christmas* goose, Watson."

"Oh, well, that makes all the difference."

"It was stolen again in the late 1990s and was missing for a decade before I assisted with its recovery."

"And now you're saying it's here, in the museum?"

Holmes turned and grinned, extracting one hand from his coat and gesturing to the front of the museum. Watson looked. The bright projection advertising the pre-Colombian gold exhibition was still on.

Then she saw the banner behind it. It hung vertically between the two columns on the left side of the façade, stopping just short of a large, ornate iron-grille door. It was bleached out by the projection, easy to miss until Holmes pointed it out. The banner advertised another special exhibition at the museum.

"The Blue Carbuncle is now the centerpiece of the Miranda Collection," said Holmes. "Quite possibly the finest privately owned grouping of rare jewels and gemstones in the world." He paused. "Actually, a lot of it is merely average in quality and value, but together"—he drew his hands together, locking his fingers to demonstrate—"they are quite the cache. But certainly the Blue Carbuncle is a remarkable mineral. The name is a misnomer—this carbuncle is actually a very rare blue diamond at least the size of, oh…"

Holmes held up a clenched fist and shook it. Watson's eyes went wide.

"Wow. Poor goose."

"Just a shame whoever had the honor of christening such a gem was far from expert at geology…"

Holmes tailed off, dropping his fist, clearly distracted by something over Watson's shoulder. Watson turned to see what he was looking at.

Dr. Lisa Harley was walking quickly toward them, her face tight, anxious, her eyes flicking this way and that as if wary of being observed. Watson tensed and took a step closer to Holmes; Holmes, perhaps sensing his partner's unease, raised his chin defiantly. Then, as Harley reached them, his face broke into a broad and not entirely genuine grin, and he bounced on his heels.

"Aren't you going to introduce me to your friend, Watson?"

Watson frowned at him, but in her moment of hesitation, Holmes seemed to change his mind and reached forward with a dirt-smeared hand.

"Sherlock Holmes, consultant to… well, never mind."

The corners of Dr. Harley's mouth twitched into a glassy smile as she slowly extended her own hand. Holmes grabbed it and began pumping it up and down with some enthusiasm, pulling himself closer and peering into Dr. Harley's face. "It is a rare honor to meet the curator of such a valuable and important exhibition. You have my hearty congratulations."

The curator leaned back a little as Holmes shoved his nose in her face, the expression on her own face fluid with surprise and disgust at the dirt-streaked, smelly individual in front of her. Holmes nodded, gave a little grunt of satisfaction, then released Dr. Harley's hand and stepped back. The curator's smile flickered back on, but she held her hand out in front of her a little, like she didn't want to touch anything else with it.

"Mr. Holmes," she muttered. Then she glanced at Watson, her eyebrows going up just a hair.

She wanted to talk.

Watson turned to Holmes to ask him for a little privacy, but before she could speak, Captain Gregson reappeared. He nodded at the curator, then glanced at his two consultants.

"Everything okay, folks?"

Holmes looked from Gregson, to Watson, to Harley, a smile fixed on his face. Watson glanced at Dr. Harley and saw the curator had her eyes downcast.

Watson let out a breath she hadn't realized she was holding, and shook her head. "No, we're fine, Captain, thanks."

A voice drifted down from the stairs by the museum entrance.

"Lisa?"

The group turned as another woman approached. She was Hispanic, mid-thirties, with black hair twisted into a long, elegant braid that curled around her head and down to her bust. She was wearing a dress of a color best described as "nude," although it was several shades lighter than her own dark olive skin. Her heels were gold leather and so high Watson didn't know how she could possibly walk in them.

And she had a companion. A large man in a tuxedo, bald, chinstrap beard. As they got closer, Watson wondered if he had a black ski mask in one pocket and a gun in the other.

And whoever the woman was, Watson could see she clearly made Dr. Harley nervous. The curator still had a smile plastered on her face, but Watson could see the muscles in her neck tense, her jaw locked as she forced the expression to stay on her face.

"Ah, Margarita, I've been looking for you," said Dr. Harley, her voice breathless. She gave the other woman a little bow, then gestured to the others. "I was just making sure our guests were all right after that unfortunate interruption." The glazed look in her eyes suggested to Watson that she was slipping back into the gala host persona; whatever opportunity there had been to speak privately was long gone. "May I introduce Margarita Caballero. Margarita represents the corporate sponsor of our exhibition. Without her generous support and assistance, this enterprise could never have got off the ground."

Holmes leaned forward, holding out his hand to Margarita. "Oh, I am quite sure of that," he said. "Charmed, madam."

Margarita extended her hand but Holmes merely touched her fingers lightly before quickly stepping back into line, his hands behind his back.

Margarita looked at him for a moment, one eyebrow slightly raised, then she nodded a polite greeting to Watson and Gregson before turning to the man in the tuxedo. "This is my assistant, Angelino," she said. He gave a bow—it was the first time he had taken his eyes off Watson. She was suddenly glad to be back in the company of Holmes and Captain Gregson, and in a public space.

"*Perdón*, I apologize for the interruption," said Margarita, her English well practiced, her accent thick. She turned to Dr. Harley and placed a perfectly manicured hand on the curator's shoulder. "We should get back to the gala and reassure the guests that this was merely a false alarm."

Watson glanced at Margarita's hand. Her grip on the curator was far from friendly.

Then Margarita turned on a bright smile. "It has been but a short pleasure. *Hasta luego*." She nodded at Angelino, and the pair turned and headed back up the steps toward the museum.

"I'm sorry, I have to go," said Dr. Harley. She looked at Watson again, the spark of fear in her eyes. Watson frowned. She wanted to say something, offer her the chance to talk... but what could she do? Margarita and her goons clearly had some kind of hold on Harley, that much was obvious.

Beside her, Captain Gregson frowned while Holmes

nodded, offering the curator a tight smile.

Dr. Harley turned to leave.

"Wait," said Watson. She stepped after the curator, opening her clutch purse. She pulled a card from inside and, moving close to Dr. Harley so nobody would see, slipped it to her.

"We can help you. You can call me if you need to. Any time of the day or night. My phone will be on. Okay?"

Dr. Harley stiffened, her eyes not on Watson or the card but scanning the stragglers still loitering outside the museum.

"I don't know what you're talking about," she said. But she palmed the card from Watson anyway, then turned and hurried up the steps.

Holmes and Gregson watched as Watson returned.

"An excellent evening's work," said Holmes, nodding at both her and the Captain. "Well done us."

Gregson frowned. "Well done? I don't know if you remember but Watson here got held at *gunpoint*."

Watson folded her arms. "Look, I'm fine," she said. "There's something going on at the museum, but I don't know how this all connects to the murder victim."

Holmes had his tongue stuffed in his cheek. He looked sideways at the Captain.

"Did you inform Liam Macnamara's next of kin yet?"

Gregson blinked. "Ah, no. Still haven't found his sister."

"I suggest you start at the museum."

Gregson and Watson exchanged a look. "The museum?" Gregson asked.

"Yes, the museum," said Holmes. "Lisa Harley is Liam Macnamara's long-lost sister."

Watson looked at him. "And you deduced that... how?"

"Her accent," said Holmes. "Actually, I was rather impressed. Not only has she spent many years in the United States, she has been putting a lot of work into it. But her American accent is mostly an affectation. There are distinct traces of her real Northern Irish lilt hidden beneath. It takes years of practice and the assistance of a voice coach to eliminate natural speech patterns."

"If you don't mind me saying," said Gregson, "that seems a bit of a leap. New York is full of people of Irish descent." He tapped himself on the chest with two fingers. "*Myself* included."

Holmes nodded. "Quite correct, Captain. New York is a melting pot. But that was merely the icing on the cake, as it were." He pointed to his own eyes, circling them with two grimy fingers. "Lisa Harley has distinctive gold flecks in her green eyes, nearly identical to those present in the irises of Liam Macnamara. Not only that, she has the most remarkable set of Darwin's tubercles that I have laid eyes on."

Gregson raised an eyebrow. "Darwin's tubercles?"

"Distinctive peaks on the inner side of the ear," said Watson, pointing to the position on her own ear for the Captain's benefit. "They're a genetic trait. Like iris coloration."

Gregson nodded. "So Lisa Harley is Liam Macnamara's sister. Which means she's the person we have to notify."

Holmes pursed his lips. He turned and looked up at the museum. Most of the gala guests had returned inside, leaving them alone on the stairs.

"I'm not sure that would be wise, at least for the moment," he said. "If Lisa Harley is under coercion, then chances are her brother was as well."

"So what do you suggest we do?" asked Gregson, the frustration evident in his voice.

"We think," said Holmes. "We *process*." He looked at the others. "We collect Detective Bell." He pulled out his phone and started typing. "I will text him to say we are coming back."

With that, he trotted down the stairs.

Gregson shook his head, then, glancing at Watson, he removed his jacket and offered it to her. She laughed, then nodded.

Gregson in shirtsleeves and Watson in an oversized tuxedo jacket, they headed off after Sherlock Holmes.

19

A MISSING PERSON

"Y'all took your time."

Bell was sitting on a park bench on the Hudson River Greenway, his shoulders hunched and his hood up against the chill. He stood as the trio of Holmes, Watson and Gregson approached.

"It's a half-hour walk," said Gregson. He glared at Holmes.

Holmes nodded. "The night air is nectar for the synapses, Captain." He looked at Bell, then turned around in a circle, his eyes scanning up and down the road.

Watson drew Gregson's rented tuxedo close to her body. "What's up?"

"Where's Judge D?"

"Who's Judge D?" asked Gregson.

"An urban explorer Holmes met online," said Watson. "He was the one who led him into the tunnels."

Bell, hands in his pockets, gave an exaggerated shrug and looked at Holmes. "Wasn't he with you? He didn't come back out this end anyway, unless it was somewhere else down the Greenway. I've been waiting for three hours out here. On my own." He turned to Captain Gregson, his expression less than happy.

Holmes paced along the road, peering into the scrubby bushes that lined the Greenway, as though expecting to find Judge D hiding in the foliage.

Bell watched him for a moment, then turned to the others. "Someone want to fill me in on what happened?"

Gregson gave his account of the night to Bell as Holmes walked in a tight, agitated circle. Watson watched him, recognizing the body language. The gushing confidence Holmes had exhibited back on the museum steps had gone, replaced by something dark, moody. And Watson knew exactly what Holmes's problem was.

He was *uncertain*.

For Sherlock Holmes, that was perhaps the one thing he was truly afraid of: *not knowing*. Knowledge was power. Knowledge was control. And that was how Holmes processed the world around him, Watson knew that. He found the world, and the people in it, fundamentally problematic. But the one way he could bear it, the one thing that allowed him to operate in a more or less normal manner, was to exert *control*. Nothing tangible, nothing *real*. But it was knowledge that gave him this control, even if it was just control over himself.

And that was what drove him, Watson knew, to solve mysteries and crimes—despite what he often said about his mind "rebelling at stagnation," his work was really his way of imposing some kind of order on the chaos of life. Once he was on the trail of a mystery, he wouldn't let go until he had solved it. As Watson had come to understand, the desire to solve a murder, bring a criminal to justice, or obtain closure for victims and their families was not necessarily her partner's primary motivator—although these *were* important to him, of course. Instead, it was the *pursuit*, the "Great Game" as he liked to call it, that was the real driving force. Missing pieces of a puzzle didn't just frustrate him, they made him angry; not at others, but at *himself*. As he saw it, an unknown variable was merely proof that he was a failure.

And now Watson recognized a new unknown variable.

Judge D had not returned.

Holmes came to a stop. He turned to Watson, his expression drawn. She knew he was worried about the missing guide—genuinely so—but she also knew that she couldn't press the matter. The more she did, the more Holmes would withdraw into his own anxious mind.

"He must have come up somewhere else," she said, as casually as possible. She looked at Holmes. His jaw was locked solid, but then he seemed to relax. He nodded.

"A logical deduction, Watson." Then he closed his eyes, rubbing them with the heels of his hands. "We are lacking data. Without data we cannot infer."

Gregson stroked his chin. "I can put in for a search warrant for the museum."

Holmes dropped his hands and opened his eyes. He gave a theatrical sigh. "An extraordinarily *bad* idea, Captain. As soon as we move on the museum, they will know we are onto them."

Watson shook her head. "I'm pretty sure they know that already." She glanced at the two cops. "We need help on this. It can't be the four of us against the world all the time, Sherlock."

Holmes rolled his neck, then he exhaled through his nose and nodded. "Very well. Captain, can you look into the exhibition itself without drawing attention to any investigation? The financial arrangements of the sponsor corporation, perhaps?"

"Absolutely."

"Excellent. In the meantime, Ms. Watson and I will do a little more digging into the late Mr. Macnamara." He turned to his partner. "I think we should pay his employer a visit."

Watson nodded. "And try and piece his last movements together. Good idea."

"Okay," said Gregson. He looked around. They were alone

on the Hudson River Greenway. "Now let's get out of here."

"This way," said Bell. He started walking, leading them back to where Watson's car was parked under the nearby overpass.

As they made their way, Bell and Holmes in the lead, Gregson dropped back to walk next to Watson.

"Hey," he said, keeping his voice low. "You sure you're okay?" He frowned at her, his face creased into an expression of concern that was quite genuine.

"I'm fine, really."

"Getting a gun pointed at you isn't fun. Believe me, I know that. And I also know *that guy* is hardly the most sensitive type." He lifted his eyebrows and nodded toward Holmes ahead of them.

Watson sighed, but she did so with a smile. "All I want now is a hot tea and good night's sleep in my own bed."

The Captain laughed. "And amen to that."

20

MR. PAUL BLACK OF THE MTA

"Wow, it's a terrible thing," said Paul Black. "I'm. I mean. Wow. Wow, that's a terrible thing. A terrible thing."

He shook his head and his elbows crinkled on the paperwork covering his desk as he turned a downcast look at Holmes and Watson, sitting in front of him.

Then the MTA supervisor leaned back in his chair in the cramped office, little more than a cupboard squeezed into the back of the Lexington Avenue and 59th Street subway station. His desk was too big for the room and was covered in papers. On the corner was a grimy old flat-panel display, the dirty beige box of the computer itself on the floor beside the desk. Next to the display was another computer, a laptop that looked, to Watson, like it was brand new.

It was early afternoon. The station—the eighth busiest on the whole New York subway—was bustling with shoppers and tourists, families out on day trips. Black's office was next to the equally tiny control room next door, where the station's signals and traffic, as well as the CCTV, were monitored. The subway system was managed from the main MTA control room elsewhere in the city—the exact location was kept secret for security reasons, as Holmes had explained to Watson on the journey over. Here, at one of the larger stations in Manhattan, the staff had minor signaling duties, but most of the system was now automated.

Black pursed his lips as he looked at his two visitors. He looked like he was in his mid-fifties, although Watson suspected he might actually be up to a decade younger; the spider naevi across his cheeks and nose spoke of a long drink habit, and she could see a stack of cigarette packets in the top drawer of the half-open filing cabinet behind him. He kept his salt-and-pepper hair trimmed neat and short, but when he rubbed his jowly face there came the rasp of unshaved skin. His eyes were a clear, bright green.

"A terrible thing," he said for what had to be the fifth time in as many minutes.

Holmes crossed his legs and linked his hands over his knees. He took a breath, then gestured with his hands to their host. "It is, as you say, a terrible thing. And as Mr. Macnamara's colleague for the last ten years at least, I'm sure you and he were quite close. I'm sorry to be the one to bring you such news, but…" Holmes tailed off, and he nodded, his eyes closed. "You have my condolences."

"Ah, yeah," said Black. "Twelve years now. How did you…?"

Holmes pointed behind Black. On the rear wall of the office was a whiteboard, next to it a large corkboard. The whiteboard was packed tight with a grid, filled in with different colored pens, while the corkboard was covered in pinned papers. There, stuck in the bottom corner, was a faded photo taken in a dark bar, the flash bleaching most of the color from the faces of those in the image. Paul Black was front and center, his hair darker, his frame slimmer, his arm locked around an equally young-looking Liam Macnamara.

"That photo," said Holmes. "The people behind you

are clad in the unmistakable pirate-themed shirts of the Tampa Bay Buccaneers, watching what is clearly Superbowl XXXVII on the television behind the bar." He turned to Watson. "The Buccaneers beat the Oakland Raiders forty-eight to twenty-one. It was *quite* the match." He faced Black again. "January 23, 2003." Then he smiled. "You two look positively chummy."

"Oh, yeah, yeah," said Black, turning on his chair to look. "He was a great guy, he really was. Nice guy. Good worker too. And now he's dead?" He turned back to the consultants and shook his head again. "That's a terrible thing. How'd it happen?"

Holmes and Watson exchanged a look. Watson frowned. It was bad enough they were breaking the news of Macnamara's death to his old supervisor themselves, before the victim's next of kin—Dr. Lisa Harley, apparently—had been informed, but it seemed they had little choice in the matter.

Especially if Dr. Lisa Harley had been involved in her brother's death.

Watson turned back to the supervisor. "I'm afraid to say your colleague was murdered, Mr. Black."

"Murdered? Wow. My God. That's a terrible thing. You said you were consultants to the NYPD or something?"

Holmes nodded.

"So, you catch the son of a bitch who done it yet?"

"We're following some leads," said Holmes. "But at the moment we're just trying to piece together the late Mr. Macnamara's movements over his final few days."

"Well, if you think I can help with that, I'm happy to," said Black.

Holmes refolded his legs and frowned. He rubbed his own chin. "I'm starting to think you *can't*, in fact, Mr. Black."

Black looked at him and blinked, then he looked at Watson. He shook his head and leaned across the desk, the paperwork shifting under his elbows. "Come again?"

"A good worker," said Holmes. "That was what you just told us. Liam Macnamara was a great guy and a *good* worker."

"Yes, but—"

"So why did the MTA let him go?"

"I... what?"

Holmes gestured to the whiteboard now, his palm open. "The work schedule," he said. "Letters and numbers across the top are dates and shifts, letters and numbers down the first column the initials of all staff under your purview. With the exception of Liam Macnamara. The space where his name should be has been wiped, as has the whole row. It would be too much effort to redo all the rows below his just to shift them up, so you are waiting for the next monthly roster before updating it."

Black's shoulders slumped. He huffed loudly, shuffled some papers on his desk, then looked back up.

"Look, he's a good guy, believe me. *Was* a good guy. Sorry."

"As you keep saying," said Holmes. He unclasped his hands and slid forward on his chair, fixing the supervisor with a steely gaze. "And while I understand it is considered poor form to speak ill of the so recently deceased, we are investigating the man's *murder*. So, as amiable as the late Mr. Macnamara may well have been, a problem had recently developed in his work, hadn't it?" Holmes raised an anticipatory eyebrow.

Watson looked at Black. The supervisor looked uncomfortable. She smiled. "We need to know, Mr. Black. It could be vital information that leads to his killer."

Black sighed. "Okay. So he was fine until maybe a couple of months ago. He changed, y'know? He was, I dunno, stressed or something. Snappy. He looked terrible too. Pale. Thought maybe he was sick, maybe he should go see a doctor. But he said he was fine—in fact, he even started taking more overtime, pulling double shifts." He spread his palms. "Hey, I was worried. We all was, but, y'know, what could you do?"

Holmes tilted his head. "Let me take a guess. A stressed, exhausted driver? A motorman who is quite possibly ill and overdoing it? Why, you would *report* him, wouldn't you?"

"Right, right!" said Black, pushing a pudgy finger toward Holmes. "Exactly. Safety first, right? And he started coming in late too, missing the start of his shifts. Caused merry havoc with the schedule."

Watson nodded. "So you took him off the schedule altogether?"

"Hey," said Black. "Look, the decision wasn't mine." He gestured to himself with both hands and a shrug of the shoulders. "But I had to report him upstairs. First he was suspended, but then he kept showing up! Hanging around, y'know? So in the end he was let go." Black shrugged. "It's a shame, y'know? He's a great guy, great motorman. *Was*, sorry. Was."

Holmes nodded. "I'm sure. And, as I said, my condolences." He closed his eyes again and nodded, like a doctor imparting bad news to an ill patient.

Then he looked up, eyes wide and sparkling. "Do you have an up-to-date map of the subway network we might make use of?"

Black took a breath, paused, let it out slowly, then gave another shrug. "Ah, sure. I mean, you can get subway maps off the website, but I guess we have some around here you can have."

Holmes's smile was tight. He held up a finger. "No, you misunderstand me, Mr. Black. I meant a map of the whole network. Tunnels, stations, service lines, rail yards. Everything the MTA administers and uses. Open, closed, used, disused, abandoned. The works."

Black sat back in his chair, shaking his head. "I'm sorry,"

he said, "that kind of information is not in the public domain." He glanced at Watson, perhaps seeing her as the more reasonable member of the partnership; she raised an eyebrow as this thought crossed her mind. "Since 9/11, y'know?" Black continued. "It's a security risk. That kind of stuff is sensitive information."

"I understand the restrictions, Mr. Black," said Holmes, "but it is that very kind of occurrence that I am trying to prevent."

Watson looked at her partner, but she bit her lip. His eyes were fixed on Paul Black.

The supervisor leaned across his desk, his eyes widened just for a second or two, then he sat back again. "What, terrorism now? I thought you was investigating a murder?"

The closed eyes, the bowed head, the patient doctor look again. "The two may well be connected, Mr. Black," said Holmes.

Black watched Holmes with narrow eyes, then clasped his fingers over his stomach.

"Look, sorry, can't help you. You'll need to go upstairs and make a request. I'm only a supervisor."

"Very well," said Holmes. He leapt from his chair, arms stiff by his sides. "Thank you for your time. This has been most revealing."

And then he turned and left the office without another word, Watson barely out of her own chair. She sighed and offered Black her hand, and he shook it.

"Thank you for your help," she said.

Black smiled tightly. "Hey, anytime, anytime, Ms. Watson."

She turned to leave, and was halfway to the door when Black spoke again. "Ah, look, Ms. Watson. About Liam. I'm cut up. Seriously. He's a good guy. *Was* a good guy, sorry. I'll have a word with the lads, maybe get a collection together. Y'know, for the motorman benevolent fund. In his honor. The lads will want to. Y'know. Make a gesture."

Watson smiled and nodded. "Thank you, Mr. Black. Goodbye."

Back down on the subway station platform, Watson looked around, but Holmes was nowhere in sight.

21

AN UNEXPECTED CALL

Holmes was standing on the corner of Lexington Avenue and East 59th Street, cellphone to his ear, apparently surveying the bustle of Sunday shoppers as they streamed in and out of the collection of upmarket department stores that crowded the broad intersection. As Watson approached, he nodded and lowered the phone, studying the screen with a frown.

"Superbowl XXXVII?" she asked with a smile. "I thought you hated football?"

Holmes shrugged. "I am completely indifferent to the sport, but memorizing games and their scores is a useful mental exercise."

He continued to stare at the phone. Now it was Watson's turn to frown.

"Everything okay?"

Holmes sniffed, then thumbed the phone's sleep button and slipped it into his pocket.

"I was just trying to reach Judge D. He encountered something in the sewer tunnels some time before the expedition he allowed me to tag along on. I need to know what—or who—it was he found."

"You think he ran into the same men you did?"

"I assumed that at the time, and, indeed, it is more than likely my belief is correct."

Watson's mouth curled at the corner into a faint smile. Holmes seemed to notice, his own mouth turning into a scowl as he glanced away, slightly embarrassed. "But, *yes*, I am also aware that making assumptions is a dangerous pastime." He nodded down the street. "Shall we?"

The pair headed down Lexington Avenue, the sunlight streaking through the tall buildings glorious, invigorating. After her experience the previous night, Watson had lain in bed for what felt like hours, staring at the ceiling, replaying the events over and over in her mind. Out here, in the city, in the streets full of people and cars and taxis and trucks and the chaos of everyday life, she felt better.

She returned her thoughts to their meeting with Liam Macnamara's MTA supervisor.

"So, what do you think he was hiding?" she asked as they walked.

Holmes smiled. "Obvious, wasn't it?"

"At first I just thought that was the kind of guy he was, but it was his reaction when you mentioned the possibility of terrorism that got me. That was a good play."

"Indeed, Watson," said Holmes. "Someone comes into your station talking about terrorism, you fly into action!" Holmes swept his arms up as they walked, like he was gathering up an armful of air. "You would be on the phone to 'upstairs' at once. The MTA is obliged to take all threats seriously. As well they should."

"But there was nothing," said Watson. "He barely batted an eyelid."

"Because he was too preoccupied hiding something else. Or because he knew I was wrong."

They walked on. Something else bugged Watson, niggled

at her conscience. She had to bring it up.

"I'm not sure we were the right ones to break the news of his co-worker's murder, though. The victim's sister doesn't even know yet."

"She may well know far more than we do," said Holmes.

Watson looked at him. "You really think Lisa Harley killed her brother?"

Holmes rolled his shoulders. "Well, why not? The killer knew the victim. The killer was also fabulously inept at using an Uzi submachine gun. And we have the museum connection."

"But her own *brother*?" Watson frowned. "Especially if they are—*were*—both in on the job?"

"Sibling rivalry? Familial feud?" Holmes shook his head. "Wouldn't be the first time. As far as the NYPD have managed to find out, they were estranged, hadn't seen each other in years. There could be innumerable reasons one would want to eliminate the other."

Holmes was right. As Watson considered the implications, her partner stopped. Watson, realizing she was walking alone, turned to see Holmes standing stock still in the middle of the sidewalk, forcing the foot traffic to part around him in two streams. He was staring at his phone.

As Watson watched, Holmes's face blanched, the blood draining, his whole expression collapsing.

Watson rushed back to him. "What's happened? Who is it?"

Holmes swallowed heavily. "Detective Bell. The police have found a body in a subway station. He says we are needed there immediately."

Watson blinked. A second murder? "Does he know who it is?"

Holmes nodded, then screwed his face tight and, with his eyes closed, he smacked his phone into his forehead three times before exhaling loudly and looking at Watson.

"It's Judge D. I fear the very worst has happened."

22

THE SECOND VICTIM

Watson descended the stairs of the subway station on the corner of West 79th and Broadway, Holmes a few paces ahead of her. He'd been silent on the cab ride over, simply staring at the partition that separated the rear of the vehicle from the driver, his cellphone clutched so tightly in his hand his knuckles were white. The station was closed when they got there, yellow police tape across the entrance, two uniformed officers on duty and three patrol cars parked along the curb. They'd had to wait by the stairs, Holmes silent, Watson trying to ignore the crowd of people gathering on the sidewalk as one of the uniforms talked into his radio. A couple of minutes later, Detective Bell's voice crackled back, and the uniform lifted the police tape and waved them through.

The platform was eerily quiet without the usual crowds, the fluorescent lights seeming to buzz and flicker, the smell of the place like that of every subway station: garbage, urine, and the sooty dust of train brakes. Watson hunched her shoulders, aware of the uncomfortable, tense atmosphere. The station was the same as most others in the city, a place so familiar, suddenly so foreign, so alien.

Bell was standing on the edge of the platform, at the end closest to the stairs Watson and Holmes had just come down. Down on the tracks, close to the tunnel entrance, a uniformed officer and two plainclothes stood, giving a CSU tech wearing blue coveralls plenty of room as she crouched over something hidden from view, under the overhang of the station platform. Glancing down the platform, Watson counted another four uniforms and one more detective she didn't recognize. He was talking to another CSU tech who was carrying a large plastic toolbox, and an MTA worker in short white sleeves, his ID badge hanging on a lanyard around his neck.

Watson turned to Holmes. He ground his back teeth as he stood with his toes over the platform edge, looking down at the crime scene. He was silent, swaying slightly, as though he might just topple straight over onto the tracks like a felled tree. Watson left him to contemplate the scene—a scene she wasn't sure she wanted to see herself—and walked over to Bell.

"What happened?"

The detective flipped open his notebook, perhaps more out of habit than necessity. When he related the facts to Watson, he didn't glance at the page once.

"The body was spotted by a passenger standing farther along the platform," Bell said, turning and pointing down the empty station. "It was tucked under the edge of the platform here by the tunnel, but it wasn't well hidden. Rush job, maybe. Station controller called it in and the MTA control center closed the station so they could take a look." He pointed with his pen toward the tracks. "Third rail is out so it's safe to go down."

Watson nodded, and turned around. Holmes was still on the platform edge.

"Sherlock—"

Then he jumped down onto the tracks, his heavy landing making the group gathered around the body turn to see. Holmes marched toward them, arms rigid by his side. The police and the CSU tech, perhaps sensing it was best not to get in his way, stood well clear.

Watson took a breath and ventured to the platform edge, then looked down.

The body was lying face-up, eyes open, stubbled face spattered with congealed blood and smeared with black brake dust. He was an older man, thin, small. He was wearing a flannel shirt that might have been plaid, but it was hard to tell; the thick fabric, acting like a sponge, was saturated with blood.

Holmes bent over the body. "Nine millimeter, multiple shots," he said.

Bell joined Watson at the platform edge and closed his notebook. "Right first time."

Watson's eyes widened. "Like the first victim?"

Holmes stood back and, his eyes still on the body, stretched out an arm toward the CSU tech nearby. The woman glanced at the police officer with her, one eyebrow arched, then shrugged and fished out a box of latex gloves from the toolkit at her feet. Holmes pulled a pair free and crouched over the body again. Watson couldn't quite see, her partner's back shielding the body from view, but he seemed to be pulling back the edges of the deceased's blood-soaked shirt.

"Not at all like the first victim," said Holmes after a moment. "Liam Macnamara was gunned down in his apartment by an amateur, one who had never handled something as powerful as an Uzi before in his or her life." He stood and looked up at Watson, gestured to the broken body on the tracks, his expression grim, his jaw set. "Victor Judd was killed by an expert. The placement of the shots, all to the center mass. Any single one would have killed him. Any more and he would have been cut clean in half."

Watson felt bile rise in her throat. That explained the blood. Who the hell would do something like that? Urban exploration was illegal and certainly dangerous, but surely harmless, in the grand scheme of things.

Wasn't it?

Bell nodded. "CSU says he was shot twelve times."

Holmes looked him in the eye. "Yes," he said, his voice barely audible. "The violence of his end was quite intentional, Detective."

Bell frowned and waved his notebook in the air.

"Do you think this has anything to do with last night?"

Holmes sighed, closing his eyes to inhale deeply through his nose. He stood like that for a few seconds, unmoving and silent. Bell and Watson exchanged a look, then Bell cleared his throat.

"All I meant was that the vic went into those tunnels of his own volition. He was going whether we—or *you*, anyway—were with him or not."

Holmes opened his eyes and tilted his head to look down at the body again. "You are right, Detective, Mr. Judd here is likely to have met his fate with or without our involvement. He knew exactly where he wanted to go. Unfortunately his own curiosity got the better of him."

Watson and Bell exchanged a look. Bell's expression didn't change, but Watson could see something in his eyes. Being a New York City cop was hardly a cakewalk, but you learned how to deal with it—you had to, or the dark side of the city would tear you apart. The job was never easy but some days... some days were just that little bit harder. Today was one of them. And unlike herself, Bell had known the victim, met him, even if it had just been the briefest of encounters.

Holmes gestured at the body. "The excessive manner of his execution is designed to serve as a warning."

Bell looked up and down the platform, like he was searching for something in particular. "If it's a warning, why hide the body under there?"

"He wasn't hidden. He was placed here, close enough

to the tunnel for his killers to come and go discreetly, but obvious enough that he would be found eventually." Holmes looked from the body to the tunnel entrance and back, then he stepped over the deactivated third rail that ran close to the platform edge and paced out the distance. At the tunnel entrance he stopped and turned around.

"Ten feet. An easy distance to creep in, place the body, then make your escape. It would have taken perhaps twenty seconds."

Bell shook his head. "Well, we're checking the CCTV now. If someone just walked in from the tunnel carrying a body then we'll have them on camera." He pointed with his pen to the ceiling above Holmes's head, where a security camera was positioned.

Holmes looked up. "Subway surveillance is woefully inadequate at many stations, Detective. That camera is pointed at the platform with a blind spot right here." He looked back at the detective, gesturing along the edge of the platform. "All you have to do is keep your head down. How do you think Victor's friends, the urban explorers, gain access to the subway system in the first place? It's remarkably easy. All you need to do is keep your eyes open and pick the right moment."

"Okay," said Watson, "so they left him here as a warning. But a warning for who?"

"For *whom*, Watson."

Watson sighed. "Sherlock!"

Holmes pursed his lips. Watson didn't like the look on his face one little bit. And she was fairly certain she didn't want to hear what she feared he was about to say next.

"For *us*, Watson. The warning is for *us*."

23

THE WARNING IS RECEIVED

Watson looked down at the body. As they had been talking, the police, CSU techs and MTA staff had gathered in a group around them. Watson looked up, noticing them for the first time, the surprise momentarily clouding her thoughts.

Judge D had been killed for a very particular reason. Just the thought of that made Watson feel sick to her stomach.

Holmes stood over the body, looking down at it. Victor Judd's lifeless eyes looked back.

"They know about us," he said. "They know what we are doing. So they left us a calling card."

Watson rubbed her forehead as she took it in. "The men at the museum," she said. "Right?"

Holmes nodded, his mouth forming a tight white line. "Easy enough for someone of their strength and athleticism to carry the body here, running between the trains. A gang of South American drug-runners, no doubt field operatives of one of the major Colombian cartels. We have walked right into the middle of a major play."

Bell said, "He never came back out at the Greenway, Holmes.

You think they got him in the tunnels, after he left you?"

Holmes nodded. "Caught on the way out. Most likely the same men I saw myself. *That* was what he must have seen on an earlier trip underground. And he couldn't resist another look, even with me in tow." He looked up at Bell, standing over him on the platform. Holmes shrugged. "Perhaps, Whitehall aside, that was why he was so easily persuaded. Perhaps he thought there was safety in numbers."

Holmes bent down again and carefully pulled the man's shirt together, straightening it out despite the gore, like he was trying to make his ruined body decent. He ran his hand over Judge D's face, closing his eyes. Watson knew he shouldn't have done that, not until CSU had given the all-clear, but nobody said anything and, she thought, she might have been tempted to do the same.

Then Holmes stood, pulled his latex gloves off and tossed them onto the tracks, then pulled himself up onto the platform on his stomach, swinging his legs around and standing.

Watson drew breath to speak, but almost immediately, and without a word, Holmes hurried for the stairs. She watched his back for a moment, then, when he was gone, turned to face Bell.

"We got this," he said, but Watson could see the muscles at the back of his jaw tense as he looked away.

Watson headed after Holmes, jogging up the stairs toward the daylight. At street level she nearly ran into his back. Holmes stood two steps down from the street; ahead, one of the uniforms standing guard was holding the yellow crime scene tape up, ready for them to pass under, but Holmes didn't move.

Watson stepped around her partner. He was staring straight ahead, staring at nothing, the corners of his mouth downturned. She placed her hand on his arm and realized he was shivering.

"Hey, are you okay?" she asked, quietly.

Holmes twitched, like her presence at his side was a surprise.

"No, Watson, I most certainly am *not* okay." He paused, glanced at the officer holding the tape up, then he ducked under it and stopped on the sidewalk. Watson followed.

"Sherlock, this is not your fault. You couldn't have seen this coming. Nobody can predict the future. Not even you. Besides, you said it yourself: Whether you had been there or not, Victor would have run into his killers. It would have ended the same way."

Holmes held his head up, inhaling deeply through his nose. Then he seemed to relax.

"Perhaps you are right," he said. "But I should have been more cautious. I was too lost in the mystery, Watson. Blasé, in point of fact. I underestimated the forces arrayed against us. Victor Judd is proof of that. I missed the bigger picture and now another man is dead."

He smiled. It was a sad expression.

Watson squeezed his arm. She looked into his eyes. They were wet.

"Then let's bring them justice, both of them. Let's catch the bastards who killed Victor and Liam."

Holmes nodded.

"Oh yes," he said, his voice a low, dark whisper. "We most certainly will do that much, at least."

24

CONTACT IS ESTABLISHED

Watson padded down the stairs and headed into the brownstone's spacious kitchen.

It was late, the house quiet, still. Outside a car cruised by, momentarily breaking the silence.

As soon as they had returned home that afternoon, Holmes had shot up the stairs and locked himself in the media room, leaving Watson alone. But that was fine. She gave him the space he needed, and—if she was totally honest with herself—she needed it too. So she spent the rest of the day and the evening pottering around, doing nothing but making tea and moving from one armchair to the next, running the events of the last couple of days through her mind over and over again. It didn't feel like a particularly healthy thing to do, but she couldn't switch it off. So instead she turned it around, convincing herself that she was merely reviewing evidence, clues. Periodically she would jot notes down as she orbited the brownstone.

She cleaned out Clyde's terrarium. She made more tea. She ordered in Thai food for dinner and ate it alone at the kitchen table. There was no sound from upstairs. Part of her nagged at her to check on Holmes, to make sure he wasn't laid out on the floor, needle in his arm. Another part of her—the more rational part—told her that was ridiculous. Holmes having a shock didn't mean he would relapse. He was not that fragile. Not anymore. And then she realized how drained she was. Emotionally, physically. She'd had a shock too—several, in fact. She'd been held at gunpoint at the museum. She'd been to two bloody crime scenes. Liam Macnamara was dead and so too was Victor Judd.

How many more would they kill? And if Victor was a warning, did that mean they had her and Holmes in their sights next? And who were "they"?

Watson allowed exhaustion to claim her. She checked out the bay window at the front of the house, reassured, even just a little, at sight of the police patrol car parked opposite, the shadowed form within of the officer Gregson had assigned to keep an eye on their place.

Then she checked the back door, and the front door, and she made two mugs of chamomile tea and headed upstairs. It was still early, but Watson felt like she had run a marathon.

On the way to her room she stopped at the door of the media room. There was no sound beyond it. None of the several television sets were on, nor the police scanner. Nothing. Watson pressed her ear to the door, that nagging worry in the back of her mind again.

Silence.

She made a decision. She would knock on the door and then open it, and make sure he was okay. He could never be freed of temptation. That was an impossibility that addicts and their friends, family and supporters had to acknowledge, to accept. Every day was a battle, and would continue to be so for the rest of Holmes's life, no matter how much progress had been made, no matter how in control Holmes appeared to be now.

And make no mistake, Sherlock Holmes was strong—the strongest person Watson had ever met. But, even so, it was her duty to check on her friend.

Watson bit her lip, raised her hand, curled a knuckle, ready to knock.

Then there was a click from behind the door, and a squawking burst of static as one of the police scanners was turned on. Another burst of static, then *fwhup-fwhup-fwhup* as the dial was spun across the radio frequencies. Moments later came the quiet, distorted murmur of police communications.

Watson lowered her hand, smiled to herself, and deposited the mug of chamomile on the floor in front of the door, the heavy clunk against the floorboards, she decided, being sufficient notice.

Then she went to bed.

Three hours later, she was still staring at the ceiling. The night was warm and she had the window open a crack, a pleasant breeze dragging the thin lacy blind around the frame in spiraling eddies. No sooner had she closed her eyes than she felt wide, wide awake.

She lay there, focusing on the strange feeling of hollowness inside. It wasn't fear, or anxiety. It was a strange sort of emptiness, borne of fatigue and shock and… hopelessness. Yes, hopelessness. Liam Macnamara had got himself in too deep in whatever it was, and had gotten himself killed. Victor Judd had been just a bystander, a victim caught in the crossfire. Holmes blamed himself for Victor's death and Watson knew that, no matter what platitudes she offered— and no matter how heartfelt they were—she would have felt exactly the same way if she were in his shoes.

But nobody could predict the future. Not her, not even the remarkable Sherlock Holmes, consulting detective to the New York Police Department. He was brilliant, gifted, a savant. But he was also human. Even that amazing brain of his couldn't deduce from every clue, foresee every possibility that branched out as events unfolded.

Watson sighed, and got up. She left her room and headed

for the stairs, passing the media room. The door was still closed, the house was silent, the police scanner off. But the mug she'd left on the floor was gone.

In the kitchen, Watson found herself making more tea. She stopped at the faucet, holding the kettle as she filled it, not even realizing what she was doing. It was amazing how the human body, the human mind, could operate on automatic. In the days—the *weeks*, even—after leaving the hospital, how many times had she got into her car and zoned out and then found herself pulling into the staff parking lot? It was crazy, frustrating. Maybe a little frightening.

And here she was, doing it again.

Okay. So what? Tea was relaxing, good for you even. She couldn't sleep, so what the hell did it matter?

Kettle on, she wandered to the table and sat down. There, in front of her, was Sherlock's mug. It was empty, and there was a bright pink Post-it note stuck to the side. She plucked it off and peered at Holmes's handwriting.

GATHERING DATA. BACK L8ER. WILL
TXT NE DEVLP.
—S.H.

Watson laughed. Holmes's predilection for outdated text speak had started creeping into his written notes now.

She stuck the note back on the mug, wondering what he meant by "gathering data," then stood to fix her tea as the kettle boiled.

There was a buzzing from the table. As she poured water into her mug, she glanced back to where she had been sitting. Her cellphone vibrated on the table as a call came in.

Maybe it was Sherlock. Maybe he'd found something.

Quickly dumping the kettle on the stove with a clatter, Watson hurried to the table, picking the phone up. She glanced at the screen and paused. She didn't recognize the number displayed.

She hit *answer* and raised it to her ear.

"Hello?"

"Ah... Joan? Joan Watson?"

"Speaking."

"This is Lisa. Ah... Lisa *Harley*. We met at the museum the other night."

Watson slowly sank into the chair, leaned on the table on her elbows. Lisa Harley's voice was pitched high, like she was worried.

Afraid.

"Of course," said Watson. "Are you okay? What's wrong? Did something happen?"

A pause. Watson thought she could hear the curator take a deep breath with her mouth away from her phone, then there was a rustling, like she had brushed the phone against her face as she brought it back up to her mouth.

"Ah, look. I can't talk long. Not now. But I think... I think there's going to be a robbery. At the museum. I've found something."

Watson's heart kicked in her chest.

"Robbery?" This was it. Watson shook her head, pressing one hand to her forehead as she closed her eyes and concentrated. "No, wait, listen. Where are you now? I can come to you."

"I... I don't know. I don't know what to do."

Deep breath. One step at a time.

"Have you gone to the police?" Watson asked.

"No," said Dr. Harley. "I can't. Look, this goes right to the top. It's an inside job. Someone inside the museum is planning all this."

"What was going on at the gala? Who were those men you were with? I was looking for you when I found someone in one of the storerooms—"

"I know. I know. Look—"

"Dr. Harley, what's going on?"

"Lisa," she said. "It's Lisa."

"Okay, Lisa. Please, we'd like to help."

Another pause. Watson strained to hear—the curator had once again pulled her phone away from her ear, but there was no other sound on the line.

The phone rustled as Lisa came back. "I *can* trust you, can't I?" asked the curator.

"Of course you can."

"Because they know about me. They're watching me. I can't go to the police. I can't do anything. They said they'll kill me if I tell anyone."

"You can trust me, Lisa," said Watson. "I said we could help you and I meant it."

"Okay."

"So where are you? I'll come to you."

Another pause. "The museum. Meet me there in half an hour. I can show you what I found."

Watson nodded in the empty kitchen. "Okay, no problem. I'm on my way."

The phone went dead. Watson stared at it for a few seconds, her mind racing. A few seconds more and the display went dark as the phone went back to sleep.

Then Watson paused. She cocked her head, considering something else.

Lisa Harley sounded scared. That much was genuine. She sounded afraid and desperate, and that was hard to fake—the pitch of her voice, the rapidity of her breathing, everything. The curator was as frightened as she had sounded.

But... did someone force her to make the call? Dr. Harley was involved, that much was clear. Holmes had even suggested she might have been her brother's killer. But it was just a theory. One of many. One Watson wasn't entirely sure of.

One thing she did know was that she'd given Dr. Harley her number and had told her to call if she was in trouble.

She had called. She said she was in trouble. More than that, she had said she was in mortal danger. And despite her suspicions, Watson couldn't let that slide. She just needed to be careful. Softly, softly, as Captain Gregson had suggested.

Watson sighed, rubbing her temples as she leaned over the kitchen table. She could sit here all night second-guessing herself. What was that about not being able to predict the future? You just had to do your best. There were two murders to solve.

Softly, softly. No, that wasn't it, wasn't the way to handle it. Softly meant tiptoeing around, meant holding back, meant being cautious, but perhaps *too* cautious. Cautious to the point of *inaction*.

No, this required care of a different kind. Lisa's call was suspicious, there was no doubt in Watson's mind about that. But that fear, that was real. It wafted down the phone almost like a physical thing.

Lisa needed help. Watson needed answers. And Watson could handle herself. She knew she could.

And she could take precautions. If she was walking into something then she could have help there in an instant. Lisa had said she couldn't go to the cops, but Lisa didn't know the ones Watson did.

She lifted the phone again and called Gregson's cellphone. Voicemail.

She tried Bell. It rang for longer, then *his* voicemail clicked in. Watson ended the call and drummed her fingers on the table, then she tried Gregson again, waited for the recorded message to play through, and left one of her own.

"Captain Gregson, it's Joan Watson. I've just had a call from Lisa Harley. She says she's found something at the museum and wants to meet me there—she seems... agitated,

I think. Anyway, I'm going there now. I thought you should know—" *how to say "I just want someone to know where I am"?* "—so… yes. That's where I'll be."

She ended the call and then looked at the phone for a few seconds. Then glanced at Holmes's note again. She wished he hadn't vanished on a mystery errand in the middle of the night. Should she call him too? No. Who knew where he was "gathering data", or what that even really meant. She could jeopardize whatever he'd gotten himself into. But she had to let him know where she was. Even a text was better than nothing.

GONE TO MUSEUM TO MEET DR. HARLEY. SAYS SHE'S FOUND SOMETHING TO HELP WITH THE CASE.

She hit send. She stared at the screen and bit her lip.
It didn't seem quite enough.
She composed a new text. She addressed it to Gregson, Bell and Holmes. It consisted of one single line:

URGENT ASSISTANCE NATURAL HISTORY MUSEUM NOW NOW NOW!

Then she hit save instead of send, then double-checked that the message was sitting in *drafts*. If she locked the phone with the message sitting right where it was, all she would have to do later is press the home button then *send*. Two simple actions she could do quickly and, hopefully, without being seen.

If she had to send it. She really hoped she wouldn't.

Watson glanced at Holmes's note again, then, wishing he hadn't vanished on a mystery errand in the middle of the night. Should she call him too? No. Who knew where he was "gathering data," or what that even really meant.

She pushed her chair away from the table and raced upstairs to get dressed.

25

THE BENEVOLENT SOCIETY OF MOTORMEN

Despite the late hour, the Alpha Inn was packed with customers, a curious mix of young hipsters exploring the brave new world of the traditional Irish pub, and an older crowd of gnarled regulars eying the former, resentful perhaps that their haven was being slowly, insidiously invaded.

Holmes stuffed his hands in his pockets as he slid through the crowd, taking it all in, observing, *collating*. Sights. Smells. Sounds. Even taste, the air thick with a fug synonymous with the serious consumption of strong, imported ales. This was no place for the craft and hobby beers that were now so common in the bars of Brooklyn. But if you wanted a proper stout served, not warm as myth would have it, but at the precise, cool temperature of the cellar, then the Alpha Inn was the very establishment.

He saw them at the back, the group of seven men squeezed into a corner booth around a table designed to seat not quite that number. Little deduction was required to confirm it was the right group—they were all drinking and there were occasional bursts of hearty laughter, as loud as any emanating from the other clusters of friends gathered in the public house, but at this table the laughter was punctuated with quiet conversation, conversation which required the focused concentration—as focused as it could be, with alcohol being consumed—of the other members of the group. As Holmes watched them nod and smile and laugh and chat, he noted at least two men from the old photo in Paul Black's office, the same photo that had allowed him to identify the Alpha Inn as the favored watering hole of the group of motormen.

The warm company of friends. Colleagues and co-workers, here to toast the memory of one they had lost: Liam Macnamara.

Holmes sidled closer, squeezing carefully through the crush of people standing four deep at the bar, his eyes firmly on his target. Given the average age of the group, some of the motormen would have been firm friends for years. A group like this was hard for an outsider to break into—and even for newer employees, like the man seated in the corner. He was at least a decade and a half younger than the two old hands jostling him with their elbows on either side, and he had his nose mostly buried in his pint glass, taking just the tiniest of sips of the dark ale, which was quite clearly not to his taste.

Two booths over was a young couple making googly eyes at each other, a half-empty tall glass of a lighter, reddish ale by the man's elbow. With the couple paying more attention to each other than the hubbub of the pub around them, Holmes deftly rolled past the table, swiping the glass and vanishing back into the crowd. Circling another group of patrons, he headed back to the motormen, and as another raucous laugh orbited their table, he stepped closer and raised his own glass.

The young man in the corner gave him a smile. The others in the group fell quiet, looking up at him. The man at the head of the table did not turn around.

"Sorry, lads," said Holmes, spinning his words into the thick lilt of a Northern Irish accent, "but Paul said I could find you all here, so he did." His eyes were as wide as his grin.

He held the glass of ale high in plain sight.

The man at the head of the table turned his impressive bulk on the small stool under him, and looked up at Holmes. He was in his mid-to-late fifties, his light gray, nearly white collar-length hair swept back from his expansive forehead, his face framed by mutton-chop sideburns. Two thick eyebrows like exotic caterpillars drew together over his sky-blue eyes as he peered at the newcomer.

"Oh he did, did he?" said the man, his own accent holding traces of his Irish roots. The rest of the group stayed quiet. Holmes gave the man a grin, and held out his hand.

"David," he said, "David Friston. I went to school with Liam's sister, so I did."

Skew-el. Sis-tar.

Holmes kept his grin up.

The group looked at each other, then the big man with the eyebrows nodded, his mouth twitching into the smallest of smiles.

"Knew Liam, did you?"

"Well, friend of the family, more like," said Holmes. "Been here a month and meant to look him up." He shook his head. "A terrible thing what happened to the lad."

The big man nodded. "It was. He will be missed." Then he turned back around on his stool and gestured for Holmes to join them. Holmes raised his borrowed glass in thanks as the rest of the group in the booth shuffled around to accommodate. With one buttock perched on the edge of the bench seat, Holmes nodded to each of the men in turn as their de facto headman introduced them.

"That's Lee, Gareth, Guy, Alex, Chuck and Nate. We all drove trains with Liam. And I'm John. John Blaylock." John raised his glass and Holmes clinked the edge of his own against it.

"To Liam," he said.

The others raised their glasses to toast the dead man. As they did, a traditional Irish band complete with bodhrán and fiddle started up in the corner of the pub.

In his pocket, Holmes's phone vibrated. He pulled it out slowly, keeping it below the table to shield the glow of the screen.

A text from Watson. She was meeting Harley at the museum. Good. Excellent. More progress.

His expression remaining fixed, Holmes looked up at the group, their eyes already bright with alcohol, their inhibitions lowered, their desire to talk about their lost companion never stronger...

As John Blaylock began tapping his foot to the rhythm of the band, Holmes slid his phone back into his pocket and Holmes settled in for a few hours of observation, collation, and deduction.

26

THE LEGENDS OF THE UNDERCITY

"And then he comes at me like this…"

Holmes balanced on the edge of his seat and held his arms out in front of him, over the table, as he lolled his head and gave a zombie-like groan. The motormen erupted into laughter, John's face bright red against the gray of his sideburns as he slapped the top of the table with the flat of his fingers.

"And then," Holmes said, dropping his arms, "and then I said, hey, Jonny, I said, you'll have to do better than that, my lad!"

More laughter. Holmes, eyes wide, mouth in an "O" of surprise, swiveled around to look over his shoulder in mock surprise, then he turned back around.

"And then Jonny comes out of the other tunnel down the other end of the platform and he calls out, 'Hey Dave, did you say something just now?'"

Holmes doubled over, his chin practically on the sticky table as he bellowed with laughter at his own story. Around him the by now quite sloshed motormen sank back against the booth walls as they joined in.

Holmes sat up and sighed, wiping the tears from his eyes.

He raised his glass, still half full after two hours of inveigling himself into the group, and stood, his thighs knocking against the table, rattling the substantial collection of empty glasses on it.

"Ah, look now," he said. "A toast. To the motormen of the world, here in New York and there in London and everywhere else, and to Liam Macnamara, the best damn driver of the lot."

The gang cheered. None noticed Holmes failed to imbibe a single drop before he sat heavily back down. He winked at old John, and nodded at him, sucking air heavily in through his mouth like he'd had far too many.

"But come on now, will you," said Holmes, the modulation in his voice pitch-perfect. "You must have some stories of your own now, eh?" He glanced around the table. "You can't all just be sitting on your fannies as you drive your little trains from here to Coney Island and back again, eh? The New York subway is the busiest in the world, so they tell me. You lads must have seen it all, eh?"

At this, John drained the last dregs of his fifth ale in two hours and, pushing the spent glass into the center of the table, followed it as he leaned his forearms on the wood. He curled his finger, inviting the others to move closer. When the others, Holmes included, were nearly touching heads, John belched.

The others complained loudly, but with laughter, as they leaned back, but moments later John was waving at them again.

"No, seriously," he said. "Listen." He turned to Holmes. "You'll know there are alligators down there, of course." He winked and tapped the side of his nose. One of the others— the young man, Nate, swore and shook his head. John jerked his head back like he'd been slapped, and narrowed his eyes at the junior driver.

"What's that now?" asked John. All eyes were on Nate. He glanced around the group and sighed.

"Come on, John. If you're going to make it up, at least

get your story straight. I thought it was alligators were supposed to be in the sewers, not the subway." He hissed through his teeth and shook his head again, slouching back into the booth.

The others muttered to each other. Holmes looked from John to Nate and back again. The youngster had dared question the old master. The friendly atmosphere had cooled a degree.

"The subway and sewers both," said John. He looked around the group, all of whom—Holmes included—were suddenly entranced by the quiet, conspiratorial tone of the man's voice. "There are places under the city where the sewers and the subway run side by side, of course. There are even some abandoned subway stations and lines, like there are in London." He sat up and nodded at Holmes. "You'll have seen what Hurricane Sandy did to the city. Overwhelmed both networks. Flooded the subway. Whole stations were underwater. Perfect for 'gators to get from one system to the other."

Lee and Gareth exchanged a look, clearly unsure what to make of John's tale. Holmes watched the reactions of the others carefully. Chuck was too drunk to notice much of what was going on. The others seemed happy enough with John's explanation, nodding to themselves and each other as they took it in.

Holmes looked sideways at John.

"Seen them then, have you?"

John frowned. "'Gators? Well, I—"

"No, I mean the old stations. The abandoned ones."

"Oh," said John, his big eyebrows going up. "Ah yeah, sure." He looked around the table. "We all have. A lot are still in use, just not for passengers. They're used as depots, store yards, that kind of thing." He turned back to Holmes and shrugged.

Chuck, sitting opposite Holmes, on John's left, sipped carefully from his refreshed pint glass of dark ale. "Yeah, most of it is still there," he said. "There might be some blocked off sections and closed tunnels, but it's all down there still, if you know what I mean. Plenty of old track used as service tunnels."

Holmes winked at Chuck. "Ever get any uninvited guests down there?"

"Yeah, well, that's a problem in itself, isn't it?" said John, raising his glass. "Hardly a week goes by I don't see someone sneaking around the tracks. Even in the tunnels. Kids, mostly. Like to call themselves 'urban explorers,' poking around. I don't know what they think they're doing. They're a damn risk to everybody—not just themselves, but to the passengers. To *us*!" He tapped himself on the chest.

"Tell me about it," Gareth said. Holmes put his age at the average of the men around the table. He had a round face and thick, short fingers which he drew in circles on the damp of the table as he spoke in a broad New England accent. "I started driving five years ago. Not a week on the job I nearly hit someone—damn kid ran across the tracks, right in the tunnel. I got the emergency brake on, but he was damn lucky."

Holmes nodded.

"Thieves too," said John. "The damn lot of them. They'll take anything metal. There're miles of copper in the tunnels and in the depots." He shook his head and sipped his drink. "They've got to do something about it. Big stations are fine, but the smaller ones? Not enough staff. Not enough cameras."

The men murmured their agreement.

Then Nate spoke up again. "That's not all they've stolen," he said. His eyes wide, he addressed Holmes directly. "I heard they took a *train*."

"Ah, come on, Nate," said John. Chuck laughed and Nate was ribbed by Lee sitting next to him. Holmes glanced around, watched the shaking heads, the frowns of disapproval. Nate was going to have to work harder to get in with this group of old-timers.

But... was he telling the truth? Holmes pursed his lips as he listened.

"Not a *whole* train," said Nate, frowning at the reaction he had just received. "Just the cab. I heard it happened three months ago. I have a friend who works the control center. He told me."

John shook his big head and spoke into his half-empty glass, his voice echoing. "Nobody can steal a train. Where the hell would you take it, anyway?"

Holmes turned to him, smiling slightly. "One of the empty stations, maybe."

The others looked at him. Holmes shrugged, but didn't offer any more.

The mood around the table seemed to darken further, the conversation hitting a dead end. It was late, the men were tired and drunk. One of the quieter members of the group, Guy, squeezed himself out from the table and disappeared into the thinning crowd at the bar.

The law of diminishing returns was starting to exert its influence, and Holmes's window for useful data-gathering was nearly up.

Time for some specifics.

He turned back to John.

"So what happened to Liam, then? Why'd they let him go like they did?"

"Ah, well, he was under pressure," said John. "Family stuff, he said. He sure was in a dark place the last couple months. Wasn't himself." He sighed. "Should have seen it coming. Paul too."

Holmes raised an eyebrow. "Paul?"

John nodded his big head. "Oh yeah, Paul. He's actually a really great manager, but he was trying too hard with Liam. I mean, I don't blame him, but they were spending a lot of time together. Even when Liam started missing shifts, Paul backed him up. I guess it was hurting him too, seeing Liam the way he was. Eventually he had to let him go. Cut Paul up. That was a bad week to be around him."

Holmes turned to Nate. "When did you say that train was stolen?"

John banged his glass down on the table. "Oh, come on, Dave! Forget it. You can't *steal* a subway train."

He laughed, but the reaction from the others was weak. Holmes kept his eyes fixed on Nate. The young driver looked nervous, his eyes flicking between Holmes and John.

His eyes settled on Holmes. "About the same time, I guess," he said. "Few months ago." He shrugged. "I don't know."

"Sorry," said Holmes, "was that before or after Paul started having trouble with Liam?"

It was John who answered, his heavy brow creased in confusion. "I'm not sure I follow?"

"I was just wondering, so I was," said Holmes. He glanced between John and Nate. "I mean was it Liam's problems that were affecting Paul so badly, or was it the rather careless mislaying of a couple of million dollars' worth of rolling stock that was playing on his mind?"

John swore. "What the hell are you talking about? You can't *steal* a subway train, okay?"

Holmes met his eye, then his face broke into a broad grin.

"Aye, you're probably right there," he said, lifting his glass high in the air. "But look, this is Liam's night, so it is. He was a great man."

The group stirred, voicing their agreement in a throaty murmur.

Guy returned, and with a *thunk* deposited an entire bottle of Bushmill's 21-Year-Old single malt Irish whiskey on the table. In his other hand he had a collection of shot glasses held carefully between his fingers.

The gang of motormen cheered. Holmes joined in, his eyes fixed on the bottle.

Time was up.

As Guy shuffled back around to his seat, and John grabbed the bottle, twisting the cap off with a single turn, Holmes stood.

"Just need to go spend a penny," he said, sliding out from the booth.

John nodded, but he and the others were now focused on the hard liquor being doled out.

Holmes walked straight past the bathrooms and headed out of the Alpha Inn and into the Brooklyn night unseen.

27

DR. HARLEY'S CHOICE

Watson skipped up the steps from Central Park West, the columned frontage of the American Museum of Natural History looming in front of her. She was alone on the broad sidewalk.

The special projectors from the exhibition gala were gone, leaving the magnificent Beaux Arts façade illuminated by the regular floodlights, making the entire structure glow in the night. On the left hung the banner advertising the Miranda Collection; on the right was a new banner for the pre-Colombian gold exhibition. Watson paused, looking up at the giant image of the gold chestplate that not only formed the centerpiece of the exhibition, but had been chosen as its symbol.

Dim light shone from the huge arched entrance. Watson frowned, unsure how to proceed. Surely Lisa Harley hadn't meant for her to come and knock on the front door?

Watson's phone buzzed in her pocket. She read the message on the locked screen.

81st STREET. LEFT SIDE DOOR.

Watson noted the direction, then unlocked the phone and checked her saved SOS. Satisfied it was ready, she slipped the phone into the front-left pocket of her black button-up tunic. Then, making her way back up Central Park West and turning left into 81st Street, she reached with her other hand into the shoulder satchel hanging against her right hip. Her fingers curled around the comforting shape of her expandable baton.

Joan Watson felt as ready as she could be.

The museum was a huge facility, nestled in Theodore Roosevelt Park, a tree-filled block that ran between Central Park West and Columbus Avenue, and stretched up from 77th to 81st. The north side of the building on 81st Street was set back into the park, which was gated; Watson wasted no time climbing the low railing and headed toward the side of the building. Here, the spherical form of the Hayden Planetarium Space Theater, elegantly encased inside a four-story glass and steel box and lit in moonlight blue, dominated Watson's view. Directly underneath the structure, tucked under a long arch, was a set of glass doors. Watson hurried forward, heading toward the left. As she got closer, she saw a shadowed figure inside the building peel off the wall next to the door and wave at her.

Dr. Lisa Harley held the door open for Watson. "Thanks for coming," she said, closing the door behind her. As it clicked shut, Watson saw the LED of the security card reader on the wall next to the door flick from green to red. Locked.

"Of course," said Watson. "Are you okay?"

Lisa looked pale, and when she rubbed her forehead, Watson saw that her hand was shaking. The curator was wearing jeans and soft-soled shoes, with a sleeveless black tank top. With her hair tied back and no make-up, Watson almost didn't recognize her from the gala. The curator looked tired, dark circles under her eyes.

Watson reached forward, touching the woman's elbow

with her hand. Lisa's mouth twitched into a smile, and she swept her stray bangs behind one ear.

Watson frowned. "I can help you, but you're going to have to tell me what's going on. You talked about someone planning a robbery at the museum? What did you find?"

Lisa took a deep breath, then nodded. "Come on, I can show you."

She led Watson up the wide, curving staircase that circled the space theater. On the next level up they headed away from the theater and into the museum proper, the curator keeping up a fast pace ahead of Watson.

Watson glanced around, taking note of the security cameras positioned at regular intervals. Somewhere in the building would be a control room, the night guards most likely keeping track of their movements. That made Watson feel a little better—as a senior curator, Lisa clearly had the authority to be in the museum after hours.

Didn't she?

Watson frowned. If Lisa Harley could move about inside the museum after hours, why had she been sneaking around during the gala? Surely she could have come in at any time.

Watson let her right hand drop over her satchel. The flap was open. Just in case.

Watson glanced up at the next security camera as they passed underneath. The red light was on under the lens. Someone was watching, somewhere.

They came to a dark door in a light wall. Lisa punched a code into the panel next to it, then gestured for Watson to enter ahead of her. As Watson stepped through, she felt Lisa bump into her as she followed. The curator sure was in a hurry.

The door led to the private working space of the museum, the rabbit warren of offices that wove between the public galleries. There was a small security desk with a dark computer screen, but no one was on duty.

The door clicked shut behind Lisa and the curator headed off down the corridor. Watson hung back.

"Where are we going?" she asked.

"I told you," said Lisa. She stopped in the middle of the corridor, but she didn't turn around. "I need to show you something."

Watson narrowed her eyes. The curator was scared for her life, and now, having seen her face to face, Watson believed it. Lisa was run ragged, and, despite the warm ambient temperature, she was shivering.

Something was up; Watson could sense it. The woman was being vague. Deliberately so.

"You need to tell me what's going on, Lisa," said Watson. "Right now."

Lisa turned on her heel. Her eyes were wide, her mouth quivering. She looked at Watson but she didn't speak.

Watson walked toward her. "If you're in trouble, I can help. But I can only help if you tell me exactly what it is you've got yourself into."

Lisa glanced to the left, to the right. The corridor they were in was lined with doors, but all was still, quiet.

"Lisa, *please*."

There was a faint creak behind Watson, then a sharp click that sounded like it was right by her ear. The sound was metallic, a spring compressed, a catch engaged. The sound was subtle and cold and instantly recognizable.

Watson slowly turned her head.

Behind her stood a man dressed in black coveralls, his face hidden behind a ski mask. He was holding a gun and that gun was aimed at Watson's face.

Watson turned back to Lisa. The curator was shaking visibly, tears tracking down her cheeks. She shook her head.

"I'm sorry," she said. "I'm sorry. But I had no choice."

Watson's left hand dived into her pocket and closed on

nothing but air. She gasped in surprise, then looked back up. Lisa smiled sadly and held up the missing phone.

Watson tensed, the fight-or-flight instinct kicking in. She calculated her options for escape. They were not plentiful.

Okay. *Fight* it would be then.

In one swift movement Watson ducked under the gunman's aim, turning on the balls of her feet as she pulled the baton from her bag. The gunman stepped back to re-aim his piece, but Watson was faster, the baton telescoping out as her thumb depressed the catch. She swung up, knocking the gun and the hand gripping it toward the ceiling, then with her footing regained, Watson stood and brought the baton around from the other side. The second hit elicited a yelp of pain as the baton connected with the gunman's exposed elbow; the third clocked his forehead, square-on, with enough force to send the man sprawling.

Aim for the pate, as Holmes would say. Watson was thankful she hadn't neglected her singlestick practice.

"Enough!"

It was a woman's voice, but not Lisa's. Watson turned, brandishing the baton with one hand and brushing her hair from her face with the other. Another office door had opened just behind where Lisa was standing with her eyes wide at what she had just witnessed. Two people had joined the party: another big man, black-clad, ski mask and all, and a woman, who stepped forward.

The woman was petite, slim, dressed in the same black coveralls as the men. She had long black hair—when Watson had last seen it, it had been woven into a long braid; now it was pinned into a large bun.

She had Watson covered with a gun of her own. She was also safely out of Watson's reach.

Margarita Caballero cocked her head and smiled. She said something in Spanish and behind Watson the first man groaned, moaned and muttered a reply that wasn't in the same language before pulling himself back to his feet. Watson didn't resist as he first tore the baton from her grip, then yanked her satchel roughly off her shoulder. He tossed both against the far wall.

Then his thick arm encircled her waist and Watson's world vanished into musty darkness as a black bag was pulled roughly over her head.

28

THE DEDUCTIONS OF SHERLOCK HOLMES

Holmes stood back from the wall and folded his arms, tapping his lips with an index finger as he studied his work pinned above the wide fireplace.

It was early morning, the light starting to creep in between the blinds in the brownstone's bay window. That was good. As adequate as artificial light was, nothing beat natural sunlight for retinal stimulation. Holmes was shirtless and barefoot. Since returning from the Alpha Inn, he had stayed up to work on his theory. The night had been unseasonably warm, and to eliminate this distraction, Holmes required fresh cool air against his skin.

And while he was eager to learn what Watson had discovered at the museum, he'd managed to resist the urge upon his return to go upstairs and wake her for an interrogation. Fresh from his meeting with the motormen, data flashing around his cerebrum, he had got straight to work.

There was a puzzle to be solved.

Center stage on the wall above the hearth was a map, hand-drawn with precision and crisscrossed with thick and thin lines in multiple colors, and covered with notations, single words, sentences, even paragraph blocks, in a mix of printed styles: Judge D's map—the map he'd slipped out of his pocket as his dead body lay in the subway station—of the undercity, compiled, collated, annotated by him and the other urban historians as they explored the hidden labyrinth of sewer and subway tunnels that even the city authorities themselves didn't know the full extent of.

That fact in itself was both incredible and yet entirely understandable. New York City—the island of Manhattan in particular—had been designed for expansion and growth at an early stage, the now-familiar grid of streets that covered most of the surface having been laid out by the Commissioners' Plan of 1811, a surprising example of forward planning at a time when the existing city didn't stretch any farther north than 14th Street. But thanks to the foresight of the New York State Legislature, the city above ground had been designed to become a metropolis.

Underground was a different story. Working under a city was, by its very nature, problematic. For the last two hundred years tunnels had been dug, opened, abandoned, closed. The major sewer lines came in 1865. The first subway in 1904. And then there were the infinite miles of pipes and plumbing and cables. Electricity. Telephone. Data. Fiber optic lines, copper wires. The complexities that lay underneath a major world city made the mind reel.

Holmes closed his eyes, took a deep breath. Then he looked at the map, his eyes drawn, as they had been nearly all night, to the top-left quarter. The map was torn, a ragged hole punched straight through the laminate.

A bullet hole.

Holmes stared at the hole for a minute, finger pressed against his lips so firmly they were white. Then he refocused his mind. Reaching behind, he flicked the switch of an overhead projector on, and stepped out of the light.

Projected onto Judge D's map was another, more familiar

one: a street map covering Hell's Kitchen, Lincoln Square, part of the Upper West Side at more or less the same scale as the other map. Overlaid like this, the match was nearly perfect. The urban explorers had been meticulous and exact, their accuracy driven by the obsessive mindset that came with being a serious devotee to the cause. Holmes nodded in appreciation. That was a quality he knew all too well.

Holmes stepped closer to the maps, keeping himself as much out of the projector's beam as possible.

Good. *Excellent.*

Then he turned and moved back to the table. The overhead projector sat on one corner; behind it another large map was laid out—this one of New York City as a whole. Three of the five boroughs were on display—Manhattan, Queens, and Brooklyn—with the bottom of the Bronx and the top of Staten Island disappearing over opposing folded edges.

Holmes bent over the map, tilting his head as he examined routes, directions, obstacles. He counted streets. He noted the subway stations marked in blue diamonds. Picking up a pair of compasses, Holmes noted the scale, checked a couple of distances, then turned back to the map on the wall and the projected overlay. Walking back to it, he peered at a spot near the center, then he stepped into the projector beam. The streets vanished, revealing just the sewer and subway lines marked by the urban explorers.

Holmes nodded to himself, and stepped back, the light of the projector warm against his bare shoulders.

It was possible. It was entirely possible.

No, not just possible. They had *done* it.

The perfect getaway.

"Watson?" he called out over his shoulder, not moving his gaze from the maps.

Silence.

"Watson, I have it!"

Nothing. She was still asleep upstairs.

"I know who killed Liam Macnamara," he called. He clicked his tongue, then turned back to the New York City map laid out on the table behind him. He dropped the pair of compasses, picked up a mechanical pencil, and began marking a line down Manhattan, starting at the American Museum of Natural History, heading roughly southwest, keeping parallel to the Hudson River. At City Hall, just over a mile north of the island's southern tip, he drew a large circle, then he continued, this time heading southwest. Across the East River. Through Red Hook. Keep going. Sunset Park, and the plethora of rail yards and piers nearby.

Holmes stopped. Tapped the map with his pencil. "Watson!" he yelled.

He looked up.

Silence.

Holmes moved through the arch to the bottom of the stairwell and called up, his mouth curling into a smile even as he spoke.

"Their plan is as audacious as it is impressive. One feels compelled to applaud their imagination, at the very least. If there wasn't so much at stake I would be very tempted to let them enact their plan, just to see if they can really do it."

He watched the stairs for a moment, then rolled his neck and padded back to the table. He called over his shoulder for the benefit of his slumbering partner.

"I made good progress last evening, while you were out gallivanting with Dr. Harley. Met some interesting characters. Liam's fellow motormen. He was well regarded among his peers, which is actually a rather fine legacy, it must be said." He tilted his head as he looked at his work on the maps. "As with the London Underground, the Moscow and Tokyo metros, and no doubt many other such systems, there are many urban legends about the New York subway." He looked up toward the stairs. "Most of which are exactly that, nothing more than mythical flapdoodle. There must be something about the act of delving into the Earth that triggers that part of the brain prone to considering fairies." A pause. "*But*—"

He stood and marched back to the bottom of the stairs.

"It seems that some tales are not quite so tall. I learned of one particular rumor doing the rounds, that a subway train itself was stolen. Sheer poppycock, I hear you say." He paused. There was no response. He waved his hands in the air dismissively. "Yes, well, I thought so too. *But*—"

He moved back to the table in long strides, a grin forming on his face. His fingers traced his penciled route. He peered closer and stopped at the first key marker—City Hall, Lower Manhattan.

"But not as impossible as it sounds, Watson. I believe a train *was* stolen by none other than our first victim, Mr. Liam Macnamara, twenty-year veteran of the Metropolitan Transit Authority. Not a whole train, passenger cars *in situ*—that would be too much to try to cover up. But just the cab, the first section. That could be achieved. Easy enough, perhaps, to fudge maintenance records, get it taken off duty, as it were. It would cause a few people at the MTA control center headaches, but it could be done. In fact, he *did* do it. He stole a subway train."

Holmes stood tall, craning his neck as he looked at the ceiling.

"But where did he hide it, I hear you ask?"

Silence.

Holmes frowned. He glanced at the clock on the wall. It was approaching seven in the morning. High time Watson was up and doing.

He went back to the stairs.

"City Hall Loop!" he yelled. "There are many older subway tunnels and stations no longer used for public transport, but are still in service for maintenance and emergency purposes. The City Hall stop is one such station. Opened on October 27, 1904. Closed December 1945. Design in the Romanesque Revival style. Very beautiful, by all accounts. But, more importantly, the station and track remain clear and in working order, and it features a large circular loop big enough to hide a single train cab in. That loop is normally still in use to turn trains around, but"—Holmes made quotes in the air with his fingers—"'extended emergency maintenance' has had it closed for the last seven weeks. Liam Macnamara stole the train and parked it there, then when it comes time for the Colombian gang to get their goods out of the museum, he drives it back up to Central Park West. They exit the museum with their booty via the water main, climb aboard their own personal subway car, then Macnamara drives them down to a disused pier in Brooklyn. Train unloaded, their filthy loot is smuggled out of the United States and back to South America by sea."

Holmes walked back to the front room. He glanced at the clock again. He frowned, then headed back to the stairs, this time climbing them with quickening steps.

"Of course," he said, as he climbed, "with the *how* resolved, the question now becomes *what*. What are they planning to steal, exactly? A cursory examination suggests the gold at the pre-Colombian exhibition. After all, Macnamara had a ticket to the gala opening and his sister is the curator. But of course that makes no sense. Most of the collection came from South America in the first place. If you wanted to steal all that gold, why not hijack it at the point of origin? Besides which, gold is heavy and difficult to move. They wouldn't be able to sell the objects as they are on the black market because there are just too many well-known pieces. And melted down, the artifacts would actually have *less* value. Not a particularly good return on investment."

Holmes stopped on the landing. He licked his lips, and nodded to himself.

"No, the exhibition is the *cover*. What they are going to steal is not gold, but *gemstones*. The Miranda Collection. Per pound weight the jewels have a far greater value than the artifacts in the next gallery over. Easy to move, and once split up, the stones recut, virtually impossible to trace."

He walked toward Watson's bedroom.

"But you can't just steal a train and drive it to Brooklyn. No. The service tunnels are extensive but they don't go all the way. You would need to pass through the regular parts of the network. So Liam needed help—he had an accomplice, someone else at the MTA who could cover his tracks, as it were..."

He flung the door to Watson's room open. He stopped short in the doorway. The room was empty, the bedclothes rumpled as though slept in.

Holmes ducked out of the room and called out in the corridor.

"Watson?"

Nothing. He checked the media room. The bathroom. Nothing.

Holmes was alone in the brownstone.

Then his phone buzzed from downstairs. He rattled down the steps and into the front room. As he grabbed the device he glanced at the screen. Watson's photo looked back at him.

He answered.

"Watson," he said, speaking quickly, dispensing with the annoying formalities of telephone conversations, such as saying "hello." "I know who killed Liam Macnamara and Victor Judd."

There was a scraping sound on the other end. Bristles—facial hair—rubbing against the plastic casing of Watson's phone. Whoever had it was not Joan Watson.

Holmes spun around, as though he was expecting the caller to be standing behind him.

"Who is this?" he asked.

"We have your girlfriend," said the man. His English was heavily accented. Holmes closed his eyes, concentrating. The man sounded Hispanic, but there was something else. An inflection. Unusual. English might not have been his first language, but, perhaps, neither was Spanish.

"Let me speak to her," said Holmes.

"You need to stop poking your nose in, my friend," said the voice. "Because if you don't we're going to send your girlfriend back to you in little pieces. Okay?"

Holmes's nostrils flared as he fought to control his temper, to keep his voice even.

"If you harm but a single hair on her—"

Beep. Off. Gone.

Holmes lowered the phone and stared at it as Watson's picture and number and the call duration stayed on the screen for a moment before they faded to blackness.

He stood and stared at the blank screen for several moments after that too.

29

THE WALKING DEAD

Watson blinked her eyes open, trying to un-gum her eyelashes. She coughed, and as she did she hit her head against the floor on which she was lying. It was hard and smooth, but covered in a fine, dirty grit. The black bag had been removed from her head, and the world she saw was sideways, all shades of cream and beige and green. It stank like damp, like dust, like something else. Something oddly familiar. Sharp, almost spicy. The floor was cold but the air was warm, close.

She slid around on the floor, but with every movement came a bass-drum thump across her temples. So instead of moving she closed her eyes and decided to lie there a while. Occasionally there were sounds, a squeal and a clatter, but they sounded a million miles away.

Then she jerked and banged her head against the floor. Had she fallen asleep? Perhaps. How much time had passed? She felt a little better, the thunder inside her skull now merely a dull ache. Her thoughts began to assemble themselves into some kind of order.

She'd been drugged. Drugged and dumped… where?

She heaved herself upright, but it was difficult, because

her arms and hands weren't working. Confused momentarily, Watson tried them again. No, they were working, they were just a little numb. They were also bound behind her back.

She sat against the cool wall, her eyes still closed. Her headache was fading but she felt ill. Nauseous. What the hell had they given her? It was a brutal knockout with a hell of a hangover. Chloroform maybe.

After a few moments, Watson felt her stomach settle. She sighed, dragging air into her lungs and then, blowing her hair away from her face, she took stock of her location.

It was a subway station.

At least... no, it *was* a station. She was sitting on the platform, leaning against the wall, her legs out straight in front of her, pointing at the tracks.

It was just unlike any station she had ever seen before.

The platform was dark stone or cement, and the walls were a light orange-ochre brick. The platform was long and curved, so much so that she couldn't see the tunnel entrances she knew must be at either end.

But it was the ceiling that caught her breath.

It, too, was curved, arching upward into great vaults, the ribs of which stretched halfway down the walls, terminating in a thick horizontal tiled divider that ran in parallel on both sides of the station—the tiles she was currently resting her head against as she sat on the platform. The vault tiles were a dirty tobacco-cream, laid in a zigzag pattern that made the ceiling look like it was woven in flax, while the great archways that repeated every few meters were bordered with dark-green interlocked tiles.

Spaced between the arches were elaborate black iron chandeliers, each holding four light globes that looked like they had once been powered by gas. Now the bulbs were electric; they were all lit, illuminating the long space in an even, flat glow.

That wasn't the only light though. As Watson moved her eyes around the ceiling, she saw that between some of the arches were three huge panels of leadlight windows, intricately laced with square, diamond, and triangular shapes. Daylight streamed in. Wherever the hell she was, the station wasn't very deep below the streets. The whole place was beautiful, an underground cathedral of architectural design, a relic from an earlier era.

The sound of trains came and went, echoing loudly down the great curve of the empty station. This station might have been long-since disused, but there were active lines very close by.

Watson felt her head clear even as she realized what exactly that meant. The station was close to a running line. Even the street above was infuriatingly near.

Both factors were in her favor, she thought. Because if she could just get off the platform, and get to the next station, she'd be okay. Hell, if the station was so shallow then maybe she could just find the exit and get out that way.

She pulled on her bindings again. She was tied tight, although they hadn't bothered with her ankles. She stopped struggling and stared at her feet, as though there was something important her drug-addled mind was missing.

As the last train rattled away and a new sound echoed around the tiled walls, she realized what that important thing was. Because, of course, she wasn't alone—they wouldn't dump her in this abandoned station and just leave her.

Watson turned toward the sound of approaching footsteps. They were heavy, soft-soled but loud enough to be unmistakable. Through an arch nearby—*The nearest emergency exit*, Watson thought, almost making herself laugh in frustration—stepped one of the big black-clad men, his face hidden behind a ski mask, an Uzi pistol in his hands. Two more followed, one of whom must have been her kidnapper, judging by the small pistol he held in one gloved hand.

The three men walked toward her, slowly, almost casually, like wolves circling in for the kill. They weren't pointing their weapons at her, but Watson thought they didn't really need to. She wasn't sure she'd even be able to stand without help.

"*Buenos días*, Ms. Watson."

Watson turned her head and winced, the sudden movement bringing her headache back. Three more people had followed the men down onto the platform: Margarita and her bald "assistant" Angelino—the only man who was unmasked—and, a pace behind, Dr. Lisa Harley.

Margarita walked over to where Watson sat, her men stepping back to give her room. She stopped by Watson's outstretched feet and looked down at her prisoner with a curl of her lip. "A heavy sleeper, huh?"

Watson said nothing.

Margarita jerked her chin at the man holding the pistol and gave him instructions in Spanish. He nodded, the pistol disappearing into a pocket as he walked away and disappeared through the arch. Watson heard his heavy footfalls scuffing on the floor. There were stairs nearby.

Watson looked up at Lisa, but the curator, standing back from the others, kept her eyes on the platform floor. She looked as bad as Watson felt.

Meanwhile, two of the men near Watson huddled together and began muttering to each other in their mystery language, the one she'd heard them speak at the museum. Watson had no idea what they were saying, but one of the men snickered at something as the other tapped him on the chest with the back of his gloved hand. From the corner of her eye, Watson saw Lisa perk up, lifting her head to watch the two men, her eyes scanning over them.

"*Bueno, ya!*" Margarita stalked over to the men, snapping her fingers. They pulled away from each other and turned their masked faces to their boss, but they didn't seem too threatened by her temper. Margarita began lecturing them in Spanish. As the group drew together, their backs to Watson, she glanced up at Lisa, nodding her head to get the curator's attention. The woman glanced at her and shuffled her feet, but then she just folded her arms and kept staring at Margarita's group.

"We can get *out* of this," Watson whispered.

Lisa moved her head a little and her mouth twitched, but that was the only reaction Watson got.

Try again.

"I know they're forcing you to cooperate with them. But I can *help*—"

"Hey, quiet!" Margarita turned and walked back over to Watson. She bent down into her face. Watson held her gaze.

"You and your friends have caused enough trouble already," said Margarita. "So you will keep that mouth of yours shut now, huh?"

She stood back and folded her arms, then went back to her men.

Watson glanced at Lisa. She could see the curator's shiver, despite the stuffy warmth of the station. Lisa was watching the others, her eyes narrowing as she listened. Given her position at the museum—her apparent expertise—it was likely she had at least a passable knowledge of Spanish. More than Watson did, at any rate.

"Okay, okay," said Margarita, apparently drawing her conference to an end. The group split up; the two men muttered to each other again in their own language, but this time Margarita didn't say anything. One of them headed back down the platform and through the exit archway, while the other, swinging his Uzi over onto his back by its long strap, jumped down onto the tracks and moments later disappeared around the curve of the station to Watson's left.

Margarita faced Lisa. "Come," she said, walking past the curator, toward the exit.

Lisa lifted her chin a little, turning with her boss but not moving. "What's going on?"

Margarita stopped and turned around. "You don't ask questions. You just do as you're told."

Lisa glanced down at Watson.

Was this it? Watson's mind raced. Lisa was being forced to cooperate with the gang, that was obvious. But she also wanted—*needed*—help. Her call to Watson had been a trap, but perhaps there was something there. Maybe all she needed was a little push in the right direction.

Because right now, she was Watson's only chance.

Watson gave Lisa a slight nod, keeping her eyes locked on the curator's.

Lisa seemed to pause, to consider something, then she turned to Margarita. When she spoke, her voice was stronger, louder. Confident. She kept her arms folded and her head high.

"I can't help you if you don't tell me what to do," she said, almost echoing Watson's own words to her.

"*Conmigo no se meta, hijueputa!*" Margarita stepped up to Lisa, her voice bouncing off the tile and brick. The curator was taller than the gang leader by several inches, but Margarita's fierce temper still made her cower. "Your own stupidity has caused this," Margarita said, her voice cracking as she barely contained her anger. "If you hadn't gone wandering off at the gala, she would never have got involved." She waved at Watson, her eyes never leaving the curator's. "And thanks to her and her boyfriend, we have to move early."

Lisa unfolded her arms, and they dropped, along with her face.

"Early? What do you mean, early?"

"Tonight," said Margarita. "We must move tonight, and be out of the city before anyone can act."

Lisa shook her head, her eyes wide, Watson sensing the

cold fear returning. "But… we're not ready! *I'm* not ready. I still need to—"

"Enough!"

Margarita took a step forward; the curator stepped back, keeping the same distance between them.

"You *will* be ready, Doctor, or you will find the terms of our arrangement suddenly altered, and *not* in your favor."

One of Margarita's men—Angelino—appeared from the archway. He walked over to his boss and whispered something in her ear in Spanish. Margarita tilted her head, listening.

Lisa stood, shaking, staring at the pair. Then she looked down at Watson. Watson took a breath, unable to do anything more than offer a slight shrug. She only hoped that the woman would read her body language, know that Watson, despite being tied up, was there for her. *They were in this together*, she wanted to say.

And they could help each other out of it.

Watson ran the situation through her mind. Holmes, Gregson, Bell—they would know she was gone by now. Whatever they were doing, Watson trusted Holmes. Trusted him with her life. Tied up, surrounded by enemies, all Watson could do was observe, and from those observations, *deduce*.

Lisa was cooperating with the gang, which was led by Margarita, her guise as a corporate sponsor clearly something put on for the gala. The curator's cooperation was far from voluntary, but if Watson was going to gain Lisa's trust and get her cooperation, she was missing one vital piece of information: *Why* was Lisa helping them? What hold did Margarita have over her? Lisa apparently had only one family member, one she had been estranged from for years. And he was dead—presumably murdered by the gang. What else did Lisa have to lose?

And what was the operation? Their original supposition had been that this was some kind of drug-smuggling ring, using the exhibition as a cover. But Margarita had said their plans were being moved ahead, and that it was going down *tonight*.

Which meant it was…

Watson's jaw dropped. She glanced around, but nobody was looking at her. Lisa had turned her back and was staring down toward the left end of the platform.

The job was a *heist*. They were planning to steal something from the natural history museum. Not the gold—there was too much, and it would be too difficult and time-consuming to move. No, something else.

The Miranda Collection. The Blue Carbuncle.

They were going to steal the gems.

There was a rattle and the harsh squeal of metal-on-metal. Another train, running close. Subway trains had passed by the disused stations every few minutes since Watson had come around; it was only when the new sound became louder and louder that Watson paid it much attention. It was coming from the left.

She turned her head as a subway train came around the sweeping curve of the platform. It was just a single car, its flat silver sides shining under the iron chandeliers. It was moving very slowly as it negotiated the curved track, then it stopped just in front of where Watson was sitting. The car's interior lights were on, but it was empty.

As Watson watched, the cab door opened and the gang member who had walked down the tracks earlier stepped out. He nodded at Margarita, then stood nearby. Watson could see there was another black-clad, black-masked man still inside, leaning over the controls like he was checking something.

Margarita walked over to the cab and, grabbing the sides of the door with outstretched hands, leaned her body in.

"Everything okay?" she asked. In English.

Margarita's body blocked most of the cab door, but with her arms lifted Watson could just see past her. The man nodded, but he didn't answer. He was still hunched over the controls.

Margarita stepped back out of the cab, keeping one hand on the door frame. She paused, cocked her head.

"Are you sure?"

The man didn't respond.

"Liam, are you listening?"

The man looked up and nodded again as Watson's heart thudded in her chest.

Margarita hung at the cab door a little longer, then turned and marched across the station, disappearing through the arch and up the unseen stairs.

Watson rested her head back against the cool wall, her eyes on the man standing in the cab of the subway train.

The man who was, apparently, Liam Macnamara.

30

JOINING THE DOTS

Sherlock Holmes flicked his eyes up from the heavy tome he was reading as the screen of his cellphone lit up on the desk in front of him. The phone was on silent, vibrate off, but the screen still woke to show the caller ID.

Captain Gregson. For the third time that hour.

Holmes frowned at the phone, then flipped it face down. He watched it a moment longer, until the thin outline of light that remained visible around the screen faded. Then he returned to his study.

He sat at a long, heavy wooden table, one of dozens that ran from one end of the New York Public Library's famous reading room in two rows, leaving a wide aisle running down the center of the room. Above each row of tables, bright chandeliers hung from the ornate ceiling, adding their warm glow to the sunlight streaming in through the arched windows that lined the walls. The reading room was busy, nearly all of the tables filled with students cramming, older visitors reading. People worked on notepads, on laptops, on tablets. At the opposite end of the room was a row of library computers, all occupied, and the book-lined walls on either side of the room were crawling with readers and librarians alike. At the other end, by the wooden framework that formed the reading room's administrative offices, a few tourists loitered, watching the proceedings within a sort of hushed reverence usually reserved for cathedrals and other places of worship.

It was driving Holmes to distraction. He turned his attention from the leather-bound volume in front of him to the laptop on his right. He moved the cursor around, turned back to the book, turned back to the computer.

Useless. Utterly useless. Everywhere he looked, there was movement; motion, light, shadow, all fighting each other as people worked and studied and read and walked around. The young woman next to him, her nose close to her yellow legal pad as she took notes on something, reached up and turned on the brass-shaded lamp fixed on the table next to her pile of books. Holmes blinked at the yellowish light, then looked up as a librarian—a large, middle-aged woman with early heart failure, going by her ankle edema—pushed a book-loaded trolley with a squeaky wheel up the center aisle.

People whispered, sneezed, coughed. The scratch of paper, the patter of typing.

Chaos fostered creativity, imagination. Peripheral stimulus enhanced the cognitive process, forcing concentration, channeling thoughts. Holmes was a firm believer in this principle.

But not today. Today he needed to focus. He needed to find what he was looking for, quickly.

Lives depended on it.

His phone lit up again, drawing his gaze. He pursed his lips, flipped the phone over, read the number. Detective Bell this time.

He palmed the phone and deposited it in his pocket.

Maybe it was an update on the financial check of the museum exhibition's sponsors. They would find nothing, of course. Holmes knew that. The corporate sponsor would be a shell company, registered in some far-flung island territory where the sunshine was plentiful, the tax laws loose, and privacy assured.

No matter. It kept the NYPD occupied, anyway.

He knew they weren't calling about Watson's abduction, because they didn't know she *had* been abducted. Holmes hadn't told them. Yet. For the moment, he intended to heed the kidnapper's warning and keep the police well away.

That didn't mean he had abandoned his own investigation. Far from it. The kidnapper's call had merely intensified his efforts.

Holmes took a breath and turned the page of the book. It was a passable nineteenth-century translation of a sixteenth-century manuscript, written, supposedly, by a member of a Spanish conquistador's entourage, recounting their journey across central Colombia as they followed a rumor of a lost city of gold. El Dorado wasn't mentioned by name, but this account was one of the earlier references to the legend.

Holmes scanned some more pages. The book wasn't telling him anything he didn't already know. There was something very specific he was looking for, and he had a very short amount of time in which to find it.

He tapped his computer to life, bringing up the library catalogue. He tried numerous searches with a multitude of keywords. After ten minutes, he had found nothing.

Holmes clenched his jaw and banged the laptop down on the table in frustration. Heads turned and there were several outraged whispers, but he ignored them, returning his attention to the screen and scrolling down the page.

And he saw it.

Memorizing the stack number, he leapt from his seat and, casting his gaze around the reading room, spied the librarian with the squeaky trolley.

"Hello, yes, librarian," he said, his words tripping out over each other. She looked at him with a wide-eyed expression. He turned on a smile. "Sorry," he said, too loudly. People turned to look. He glanced around with a frown, then lowered his voice.

"I need access to a special collection, if you please."

The collection was housed in a small locked room somewhere off one of the cavernous marble corridors of the library building. Holmes had to check his speed as the librarian led him with infuriating slowness to the door, then spent a good deal more time trying to find the right key. Holmes buzzed beside her, clenching and unclenching his fists, rolling his neck, his laptop wedged under an armpit. Perhaps seeing him twitch out of the corner of her eye, the librarian turned and looked at him with a puzzled expression; Holmes stood stock still and turned on his smile.

The room was filled with shelves, on which were neatly arranged rows of box files. The librarian made Holmes sign in, then offered him a pair of cotton gloves.

"You'll need to wear these," she said.

Holmes bit his tongue, desperate not to argue, not when he was *this close* to getting what he needed. He placed his laptop on the collection register near the door and took the gloves. He slid them on, smiling tightly at the librarian. White cotton gloves, a common sight when dealing with original antique documents, actually posed a far greater risk to precious manuscripts than the oil and dirt of bare skin, the significant reduction in manual dexterity caused by the protective fabric resulting in a much higher chance of accidental tears.

Holmes kept his mouth shut. The librarian seemed satisfied. She gave him some further instructions, then left him alone in the room.

Holmes pulled the gloves off and dumped them on top of

his laptop, and turned to the shelves. He brought the stack numbers to mind, and began to search.

He found the box quickly. He pulled it from the shelf and took it to the small reading table at the side of the room. Inside the box was a manuscript, bound with string, the cover annotated in pencil around the thick, black printing of the title.

The Peoples and Tribes of the Upper Reaches of Northern Ecuador and Southern Colombia, Their Cultures, Peculiarities and Dialects, with Special Reference to and Annotations on Certain Legends, Beliefs, Myths and Superstitions Prevalent to the Region

By the Reverend Ernest Matthews

~ Perivale, 1883 ~

A primary source. The only kind to be trusted. Holmes began to read.

31

BATTLE STATIONS

Two hours later, Holmes tilted his head as he regarded the sepia photographic plate, retrieved from another box in the stack. There were several others, none of which, he was quite sure, had seen the light of day for a century at least.

But... he had found it.

He then pulled the cellphone from his pocket, and, thumbing past the list of missed calls, dialed the NYPD. He was answered on the first ring.

"Holmes!"

"Captain."

"What the hell is going on? Where are you? We've been trying to reach you all day."

Holmes closed his eyes. "I am aware."

"We came up blank on the financial search. Shell corp registered in the Caymans."

"I suspected as much."

"We also ran financials on Liam Macnamara and Lisa Harley," said Gregson. "Macnamara cashed out his 401k for $18,000 two weeks ago. But get this. Lisa Harley made a bank withdrawal the next day. Forty thousand. Arranged to have it in *cash*."

Holmes opened his eyes. "Substantial savings for someone of her age."

"Exactly. And when you add them up—"

"You get fifty-eight *thousand* dollars," said Holmes. "Don't tell me, the exact amount stashed in the late Mr. Macnamara's bread bin, correct?"

"To the dollar."

Holmes ran his tongue along his top teeth. "Interesting."

"Sure is. But look, we've got a warrant to search the museum. I'm just getting a team together. You and Watson want in?" There was a pause. "Is she with you? I've been trying to reach her—she left a message last night saying she was going to meet with Dr. Harley at the museum. Did she come up with anything?"

Holmes turned from the reading table, drawing the phone close to his mouth, as though trying to make sure nobody else in the empty room could overhear him.

"On no account are you to go anywhere near the natural history museum."

"What? You have any idea how long it took to—"

"Keep the warrant, but wait. *Please*. Do not send anybody to the museum. We must keep our distance."

Gregson paused. Holmes heard him sigh away from the phone.

"Okay," said the Captain, "I don't like the sound of this. You want to tell me what you've been doing all day?"

"Forgive me, Captain, but I will have to leave explanations for a later, less urgent moment. Please be assured that I have matters under control, but also remember that we must proceed with extreme caution."

"You called me to say you have 'matters under control'?"

"I called to give you instructions, Captain."

Another sigh, then: "Go ahead. What do we need to do?"

"For the moment, nothing," said Holmes. "However, I will

require your assistance very shortly. You will need to wait for my call, but it would be prudent to have not just the NYPD standing by, but every agency you have at your disposal."

"Okay, I'll call the Feds." There was a scraping sound from Gregson's side as the Captain moved the phone from his mouth. "Bell, stand by. We're going to need to put some calls out."

Holmes nodded to himself. "Not just the FBI, Captain. All of them. ATF. DEA. ICE. Even Interpol. They all need to be ready."

"Got it. Holmes, that's quite a list. Is everything okay?"

"I sincerely hope so, Captain."

"You sure you don't need assistance now? Bell and I are ready to move."

"No, but thank you. All I ask is that you be ready for when I contact you again. I fear I am about to do something rash, but—"

"I don't like the sound of that…"

Holmes closed his eyes, pinched his nose.

"*But*," he said, "if my plan is successful, I will not only have solved the murders of Liam Macnamara and Victor Judd, but will perhaps have prevented the deaths of many others, not to mention performing the city, county and even state of New York a great service."

"Holmes, I—"

Holmes cut the call. He sat at the table, staring into the middle distance as he thought, running the plan over in his mind again, and again, and again.

He glanced down at the table, at the Reverend Matthews' manuscript. New page, new chapter.

Annotations on the Legend of the Return of Ambu Pá, the Sun Man, and Description of the Lost Reliquary Thereof

Then Holmes lifted his phone again, and activated the audio recorder. Laying the phone next to the manuscript, he pulled a small notebook and pen from his pocket.

He hit play, and the slightly distant, slightly hollow sound of the men talking in the sewer tunnel filled the room.

Holmes listened carefully and began making notes in a fast, small hand.

32

AN OLD FRIEND

The man sauntered around the corner, kicking his heels, bobbing his head as will.i.am laid down the beats in his headphones. It was early evening—strictly a little too early for a dinner break, given the schedule he'd worked up over the past couple of days, but he couldn't resist the pull of the extra-thick, white-chocolate, mocha, banana, and curry milkshake from the Bad Belly Burger just down the street. Damn, when that place had opened just five minutes from his workshop, he knew he was in trouble. Especially when they started doing artisanal milkshakes. See, adding something like curry to a shake sounded crazy, but the result was Off. The. Charts. Now he was addicted to the damn things.

Alfredo, he thought to himself, *Alfredo, you are going to get a bad belly yourself if you keep this up.*

Not to mention the fact that he had a long night of work ahead and was not only sucking down a milkshake but had a big burger (emphasis on the big) and a large fries (emphasis on the OMG) weighing down the paper bag hanging from his other hand.

Carb coma incoming, twelve o'clock.

He stopped at his lockup, keyed the code into the small door set into the large rollered frontage of his garage (working for the big guns of the automotive industry came with some perks, including a state-of-the-art security system to keep their assets sitting nice and tight while in Alfredo's custody), and stepped into the darkness.

He reached for the lights and dumped the bag of takeout on his desk and sucked on his straw as he idly flipped through the stack of pages on the desk, reminding himself of where he had got up to before he had been unable to resist the call of Bad Belly Burger any longer. He was supposed to get his report back to the company in the morning, but, he had to admit, they'd outdone themselves with the upgrades to the new alarm system. Upgrades *he* had suggested—man alive, had he argued for them too. Bunch of pen-pushers with thin ties so tight their heads were going to pop off kept gabbing about the added cost, lecturing about return on investment in slow, ponderous voices like they didn't think their security consultant could understand them. Man, those guys would argue that the sky was just the wrong shade of blue if it meant shaving another penny off the bottom line.

Two words. *Up* and *tight*.

Alfredo sighed. Oh well. That was their job. Just like this was his.

He turned on his heel, adjusted his baseball cap, and drained the last of his milkshake as he cast a long eye over the current project.

The car parked in the garage was white and angular, all lines and right angles, not a curve in sight. The machine almost looked clinical, designed to appear fast and angry even standing still, the whole thing angled like a razor ready to cut through the air at a top speed of 225 miles per hour.

Yeah, well, good luck reaching that in Manhattan,

thought Alfredo as he rattled the straw in the plastic top of his drink.

But, he had to admit it, it was beautiful: less a car, more a work of art. A work of art with, thanks to his suggestions, one hell of a security system.

He wandered closer, nodding in time to the music being pumped into his ears, admiring the sweet, sweet ride; the way the tinted windows were angled up like the stylized wings of—

Alfredo opened his mouth in surprise. His milkshake straw popped from beneath his teeth, sending a white-chocolate-mocha-banana-curry droplet flying against the immaculate side of the supercar. He yanked the headphones from his head and reached down, gently tugging on the door handle. Catch released, the scissor door moved out an inch from the body then slid up smoothly.

Alfredo shook his head.

"Dude, you *really* need to stop doing this."

Sherlock Holmes sat in the passenger seat, staring straight ahead, hands on his lap. He didn't seem to notice Alfredo was there, or that the door had been opened. Alfredo shook his empty milkshake container.

"I've been gone a half-hour at least. You been in here all that time?"

He leaned into the car, one arm resting on the roof.

"Holmes?"

Holmes took a deep breath through his nose, then blinked, as if waking from a deep sleep. He looked around the interior of the car and Alfredo found his eyes making the same journey. Everything inside was charcoal gray, done out in a matte finish. With the engine off the dash was a solid dark block, devoid of any display or even obvious controls, save for the wheel itself.

Then Holmes looked Alfredo in the eye. Alfredo frowned.

Holmes was acting weird. Okay, so acting weird was the default with his friend, but there was something else in his manner that was freaking Alfredo out just a little.

"I needed a… place," said Holmes. "Somewhere to think, to make sure I was doing the right thing, considering every option available, making the correct choice." He rolled his hands in front of himself as he spoke, craning his neck forward. He looked at the car's dark ceiling. "This environment, it is a cocoon, a womb. Practically a sensory deprivation chamber." He closed his eyes and drew in a deep breath, sweeping both hands toward his face like he was inhaling the aromas of a Michelin-starred kitchen. "And while I know far better than to admit this to a fellow addict, I must admit to finding the new-car smell to be quite… alluring."

Alfredo shook his head. "Uh-huh. Well, maybe you need to get yourself your own sensory deprivation chamber. One that doesn't cost a rock and a half."

Holmes glanced up at his friend. "Seventeen minutes."

"What?"

"I've been sitting here for seventeen minutes. It took eight to disable the alarm, four to gain access to your workshop. Your journey to Bad Belly Burger and back took thirty-six minutes."

Alfredo sighed and wandered back to his desk. He glanced down at the pile of paperwork again. Well, at least he'd be able to finish his report now. The car's security system, despite the upgrade, had a vulnerability. Whether Holmes would tell him what it was was another matter.

He sat at the desk and tore open his takeout bag. The burger was lukewarm, the mountain of fries even cooler. He grabbed a few, savoring the burn of salt on his tongue. Then he glanced over at Holmes. His friend hadn't moved from the car, and was once again staring into the tinted windshield.

"So, you going to tell me why you're here or not?" he asked, angling another handful of fries into his mouth. "You know you could just pick up the phone, right?"

Holmes rolled his neck. "As much as I advocate the use of electronic communications, sometimes difficult discussions require a face-to-face encounter."

Then Holmes looked at Alfredo. A smile flickered across his face, one that had Alfredo worried. It was nervous, almost like Holmes was embarrassed by something. The pair held each other's gaze for a moment, then Holmes looked away, his eyes scanning the lockup's floor.

"Look, Holmes, whatever it is, just say it. I'm here for you, man. You know it. So do less thinking and more talking, man. I'm all ears."

Holmes nodded, and gave Alfredo a tight-lipped smile that might have been a thank-you.

"The fact is," said Holmes, "I wish to employ your services."

Alfredo raised an eyebrow, and reached for a napkin to wipe the grease from his fingers.

"You want to hire me?"

"I do indeed."

Alfredo winced in disbelief. "I'd like to think we were friends, Holmes. You know that. You don't need to *hire* me. You need a favor, you just ask. I'm happy to help."

"This is more than a simple favor, I'm afraid. I do not wish to intrude upon our friendship, hence the formal approach, one professional to another."

"The only thing I'm professional about is jacking cars," said Alfredo.

Holmes nodded. "Indeed."

Alfredo held up his hands. "Wait, you want me to steal a car?"

"There will be no theft involved, but the job is not quite above board. I have need of your expertise with electronic alarms."

Alfredo shook his head and returned his attention to his

rapidly cooling meal. "Look, I don't know what you've gotten yourself into, and you may not have noticed but I've got my life turned around now. Took hard work and hard decisions, but here I am. What's past is past. I'm not going to throw all that away." He turned to face Holmes. "Hell, you know that more than anyone else, Holmes."

"I am aware your previous career is very much ancient history," said Holmes. "We have much in common, you and I. We have both fought many battles. Some we have lost. Some we have won. And we also know that there are many more in store for us both. In a way, we are brothers."

Alfredo frowned. "You want to go to a support meeting tonight?"

"Will you take the job?"

"Holmes, you haven't even said what it is, man. You sure it's me you need and not your friends at the NYPD?"

Holmes pursed his lips, then looked down into his lap. "My father is a wealthy man. He owns five properties in New York City. The trust fund I am able to draw from supports my work here."

"I know all that."

Holmes snapped his head around. He stared at Alfredo, wide-eyed, white-faced.

What the hell had got into his friend? He wasn't using again, Alfredo could see that. An addict was always an addict, but both he and Holmes had been sober for going on three years now.

No, something else was up.

Alfredo sighed. "Holmes, I—"

"It's yours."

"Uh. What?"

"The value of the trust fund," said Holmes. "There will be some paperwork to arrange, but I should be able to transfer the funds to you within a few days."

Alfredo stood from his desk and stalked back to the car, rolling his shoulders like a prize boxer going in for the big fight. He leaned on the car roof again.

"What the hell is going on, Holmes? That's the most ridiculous thing I've ever heard."

Holmes looked up at Alfredo. The weak, fleeting smile returned. "Sufficient compensation, I hope, for you to put your... skills, shall we say... to use outside of this lockup."

Alfredo slapped the car. "I'm not breaking no laws, man. And you need to tell me what the hell this is all about before I pick you up and throw you out myself. What the hell is so important that you'd be willing to lose everything, man? *Everything*."

Holmes closed his eyes again. When he opened them, he looked up at Alfredo.

He looked afraid.

"The very life of Ms. Joan Watson hangs in the balance. I need your help, before it is too late."

Alfredo shook his head, curling one hand into a fist and thumping the roof of the car.

"*What the hell*, Holmes! Who do you think I am, exactly?" He waved at his uninvited guest. "Why didn't you just come out and say that in the first place?"

Holmes's jaw went up and down a few times. Alfredo shook his head again and reached into the car. Holmes stared at the offered arm, then took it. Alfredo pulled him up, then clapped him on the shoulder.

"Whatever you need me to do, I'm in."

Holmes nodded.

"And don't ever try that again," said Alfredo. He pointed a finger in Holmes's face, then he turned and went back to his desk. "So lay it out. Tell me what we need to do, and we'll go and do it."

Holmes cleared his throat. "You're a good man, Alfredo,"

he muttered, looking at the floor again. "I once told her—Watson, I mean—that I was lucky to have you in my life."

Alfredo smiled. "The feeling is mutual, believe me. Now, Watson is my friend too. Time for you to tell me what's going down."

33

LISA'S SURPRISE

Watson paced the small storeroom for the millionth time, arms folded.

Thinking.

She was actually grateful that they'd decided to dump her here, instead of leaving her trussed up on the platform. While she had managed to walk out the cramp in her legs, her wrists were still red and burning from the tight bindings. But at least in the storeroom she could move around, even if her freedom was limited to barely twelve square feet. They'd dragged her up and through the archway, which led to a short flight of steps and a vaulted atrium, the ceiling curved and tiled like the platform proper. In contrast, the storeroom they'd found for her was clearly less serviceable. It was completely empty, the tiled walls black with mold, the air damp and heavy with the scent of decay. There was a single overhead lamp, another piece of period ironwork like the chandeliers over the platform, only here the single bulb was smashed. The only light she had came through the two long rectangular windows of wire-reinforced frosted glass in the door.

Watson had lost track of time. She wasn't wearing a watch

and her phone was long gone. She felt like she'd been in the storeroom for hours, either pacing or leaning against the door, trying to see through the rippled glass of the windows, listening for what was going on. But the platform was too far away and only the faintest rumble of the active subway lines reached her. Occasionally dark shapes would move past, the various members of the gang carrying out whatever tasks their boss, Margarita, had assigned them. With Watson safely locked away, they could get on with the job.

The *heist*.

Okay. Think. *Think*.

She was alive—unlike Macnamara and Victor Judd. That was a definite tick in the *pros* column. The fact she was still alive, and being kept hostage, meant that she must be useful to them in some way—perhaps as a bargaining chip, to be used later as a back-up to guarantee their safe escape? If so, they would have told Holmes, sending him a threat, probably using her own phone.

The heist had been brought forward because of the interference of her and Holmes. Lisa Harley had been surprised at this change, as she had some task which she had not yet carried out. Clearly, she was their person on the inside at the museum, getting them access to the Miranda Collection. That exhibition would be under tight security, guarded and alarmed. Which meant they had some way of dealing with all of that. Perhaps that was where Lisa came in.

Okay, progress. A useful deduction.

The question was, why was she helping them? What was the hold Margarita had? Lisa's brother, Liam, was already dead, killed by the gang.

Which meant the *other* man, the one in the black coveralls and ski mask who had driven the subway train into the station, wasn't him.

Except Margarita thought he was.

Which meant the rest of them thought he was too.

Including Lisa. She had no idea her brother was dead. True, there was the possibility that she had killed him herself, but that meant she was working with someone else, the man who had taken Liam's place.

Wait. Stop.

Watson closed her eyes, rubbed her temples. Occam's razor. The fewer assumptions made, the better. The simplest explanation was most likely the correct one.

Which meant—

Watson opened her eyes, turning toward the door. Footsteps and a dark shape approached.

There was a rattle of keys, then the old storeroom lock clunked as the bolt was slid back. Watson stepped into the middle of the room as Lisa Harley swung the door open. She stood in the doorway, and held out a plastic bottle of water. Watson looked at it for a moment, then took it.

"Thanks."

Lisa looked her in the eye, but she didn't respond. Then she began to pull the door closed.

"Wait!" said Watson. Lisa pulled the door half-closed, then stopped. The two women regarded each other for a moment, then Lisa looked over her shoulder, back down the foot tunnel. Watson could see the green and cream tiles of the station atrium, and heard the faint rumble of a distant train. Other than that, it was quiet.

"Are you alone?" asked Watson.

Lisa pursed her lips, like she was steeling herself for something. She lifted her chin and didn't say anything, but she pushed the door fully open. She kept her hand firmly on the handle.

"I know you don't want to do this," said Watson. Lisa looked at her, said nothing. "I said I can *help*," Watson continued. "You have to believe me. I can get you out of this, if you'll just let me. We can *both* get out of this. I can take you somewhere safe."

Lisa glanced at the floor. Watson could see she was shaking again. When the curator raised her head, there were tears in her eyes.

"*Please*," said Watson. "Let me out of here. Together we can stop them. I know they're going to steal the gem collection from the museum. We can stop them. We *have* to stop them."

"I'm not supposed to talk to you," said Lisa. She looked over her shoulder again. Her shivering seemed to increase.

She was crumbling under the pressure. Watson could see it. Lisa was in over her head with dangerous people. There were two paths open to her—she could either finally surrender utterly, her spirit breaking, allowing Margarita to control her completely. Or she could fight it. She could make the decision and she could *fight*. And maybe all she needed was a tiny ray of light, a flicker of hope. And then they could both get the hell out and bring the entire New York City Police Department back with them.

Watson took a breath and took a step forward, toward the door. Lisa adjusted her grip on the handle and the door wobbled. But she didn't close it. Watson looked at her but Lisa looked at the floor.

"What have they got over you, Lisa?" asked Watson. "Why are you helping them?"

Lisa looked up and blinked back tears.

"You have no idea," she said. "You have no *idea* what these people are capable of. What *she* is capable of."

Watson shook her head. "I think I might. They've already killed two people. They're going to kill more. You might think you're safe, but you're not. They're just using you. What do you think is going to happen once the job is done? That they would just let you go back to your old life? You can't stay here, but they won't take you with them either."

Lisa's mouth curled into a snarl. "We have a plan. Me and Liam. We have a way out."

Watson sighed, shook her head.

So she didn't know. Which also meant she wasn't his killer.

"Lisa, listen to me," said Watson. She paused. There was no way around this. "I'm so sorry, but they killed Liam. Just as sure as they will kill you when this is all done. They won't leave anyone behind."

Lisa blinked. Then she stepped into the room. Watson gave a tight smile she hoped looked reassuring. She'd dealt with grieving relatives many times—all part of being a doctor. But here, today, in a musty storeroom in a disused subway station, she'd broken the news of Lisa's brother's death in the worst possible circumstances. Lisa would fall into shock, denial, anger.

If she even believed Watson in the first place. There was a chance she wouldn't.

"Liam?" asked Lisa.

Watson nodded. "I'm sorry—"

"What are you talking about?" Lisa's voice rose in volume, in pitch. Here came the anger, the denial. "Liam's in charge of the train! He drove it in here earlier."

Watson made the decision. There was no time to pull any punches. It felt like everything was riding on this single moment. She reached for Lisa, held her by the arms. Lisa didn't resist. She just stared at Watson, her jaw slack.

"I'm so sorry, Lisa. I'm truly sorry. That's how I got involved in the first place. I work with Sherlock Holmes. We consult with the NYPD. But whoever is in that train, he's not your brother. He's not Liam."

"I... I don't understand."

Watson took a breath. "Liam was shot in his apartment."

"What? When?"

"Two days ago."

Lisa pulled away from Watson, ran her fingers through her hair, shook her head, stepped backward out the storeroom door.

Watson followed her. Now she was out of her improvised cell and in the foot tunnel. "That's how we got into the museum gala. Captain Gregson and I used Liam's invitation. We found it in his apartment."

Lisa shook her head, again and again, tears flowing freely down her face. "No," she said. "No, no, Liam was just late. He didn't show up until later, I'm sure. And with the alarm and everything I just didn't see him. I meant to call after but…"

Watson frowned. "I'm sorry. I really am."

"No, no…"

"But he was killed by these people. They're not just thieves planning a heist. They're *murderers*. Liam wasn't the only victim either. They killed someone else too. Someone who had nothing to do with any of this. *Any* of it."

At this revelation, Lisa's expression changed. She screwed up her face, bared her teeth.

"Lisa, I—"

"Get *away* from me!" Lisa yelled, then she turned on her heel. She fell toward the wall and leaned on it heavily, gasping for breath, then she pushed herself off and ran down the foot tunnel toward the station atrium and the platform stairs.

Watson cursed under her breath. This was her chance to get away. She was free. She could get out of the station, get to Holmes, Gregson, Bell. She could bring back the police, SWAT teams, the works.

No, she couldn't. She couldn't leave Lisa Harley, not now. She was vulnerable, more than ever after learning about her brother's fate, what the gang had been doing behind her back. Watson felt she was responsible. She had promised to help. Lisa needed her. Watson had to get them both out of this.

Alive.

Watson ran after Lisa.

34

THE TRAIN DRIVER

Watson crept down the stairs that led to the station platform, the century-old tiles cool beneath her fingertips as she hugged the wall. She was exposed here, the atrium and platform brightly and evenly lit, but at least that meant she didn't cast a shadow that would give her away. She had to be careful. The gang had apparently assembled again on the station platform. Lisa had disappeared through the archway and down the stairs just as Watson had reached the end of the foot tunnel.

Watson came to the bottom step. With her back against the wall, she was just close enough to risk a cautious glance around the edge.

Margarita was halfway down the platform, talking to Angelino. Lisa stalked straight toward her. The other members of the gang, all of whom had discarded their ski masks now, were sitting around, two leaning up against the wall, two sitting on the platform edge, their legs swinging over the gap. As Lisa approached, they stirred, unsure what was happening, their hands reaching for the weapons lying on the floor beside them. The subway car sat idle a little farther down the tracks.

"Margarita!"

The gang leader didn't turn around. She kept her back to Lisa and kept her attention on Angelino, even if Angelino was now looking over his boss's shoulder, watching the curator approach. When Lisa was within touching distance, she grabbed Margarita, pulling her around by her shoulder. Margarita snarled and gave Lisa a heavy push, sending her careening backward. Lisa kept her footing. The two women looked at each other, hands hanging loosely from their sides, each looking like they were ready for a fight.

"What is the meaning of this, huh?" asked Caballero, her thickly accented voice echoing around the cavernous station.

"You lied to me!"

Margarita hissed. "What are you talking about?"

Lisa turned, pointed at the subway train. Watson risked leaning out a little farther, trying to see what she was looking at. The train's engine was off. The doors to the driver's cab were open, but there was nobody at the controls.

Lisa stalked over to the cab and stepped over the threshold, holding onto the door frame with both hands as she leaned in. After a moment she pulled herself out and turned back to Margarita. Two of the gang members stepped into her path, one raising his gun, the other pulling on Lisa's bicep to keep her away from their boss.

Lisa let herself be held. "Where's Liam?"

Margarita grimaced in confusion. "He will be here soon."

"What did you *do* to him?"

The gang leader shook her head and took a step forward, Angelino at her shoulder. The man holding Lisa yanked at her arm again. *Just to remind her who's in charge*, Watson thought.

"What's the matter with you?" asked Margarita. Lisa clenched her teeth and lifted her chin as the petite woman looked up at her. Lisa's lips were drawn back, her nostrils flaring as she panted with anger.

Margarita cocked her head, a faint smile playing over her lips. "*Nea*, you are cracking up, huh? Don't worry. Your brother has gone to check that everything is in place for tonight. With the plan brought forward, we need to make sure the route is clear. Once he confirms this, we can proceed."

Lisa hissed, and shook her arm free of her guard. She stepped up to Margarita. The other woman didn't move, didn't flinch, despite the six-inch height difference. She had the power. She had the control. If anything, her smile just widened. She regarded Lisa as though she were someone else's child having a particularly amusing temper tantrum.

"Did you kill him?" asked Lisa.

Margarita's smile flickered, but did not fade completely. Her eyebrows drew together in confusion.

"What?"

"I said, did you *kill* him?"

Margarita snorted. "I have no idea what you are talking about. Liam is our *driver*," she said, waving at the subway car. "Why would we kill the man who is to drive us away, huh?"

Watson shrank back into the stairwell. That confirmed it. The gang—Margarita anyway—thought that Liam was still alive. And Margarita was right, too. Why would they kill their getaway driver? Their plan was complex, requiring extensive preparation and organization. If just one link in the chain failed, the whole thing would come crashing down around them. There was no way they would jeopardize it. No way.

But... Liam *was* dead. Victor too. Both shot with Uzis, the very weapons the gang members were carrying. Victor's murder, at least, had some logic to it, as much as it sickened Watson to think this way. The urban explorer had stumbled across the operation, been caught and killed—*murdered*—as a warning.

But Liam? Nothing about his death made sense. He'd

been shot by the gang, all of whom thought he was still alive. Besides which, the men standing on the platform were experts, trained soldiers, mercenaries. Liam's execution was sloppy.

Okay. Time to go. As Watson watched Lisa and Margarita continue their heated exchange down by the train, she realized there was no way she would be able to get the curator out now. All she could do was take the opportunity that had been offered. She was free. She could find the exit, get out, get to Holmes, get to the NYPD. Lisa was in danger, but Watson had to take the chance, a calculated risk that Margarita would keep her alive for the moment, at least until the job was done—given the abbreviated timeline, they wouldn't want to complicate things further. Watson just hoped that it was easier for them to keep Lisa alive than to kill her and dispose of the body.

That's when Watson was grabbed from behind, a thick, strong arm encircling her neck, a heavy hand stifling her cry of surprise. She struggled, kicking, and felt her feet leave the stair beneath her as the man dragged her out onto the platform. She scrabbled at the arm, managing to twist around to get a look at her captor. He was wearing the standard black coveralls of the others, but he still had his ski mask on. This close, Watson could see his eyes were bright green, nothing like the brown of the other men.

Everyone on the platform froze as the man pulled Watson toward the group. Margarita looked surprised, then her expression twisted in anger as she gestured to Lisa and barked an order in Spanish. The gang member holding Lisa's arm reached around and took hold of her other, yanking them behind her back. At once Lisa cried out and tried to pull away, but her captor kicked out the back of her legs and she fell onto her knees in front of Margarita.

The man holding Watson released his chokehold and quickly pushed her forward. Watson's ankles tangled and she too dropped onto the hard platform floor next to Lisa. Whooping for breath, Watson looked sideways at the curator. Lisa was staring up at the newcomer.

"Well done, Liam," said Margarita. "*Bien.*" She nodded at the ski-mask-clad man, then she stepped closer to Lisa, bending down to look her in the face. "I should have known better than to put you in charge of the prisoner. Been putting ideas into your head, has she, huh?" Margarita stood tall. "You need to be careful and do what you are told like the *niña buena* you are." She nodded her chin toward the newcomer. "At least your brother knows his place, huh?"

Lisa screamed and pulled herself to her feet, lunging for Margarita. Margarita sidestepped swiftly as the men around her reached for Lisa. Watson's captor—the man Margarita had addressed as Liam—was closest and got hold of her first, tackling her in a bear hug. Lisa pounded his chest with her fists, then, screaming again, she managed to pull her arms free. She went for his face, grabbing the ski mask. Pulling it free. The man immediately released her, scrabbling at his own face, but it was too late. Lisa toppled back onto the platform, the ski mask in her hands.

Margarita froze and stared at the man. Everyone did. Including Watson.

Panting heavily after his struggle, the man ran a hand over his face and through his hair. He looked at Lisa, then at Margarita.

Then Paul Black, the MTA supervisor, looked down at Watson, still kneeling on the platform.

He smiled.

35

A CHANGE OF PLANS

"**N**o!"

Lisa crawled backward on her hands, staring at Paul Black in shock. She pushed herself away, the ski mask sliding out from under one hand, until she hit Margarita's legs. As Watson watched, Lisa half-turned on her hip as she lay on the floor, and stared up at the gang leader.

"What the *hell* did you do to my brother?"

Margarita ignored her. Instead, she stepped around Lisa's sprawled form and walked up to Black. Older, not nearly as fit as the other black-clad men, he was still puffing as she pushed him in the chest. He went with the contact, letting himself take a couple of steps back as Margarita yelled into his face.

"What is this, huh?" she asked, her face a mask of barely contained fury. "*Pirobo!* Where is Liam?"

Black held out his hands, palms toward Margarita, pressing against the air as he made an attempt to calm her down.

"Don't worry," he said with the quiet, calm tones of someone who, Watson thought, knew he was suddenly on very thin ice indeed. "Everything is still going to plan."

"*Coma mierda!*" said Margarita. She pushed Black in the chest again and swore at him in Spanish a second time. Then she motioned toward the subway train. "Who is going to drive the train, huh? You were supposed to be in your control room, guiding the signals."

"It's *fine*," said Black, sharper, his mouth twisting as his temper rose. "The route will be cleared according to the schedule. Nobody will see us. You don't need to worry."

Margarita sighed, gave a despairing laugh, and pushed the heels of her hands into her eye sockets. She bent nearly double at the waist, muttering something to herself, then she stood tall and took a deep breath as she craned her neck to the ceiling. Then she looked again at Black.

"Okay," she said. "Okay, okay, okay. So where is Liam? Is she right? Is he dead?"

Black sighed, then he paused, then he nodded. "I had to take matters into my own hands." He nodded again. "It was the right decision."

Watson wondered who he was trying to convince more, himself or his angry boss.

That was when Lisa leapt to her feet, making a dive for Black. He jerked back, clearly surprised—frightened?—but Lisa was grabbed by one of Margarita's men and was left swinging in the air as she was held by both arms, her feet slipping out from under her. She let fly a stream of obscenities at Black, who first looked her in the eye, then pursed his lips and looked away.

Margarita nodded to the man holding Lisa. "Lock her in the storeroom." She glanced down at Watson. "Her too."

The guard next to Watson reached down and pulled her by the arm. Watson didn't resist.

"No!" Lisa yelled. She struggled against the man holding her, leaning as far as she could toward Black. "What did you do to him? *What did you do to him?*"

Her guard yanked Lisa back, swinging her right around so he was now between her and Black.

"Enough!" said Margarita. She nodded at Lisa's guard, who held her tight, but stationary, on the platform. The man holding Watson's arm adjusted his footing, but he too stayed right where he was. Margarita licked her lips, then turned to face Black.

"So?"

Black looked at each of the people on the platform, one by one. To Watson's eye he looked nervous. His face was covered with a sheen of sweat, and one eyelid was twitching.

No, not nervous. Afraid. Whatever he'd done, it was most clearly *not* part of the plan.

After another beat he shifted on his feet, the creak of his boots suddenly loud in the echo chamber of the station. He took one step closer to Margarita, and looked down at her from under his heavy eyebrows. He took a breath before he spoke, and seemed to hold it. Watson hoped he realized just how much was riding on the answer he was about to give.

"I had to take *action*," he said. "Liam was unreliable."

Margarita said something else in Spanish. Black held up his hand and bowed his head, like he was acknowledging his boss might, just might, have a legitimate problem with the executive decision he had apparently taken.

"Look, he wasn't *needed*," he said. He pointed to the train. "The signals are all set—you can control them yourself. Trust me, the route will be clear."

Margarita just looked at him.

Another breath.

"Look, we don't need Liam. *I* can drive the train. And"— Black glanced around the others, like he was trying to convince them all—"with one less person, the split goes up, right?"

Watson frowned. The split? Black thought it was about money? Thought he would get a bigger split if he removed Liam, allowing the proceeds to be redistributed in a better ratio? His comment about the signals didn't make sense either. How could Margarita control them herself? Surely the signals—the whole route—had to be set from the MTA control center. Wherever that was.

And when Margarita's angry grimace softened into a smile, Watson knew that Black had made a mistake. A terrible, terrible mistake.

"Sure," said Margarita. "You want more money, huh? Huh?" She turned, looking around at her men. Watson followed her gaze, followed the smiles of the men surrounding her. By the time Margarita's eyes fell on Black again, he was grinning too, his own gaze flicking around the group.

Part of Watson wanted to say something, warn him. But she couldn't interfere, not now. Things were on a knife edge and she was in no position to do anything. Not yet.

Margarita laughed. Black laughed too. It sounded fake to Watson, like he was testing the waters. Then Margarita reached forward and tapped Black on the arm. "I think we can arrange the money. But, come. Show me how to operate the signals." She nodded at the subway car. "The train too."

Black's face creased into a frown. Margarita shrugged.

"Just in case someone else needs to help. It always pays to have a back-up, huh?" She patted his arm again. "Like yours, huh?"

Now Black's smile was genuine.

"Wait," said Watson.

Everyone turned to her, but she didn't take her eyes off the MTA supervisor. She jerked her chin toward Margarita.

"You can't trust her."

Black hissed through his teeth. "That really the best you can do?"

Watson shook her head. "Paul—"

"It's not about *money*," Lisa said. Like Watson, she was letting herself be held, her arms pulled behind her back. "You don't get what you've walked into—"

"I think I can handle it," said Black. "But thanks all the same." Sarcasm now. Then Black turned back to Margarita, and motioned toward the train. "Shall we?"

She nodded. He led her over to the cab.

Watson and Lisa exchanged a look.

"You made the right decision, Mr. Black," said Margarita, her hand on the small of his back, guiding him. They stepped into the cab and Paul reached down behind the seat. He pulled out a laptop, set it on the train's control board, and flipped the lid. His fingers moved over the keyboard, then he pointed at the screen. It was the wrong angle for Watson to see properly.

"This is the route, and the signal sequence is here," he said, as Margarita peered at the screen. He unzipped the top of his coveralls and pulled a square of paper from within. Unfolding it, he handed it to his boss. "Login details, and the command list. Should be easy to follow, but you might want to read it over a couple of times."

The paper, Watson could see. The top half was printed, something like an email with a few blocks of text. Below that, jotted in black pen, was a list, each item a line of text running across the page. It was too far away for Watson to read.

Margarita nodded as she studied the paper. "I understand," she said. Then she dropped the arm holding the paper and nodded at the train's controls. "Now, show me this."

Black gestured to the controls on the train's panel and began to explain how to run the train when Margarita motioned for him to stop. She turned and waved at one of her heavies to join them. As the man peeled off the group and went to stand by the cab door, Margarita told Black to keep going. Black laid his fingers on a horizontal bar mounted on the control panel.

"Throttle and brake is easy. Push forward to accelerate, back to slow. Emergency brake is down here. All the trains use a dead man's switch—you have to keep pressure on the handle or the emergency brakes kick in automatically. Okay?"

Black moved back to give Margarita room as she moved in front of the handle. She rested her hands on it, getting a feel for the system, Watson thought, as Black continued his tour of the cab. The system was simple; even Watson thought she could probably drive the train now.

When the supervisor was done, Margarita clapped him on the back, nodding, her white smile appearing again.

"Excellent, Mr. Black. *Bien, bien, bien*. You have done well. Good work."

Black stood by the controls, a self-satisfied smile on his face, as Margarita, still nodding, stepped out of the cab.

Then her man standing at the door handed her something. Something black.

"No!" yelled Watson.

Black looked confused.

Then Margarita raised the pistol and shot him in the head.

Watson jumped at the report, appallingly loud in the curved subway station. Lisa screamed, her legs going out from under her. Only the man holding her arms kept her from hitting the floor.

Black's body hit the deck. The cab's walls, the control panel, and the laptop were covered with a curtain of blood and brains. Margarita swung the pistol in her hand and stepped into the cab, looking down at the mess she had just created, then she turned and nodded to the man who had given her the gun. As his boss left the cab, he moved inside and grabbed Black's ankles. Margarita waved another man over and gave instructions in Spanish. As the first gang member pulled Black's feet toward the door, the other man stepped around the body and grabbed it under the armpits.

The cleanup had begun.

Watson felt lightheaded, like she was asleep and this was

just one long crazy nightmare. Beside her, hanging from her captor, Lisa was sobbing.

Margarita moved to Lisa. She grabbed the curator's face between her fingers, and, squeezing, pulled Lisa's head up so they were eye to eye.

"Is everything ready?" asked Margarita.

Lisa just stared at her, her eyes red and wet.

Margarita raised her pistol with her other hand, her thumb flicking the safety off, the barrel just an inch from Lisa's face.

"I asked you if everything was ready?"

Lisa sniffed. She nodded.

Margarita smiled, and flicked the safety back on. She pushed Lisa's face away and turned to the others.

"Excellent," she said. "The operation will go ahead as planned."

36

A LITTLE WETWORK

Alfredo, on watch, glanced back over his shoulder to see Holmes heft a long metal pole with a curved, forked end, sliding it into the slot on the manhole cover on the sidewalk. They were in a narrow residential street somewhere in Hell's Kitchen, the wet roadway glowing with the dull sheen of streetlights and of the moon when it appeared from behind a cloud. There had been a light shower, lasting just a few minutes; Alfredo hadn't asked, but he didn't think that was going to make things any easier for them. He and Holmes were about to enter the sewer system, after all. Alfredo was pretty sure that channeling storm water funneled from the Manhattan streets was one of the sewer's primary functions.

Holmes levered the manhole free. The sound of rushing water below was just a little *too* loud.

Alfredo returned his attention to his duty. The residential street was pretty dead, which must have been why Holmes had chosen it. It was lined with old brownstones that looked like their glory days had long since passed. Cars moved across the intersection ahead, their tires hissing with the familiar sound of rubber on wet tarmac. So far none had turned down toward them. Just as well.

Alfredo turned back to Holmes. "We good?"

Holmes sank to his haunches, the metal tool by his feet as he gripped the circular manhole cover with his hands and slid it onto the street. The narrow opening it had revealed was dark. A ladder with small, awkward-looking square rungs descended. The roar of water echoed.

Alfredo peered down into the gloom. He frowned. "I don't like the sound of *that*."

Holmes stood, kicking his crowbar-like implement into a gutter with a clang that made Alfredo turtle his neck into his jacket. His friend dusted his hands off, then pointed down into the hole with an open palm.

"Don't worry," said Holmes. "We won't be following the main course of the tunnel." He turned, looking up and down the street, as though getting his bearings. "The museum is one mile northwest from here. I have the route planned using the map prepared by the urban explorers." Holmes patted his bulging coat pocket.

Alfredo relaxed his shoulders and sighed. "A mile? Man, that's a long way to be crawling through the dark. Can't we get in a little closer maybe?"

Holmes shook his head. "No. There may be a better route, but it is one I don't know and have not had the time to prepare." He pointed down into the manhole. "At least here we will know where we are going. Better that than to get lost—from here we will be able to join the main route back to the museum and follow the path laid out by our opponents. They have planned their entry and exit routes to the minutest detail. The easiest way in is to follow their lead. Here."

Holmes reached into a pocket and yanked out two headlamps with elasticated straps. He handed one to Alfredo. Holmes fitted his around his head, then flicked the lamp on. Then he stepped onto the ladder in the manhole, and began to descend. When his chest was level with the street, he paused and looked back up at Alfredo, spotting him with his headlamp. "Make sure you slide the cover back," he said. "We don't want anyone discovering or following us, least of all the police."

Then he vanished into the gloom.

Alfredo turned the headlamp over in his hands; then he pulled off his baseball cap and fitted the strap around his forehead. Satisfied that it was firmly in place, he pulled his cap back on, resting the peak on the top of the flashlight protruding from his forehead.

Flicking his own light on, Alfredo followed Holmes into the undercity.

Holmes was standing near to the bottom of the ladder, turning a folded, laminated sheet of paper around in his hands, the shiny surface bouncing his light around the wet brick of the tunnel. Alfredo descended the narrow ladder, then hopped off the bottom, his sneakers sinking into an inch of water. He looked down at his feet and sighed, then looked at Holmes. His friend was wearing his usual boots, the black ones with brown suede panels. They were clearly going to get wrecked down here. Alfredo sighed again, rolled his shoulders. That was the least of their problems.

The tunnel was made of brick, the walls on both sides semicircular, curving up to meet a flat ceiling that looked more like concrete. There was about seven feet of headroom, Alfredo guessed. Plenty of room to stand up in. Still claustrophobic and close like nothing else, though.

The sound of rushing water was loud, but apart from the inch-deep stream at their feet, the tunnel was pretty dry. There must have been a storm-water conduit nearby though. For that, Alfredo was thankful. A close, dark tunnel was more than enough to deal with. A close, dark tunnel filled with water was something else entirely.

Then a thought occurred to him. He turned to Holmes, who was still checking the map.

"Hey," said Alfredo, keeping his voice to a low whisper that seemed appropriate. "What happens if it rains again while we're down here?"

"We get wet," said Holmes, turning the map as he studied it.

Alfredo adjusted his cap. "Gee. Yeah. Great."

Holmes looked up, and pointed ahead. "This way," he said. He folded his map and pocketed it, then took something else out. Alfredo wondered how much junk his friend was actually carrying.

In one hand, Holmes held what looked like a fat marker pen. In the other, he had a black plastic box, rectangular and thin. Then he looked up, scanning the ceiling near to the ladder they had come down. Alfredo followed his gaze, his own headlight playing over the surfaces. There was metal pipework running along the ceiling.

"Hold this." Holmes handed Alfredo the plastic box, then he stepped onto the ladder and went up so he could reach the pipework. He leaned out from the ladder and wiped the pipe with his hand. Then he turned back down to Alfredo.

"Switch on the back, light at the front. Shine it up here."

Alfredo frowned, turning the plastic box over in his hands. He found the switch, and when he turned it on, one of the narrow edges of the box lit in an eerie white-purple glow that hurt Alfredo's eyes. Alfredo turned the UV lamp away from his face and held it up at arm's length, shining it on the pipe.

"What are you doing?" he asked Holmes.

"Leaving breadcrumbs."

Holmes uncapped the marker pen with his teeth, which glowed electric bright under the UV light. He began writing on the pipework in brilliant fluorescent blue ink. Then he withdrew his arm and hopped back down the ladder.

Alfredo read the message out loud. "The only way is up?" He raised an eyebrow and looked sideways at Holmes.

Holmes took the UV lamp from Alfredo and turned it off. Immediately, the message on the pipe vanished. He looked up and down the tunnel.

"Let's go."

Holmes led the way. Alfredo followed.

The tunnel seemed straight, felt endless. Ten minutes. Fifteen. Finally, they took a side tunnel, then another. Twenty minutes, and Holmes stopped.

The tunnel had opened into a larger chamber. The way ahead was impassable, the stream of water at their feet disappearing into a low arched culvert in the solid brick wall in front of them, from which came the roar of rushing water.

The wall on their left bulged inward, and farther along was broken completely, the chamber floor scattered with debris. Holmes moved to the gap in the wall and peered through, then he turned back to Alfredo.

"The coast is clear. Follow me."

Alfredo adjusted his cap and headed through the gap after his guide.

37

NIGHT AT THE MUSEUM

They emerged into a construction site, a set of new offices being fitted out. It was obvious to Alfredo that Holmes knew the way, and he followed him wordlessly out into and then down a carpet-tiled corridor. The whole place was quiet, dark. Alfredo looked around, his headlamp glinting off the windows of office doors. Holmes hadn't spoken, but Alfredo assumed they were in the right place—some kind of back-office space of the American Museum of Natural History. Alfredo was familiar with the public galleries. Hell, just about everyone was, he assumed, even if they hadn't been here themselves, thanks to Hollywood. As they crept forward, he imagined the exhibits somewhere above their heads coming to life, having a hell of a party.

If only. At least then they might have had a little help. As it was, the two of them creeping through the dark, Alfredo's wet sneakers squishing as he walked, was starting to feel more and more like the bad idea Alfredo had suspected it was.

But… he trusted Holmes. Guy was a freaking genius. Not only that, Alfredo knew that they had each other's backs. They were here, he assumed, to get Watson. And that was exactly what they were going to do.

Alfredo gritted his teeth, filled with a new sense of determination.

Holmes led them on and up some stairs. They proceeded with the utmost caution, pausing at intersections, checking around corners. The museum was closed, the office spaces locked—but that didn't mean they were alone. Alfredo assumed there would be security guards patrolling the public galleries, while, elsewhere in the building, more guards would be stationed in a control room, no doubt watching every corner of the museum on a bank of monitors.

Or maybe that was just what it was like in TV land. Okay, he'd seen the winking red lights of motion detectors as they crept forward, but only through the glass of the office doors. The corridors themselves were unchecked. Which made sense. No point alarming the whole damn thing—anyone wanting to work late would only need to key in their code for their own office, leaving the rest of the place secure while allowing free movement in the corridors.

They came to a corner. Holmes motioned for Alfredo to wait while, flat against the wall, Holmes turned his headlamp off and risked a look around the edge. He pulled back quickly.

"There's a camera at the end of the corridor."

Alfredo frowned. "Camera?" His theory about the security systems had just been blown out of the water.

Holmes nodded. "Covers a door leading out into the galleries. Extra security measure."

"Oh, okay," said Alfredo, nodding as he thought it over for a second. "Wait, *where* are we going?"

"We have to cross the galleries on this floor to reach our final destination. It is by far the quickest route."

Alfredo shook his head. "What about the security? There's a camera here, but won't there be guards patrolling the galleries?"

"Undoubtedly," said Holmes. "However, we are at an advantage. The museum consists of forty-five exhibition halls spread out over four city blocks. While there will be security patrols, they should be few and far between, if I have calculated correctly."

"And if you haven't?"

Holmes glanced at him. "I am always correct."

Oh great. Holmes was in one of *those* moods. Alfredo had seen enough of that side of him already for one day.

But instead, Alfredo just gave a slight shrug. "Whatever you say, chief." He nodded back in the direction of the camera. "How do we get past this one? You pack some spray paint to coat the lens or something?"

"Nothing so complicated," said Holmes. "We just need to be quick."

Holmes went first, checking the corridor again before darting ahead and to the right, disappearing into the shadow of a large arched doorway. Alfredo followed the same route, then pressed himself against the wall next to Holmes. He exhaled hotly.

"They must have seen us."

Holmes didn't answer. The archway housed a big set of dark double doors. Holmes was already bent over the lock. A moment later there was a click; Holmes pocketed his tools and cracked the door open an inch, first checking that the coast was clear, then squeezing himself through. He ran at a crouch until he was hiding behind a freestanding display case just a few meters away, then he waved Alfredo over.

The pair huddled in the dark space behind the case.

"So, how do you know when the patrol is coming?" Alfredo whispered.

Holmes shook his head. "I don't."

They waited a few minutes. Holmes checked his watch periodically.

"Okay," said Alfredo. "So... now what?"

"Just another minute."

"You said you didn't know the patrol schedule."

"I don't."

"So—"

Holmes dropped his wrist. "I do know something about museum security in general. This place is not dissimilar to other facilities with which I have some personal experience."

"Broken into museums before, huh?" asked Alfredo, one eyebrow heading for the sky.

Holmes nodded. He rose up a little so he could peer through the glass of the display case.

"Back in London," he said, eyes scanning the gallery. "New Scotland Yard had liaised with Department 19 on a particularly fascinating case at the British Museum involving an exiled king from Eastern Europe, a scuttled German U-boat from the Second World War, and an Egyptian mummy."

"A mummy?"

Holmes nodded, ignoring the incredulous tone of Alfredo's voice.

"What's Department 19?" Alfredo asked. "Some kind of secret service?"

"Something like that."

Holmes ducked back down and checked his watch again. He tapped the dial with his finger, repeatedly, but he remained silent.

Alfredo adjusted his position. His calves were starting to get stiff. He stretched his neck. He was sure only a few minutes had passed, but it felt like they'd been hiding for hours.

He listened. He could hear nothing at all. The place was as quiet as a morgue. Alfredo sighed.

"Okay, let me take a look," he said. He went to move, but Holmes grabbed his arm.

"I'm not sure that would be an entirely good idea."

"Hey, you wanted me in on this for a reason, right? Trust me, Holmes. Time I started doing some of the heavy lifting. I'm good at sneaking around. Okay? Okay."

Holmes released him and Alfredo hopped up. Following Holmes's example, he used the display case as a shield as he checked the coast was clear, then, nodding back down at Holmes, he ran at a duck and crouched at the next case.

Within moments he was out of sight, and Holmes was alone.

Holmes jumped as Alfredo clapped him on the shoulder. Alfredo stood back, thumbs hooked into the belt loops of his jeans. He gave Holmes a shrug.

"Doesn't look like the security team here has the same manual they use at the British Museum."

Holmes's eyes darted left and right. Then he stood, slowly, looking around. Alfredo shook his head.

"Ain't nobody here, Holmes. I walked straight down two galleries. And that's not all."

Leaving Holmes at the case, Alfredo walked out into the middle of the gallery. He turned to face one of the corners of the room, where there was an alarm sensor, painted the same beige as the wall but still clearly visible, thanks to the light shining a solid red on its front.

Alfredo lifted his arms, scissoring them over his head like he was guiding an airplane down a runway. The light on the motion sensor stayed a solid red.

Alfredo dropped his arms. He glanced at Holmes and gave another shrug. "Shouldn't that little red light flicker as it picks up movement?"

Frowning, Holmes joined Alfredo, staring up at the sensor. The device worked just like the kind of domestic sensors used in home burglar alarms, although Alfredo guessed it was more likely a microwave scanner than a passive infrared one, given the size of the space it had to cover. But one thing he was sure of—the sensor might have been powered, but it sure wasn't sensing anything.

Holmes, hands hanging by his sides, rolled his fingers. Then he glanced around at the other corners of the gallery. Alfredo pivoted on one heel.

"Same all over," he said. "The alarms are on, but they're not active. I'm guessing the CCTV is probably the same. No foot patrols either. Ain't heard nothing. This place is deserted."

Holmes turned to Alfredo, his face blanching, his expression drawn.

"What?" asked Alfredo.

"We have far less time than I thought."

"How do you figure that?"

Holmes waved his arms, perhaps more out of frustration than any particular desire to explain his thinking. Alfredo frowned. He recognized that body language well.

"The alarms are deactivated, the security patrols absent," said Holmes. "You were quite incorrect in your observations."

Alfredo glanced up at the motion sensor again. He waved at it, looking at Holmes out of the corner of his eye.

"Holmes, the alarms *are* off. You just said—"

"I meant you were wrong when you said the museum was empty."

Alfredo felt his jaw go slack as he realized what his friend meant.

Holmes gave a small, tight nod.

"We are not alone," he said. "Time has run out. The gang is here. Their plan is in motion tonight. *Now.*"

Alfredo spread his arms, looking around. The gallery was dark and quiet, the cases filled with the costumes, objects, relics of what looked like the Inuit. The thought that elsewhere in the very same building an armed gang of organized criminals was staging a heist was almost impossible to believe. The place seemed peaceful, almost serene.

But Alfredo also knew that the museum was a hell of a big place. And he also knew that Holmes was never wrong.

"So... we have to stop them!" said Alfredo. Then he paused, letting his arms flap against his sides. "*How* do we stop them?" The thought of confronting armed criminals filled him with a cold, creeping horror.

"By continuing with the plan," said Holmes. "Alfredo, we have not a single moment to lose. Come on."

38

THE CONTROL ROOM

They were soon back in the museum offices. Able to disregard the CCTV and motion sensors, and without fear of being found by any patrol, Holmes had led Alfredo at a brisk pace across the polished marble floors of the public galleries. At a recessed door, Alfredo had hotwired a security keypad in two minutes flat, happy at last that he was being of some use to his friend. As they rushed down the carpeted office corridor, Alfredo was sure the bad guys would be able to hear his heartbeat from the other side of the museum. Holmes had fallen silent again. Alfredo didn't like it when Holmes didn't talk. When Holmes didn't talk, things were bad, bad, bad.

Holmes stopped, so abruptly that Alfredo, lost in his thoughts, nearly ran into him. Holmes, his back ramrod straight, pointed to the door on the other side of the corridor. It was a nondescript gray, and unlike most of the office doors they had seen, had no window. Large black letters were stenciled across it.

SECURITY
STRICTLY NO ADMITTANCE TO UNAUTHORIZED PERSONS

The door was an inch ajar.

The two men exchanged a look. Holmes stepped up to the door, pushed it gently open. Alfredo glued himself to his friend's shoulder.

The control room within was not a million miles from the Hollywood image Alfredo had in his head, maybe just a little smaller in scale. The main lights were off, but the room was lit by the flickering TV glow of a dozen video monitors that covered most of the far wall, each cycling periodically through a different view of a public gallery. In front of the monitors was a wide desk with a bank of controls for the monitor feeds. Four vacant office chairs were arranged in front of it. At either end of the long desk was a computer terminal with its own smaller display. Those screens were both dark, the faint blue dot on the bottom corner of their frames suggesting the computers were asleep rather than shut down.

Holmes walked up to the bank of monitors, casting his eyes over the screens. Alfredo looked around the room, checked behind the door—yeah, like a security guard was waiting to jump out at them, catch them by surprise—then he walked over to the desk. Holmes seemed to be absorbed by the security feeds, so Alfredo pulled out one of the office chairs, turned it around, and sat on it backward. He folded his arms over the back, and rested his chin on his forearms.

"So the cameras are on," he said, pointing with one finger to the displays. "Just that there's nobody here to watch them."

"Not all of the cameras," said Holmes. He pointed down to the bottom of the wall of monitors. Alfredo sat up to get a better view over the top of the security desk.

The monitor wall was actually bigger than he had realized—there was a whole extra row of screens at the bottom, but they were all dark.

Holmes, not taking his eyes off the displays, pointed now to the computer terminals near the end of the desk.

"Time to put your admirable skills to good use, Alfredo," he said. "See if you can get into the security system and turn these cameras back on. Let's see what they're hiding."

Alfredo stood, spun the office chair back the right way around, then sat down again and wheeled himself over to the terminal. One tap of the keyboard and the display came to life, revealing a login window. Alfredo whistled and began tapping at the keys.

"This isn't the kind of security system I normally deal with, Holmes. It's going to be pretty difficult."

"Of that I have no doubt," said Holmes. "I also do not doubt your expertise. You, my friend, are a maestro; you possess a genius of which the greatest minds of the Renaissance would have been proud, if only Twitter had been around in the late fifteenth century."

Alfredo stopped typing. He looked back over his shoulder. Holmes was still staring at the monitors, his fingers twitching by his sides. Then he turned his head and looked at Alfredo. He didn't smile, he didn't blink. But he did give a tiny, almost imperceptible nod of the head.

Alfredo turned back to the computer. Dammit, Holmes was right. He *was* good. Man, he was more than good. He was a *bona fide* genius. Why else did European car companies let him work on million-dollar cars, right? Right. And there was a lot at stake here, too. Somewhere, perhaps somewhere nearby, Joan Watson was being held hostage. It was up to him—and Holmes—to save her.

Buoyed by Holmes's confidence, Alfredo interlinked his fingers, cracked the joints, and got to work. All that stood between them and rescuing Watson was a crappy old computer stuffed in the back of a dusty old museum.

Right? Right. No problem. Let's go.

Alfredo rifled in the front pockets of his jeans, and pulled out a USB stick. He ducked under the desk to slot the stick into the computer, then he returned his attention to the screen as his little Python hack script went to work on the login window. A few moments later Alfredo's fingers were flying across the keyboard as screeds of text scrolled by.

Bingo. Alfredo rolled his neck. Damn, he *was* good.

Now he was logged in as a super-user, it took only a few moments to bring up the entire museum's security system interface, including schematic floor plans of all the galleries and offices, showing alarm and sensor positions. Alfredo paused in his work as he cast his eye over the diagrams.

"Holmes, take a look."

Holmes moved to the computer, leaning over the desk to peer at the screen. Alfredo pointed to the display as he spoke. The floor plans were white outlines against a dark blue background. Scattered over them were dozens of small red icons.

"Motion detectors, here, here, and here. CCTV too. All over, all floors."

He alt-tabbed to bring up a small window, typed a command, then hit enter. On the schematic in the background, the red indicators were each overlaid with a new flashing icon, a white circle with a diagonal line running through it.

Alfredo glanced up at Holmes. "The whole security grid has been shut down. Look." He clicked with the mouse again; the floor plan flipped through gallery after gallery. On each, the flashing white icons over the alarms.

Alfredo whistled. "Man, the whole place is *wide* open. They can waltz in here and take anything they want."

Holmes rubbed his face. "Someone must have accessed the system and turned the grid off manually," he said.

Alfredo nodded. "Checking the log now." A new window, showing a long list of time-stamped entries. He ran his finger down the screen as he quickly scanned the log.

"Nothing."

Holmes sighed.

"Wait." Alfredo leaned in to the monitor, then he tapped it with a fingernail. "Here. There's an entry missing. The log is time-stamped but each line is also numbered. Here, it jumps from twenty-five to twenty-seven. Looks like... three hours ago." He sat back and shook his head. "Man, deleting an entry from the admin log is more than I could do."

Holmes stood back. Alfredo watched him, wondering what was going on in that brain of his. He felt like they'd spent enough time in the security office... but now they were here, it seemed they had a little more power, didn't they?

"We could turn it all back on. Set the alarms off, call for help. I mean, if they're here, now, stealing whatever it is they're stealing..."

Holmes shook his head. "No. Remember, they have Watson, and they are not afraid to kill." He pointed again to the inactive displays. "Can you bring these cameras back up?"

Alfredo turned back to the computer. "Let me try," he said. A moment later, the first monitor flickered back into life, then the next, then the next, until the entire row of six was back in operation. Alfredo turned to look, pulling himself around on the chair, his stomach pressed into the desk.

"Okay," he said, a pulse of adrenaline surging through his body. "So that's what happened to the security patrols."

The two screens in the middle showed a top-down view of what looked like a storeroom. The screen, like all the rest, was monochrome and washed out, as seemed to be standard for most CCTV. But the events it was relaying from somewhere else in the museum were crystal clear.

Kneeling on the floor of the room was a group of men, arranged in a four-by-four square. They were wearing police-like uniforms; light shirts with epaulets, dark pants. They each had a black bag over their head and it looked like their hands were bound behind their backs.

There were two other men in the room with them—big

men, in one-piece dark coveralls. They both wore ski masks, and were carrying small, angry-looking submachine guns. *Maybe Uzis*, thought Alfredo, as he watched with wide-eyed horror. One man stood at the back of the room, behind the kneeling security guards. The other paced slowly down one side, his masked face surveying the prisoners.

Alfredo pushed his chair out and stood from the desk, shaking his head, unable to take his eyes from the scene. This *was* like something on TV. *News at Ten*. Only here it was, now, playing out right in front of his eyes. Worse, the men with guns were somewhere in the same building they were standing in.

He took a step back, almost despite himself, then stopped and turned to Holmes. He threw his arms wide.

"Man, we gotta fly outta here."

Holmes appeared to ignore him, his eyes glancing around the other monitors. Two of the displays Alfredo had managed to turn back on showed the prisoners. The other four showed apparently featureless, quiet corridors.

Holmes pointed at the monitor showing the bound security guards. "The cameras are on, but they are not recording onto the security server's hard drives. Correct?"

Alfredo adjusted his baseball cap and blew out his cheeks. "Uh… yeah," he said. "We can see what the cameras see from here, but that's it."

"And likewise the motion sensors? The system is powered up, it's just not connected to the alarms?"

"Right."

Holmes waved at the computer. "Cut those feeds again. We don't want to leave a trace should someone come back here. As far as our opponents are concerned, they have the museum to themselves."

Alfredo went back to the computer. A few taps and a mouse click and the bottom row of monitors were dark again. He felt the energy leave his body, the adrenaline fading, leaving behind a hollow emptiness.

"You'd better have a good plan for getting us out of here, Holmes."

Holmes nodded. "I do. But we must not leave empty-handed." He moved back to the computer, this time operating it himself to bring up the security schematics and floor plans. Alfredo watched as he cast his eyes over the images. Then Holmes stopped, and stood back.

"There," he said.

Alfredo peered at the display. Whatever Holmes was after, it was on this level at least.

"You gonna tell me what it is *we've* come to steal yet?"

"The less you know, the better."

"Come on," said Alfredo. "What's the difference now? The museum is full of people with machine guns, Holmes. *Machine guns*. This is *very* bad news, man. We're going to be lucky if we get out of here at all!"

"All I ask is that you have a little faith in me, Alfredo."

Alfredo huffed in disbelief. "Oh, right, yeah, okay, fine. Good."

Holmes turned to face his friend. He paused, then he nodded. "I'm sorry I got you into this."

Alfredo grimaced. Now *that* didn't sound good. Surely Holmes knew what he was doing? What he just said about the machine guns, about getting out of this alive. He hadn't meant it, not really. Holmes was going to get them through this. They were going to win.

Weren't they?

"Hey, look," said Alfredo quietly. "We're in this together, man. Right? Watson needs our help. We gotta get her out of here." He laughed. "Us too, right?"

Holmes gave a little nod. "Watson does indeed depend upon us. But I feel obliged to release you from any responsibilities I may have burdened you with. I believe you know the way back down into the tunnel if you wish to make your exit now."

Alfredo stuck his tongue into his cheek. He looked at Holmes—his fellow addict, his former charge as sober sponsor. And now, his friend. Brilliant, ingenious, his mind sharp and honed beyond anything Alfredo was fairly sure he could even guess. The man was formidable, unstoppable.

And also, right now, in the middle of the night, in the middle of a museum filled with gun-toting drug-runners, he was—without Alfredo—completely on his own.

Alfredo adjusted his hat. He jutted his chin out at Holmes. "A little faith, right?"

A small smile crept across Holmes's features.

"Besides," said Alfredo. "What happens when you get to another keypad lock? You can't pick that with a hairpin."

The smile widened. Holmes gave his little nod again. "Thank you."

Alfredo sighed as he looked around the security control room. "So, we done here or what?"

Holmes glanced around. "Time we moved on."

Alfredo nodded. "A'ight." He stuffed his hands into the pockets of his capacious hoodie. "Autobots, transform and roll out," he said, then he pointed to the door with his shoulder. "Lead the way, Optimus."

Expression dark, Holmes marched out of the room, Alfredo following close behind.

That was better. Holmes was back in the game, and Alfredo was right there with him.

39

LIKE A THIEF IN THE NIGHT

Alfredo paced outside the storeroom, keeping watch while Holmes searched inside. It was weird, creepy even—this corridor, like every other they had walked down, was eerily quiet. Every movement Alfredo made, every rustle of his clothing, every footfall on the soft carpet, sounded to him as loud as a gunshot. He'd even kept his headlamp off. Enough of the city's glow came in through the high-set windows to see by. That would do. Anything more would surely be a homing beacon for the gang currently at work somewhere else in the museum. It didn't matter that they were most likely on the other side of the huge complex. Alfredo thought back to the image on the security monitor in the control room, and shuddered.

This wasn't the usual kind of thing Holmes got involved with. Alfredo didn't like to pry into Holmes's business—it was none of his, after all—but, tonight, homicide felt so easy, so simple. Means, motive, opportunity. Investigate the evidence. Collar the suspects. Give them a grilling. Make the case.

But this? Alfredo blew out his cheeks as he watched the dim, empty corridor. This was big. This was Something. Else.

They were up against an entire criminal organization.

Heavily armed. Uzis. Uniforms, like they were an army. It was incredible—just amazing, man—that they were *here*, in the heart of New York City, hitting a cultural institution famous *internationally*. Holmes had at least explained a little more on their journey from the control room to here: his theory that the gang were in fact drug-runners, part of one of the Colombian cartels, one that had the means, the resources, to steal right from under the noses of eight and a half million sleeping New Yorkers.

They'd killed already. Two people, Holmes said. One of them an innocent bystander. Nothing to say they wouldn't kill more to ensure their plan went ahead.

And they'd taken Watson. Alfredo hoped—*prayed*—she was okay. But Watson was tough. She was on it. He knew how much respect Holmes had for her, and coming from Holmes, that meant a hell of a lot.

So all they could do was trust that she could handle her end of the situation, wherever she was.

Alfredo reached up and flexed the peak of his baseball cap, more out of habit than anything. Realizing what he was doing, he dropped his hands to his side and sighed. What the hell was taking Holmes so long? He'd been in the storeroom nearly ten minutes now. And man, was ten minutes a long time on a night like this.

Alfredo blew his cheeks out again, trying to put the image from the security monitor out of his mind.

Oh man.

Bad, bad news. If anything, the poor quality of the security camera feed made it even worse. Bleached out, low-contrast black and white, the way it rendered everything so… distant. Dreamlike.

This was no dream. Alfredo felt his stomach do a flip.

Come on, Holmes. Come on!

And there was the rub. It was just them. Alfredo Llamosa,

Sherlock Holmes. Two guys against the world. If they were caught in the museum, nobody would ever see them again. Of that, Alfredo was quite sure. The gang wasn't going to let anyone stop them.

Alfredo stopped pacing, rolled his shoulders, took a deep, deep breath.

Change the tune, man, change the tune.

He closed his eyes, trying to clear his thoughts.

And then he allowed himself a small smile.

So, Alfredo Llamosa and Sherlock Holmes versus the Evil Empire, a'ight? Yeah. Well. About that. Lemme tell you something, right now. You don't have a single clue about who you're up against. Not. A. Clue. Because you might think it's just two ex-junkies trying to save the world, but, brother, believe me, that's more than enough. Holmes could take on the Devil himself and come out on top.

Just a little faith, Holmes had said. Well, he was in luck. Because that was exactly what Alfredo had in his friend. Faith.

More than a little.

The storeroom door swung open six inches and Holmes slid through the gap, hunched over. As the door closed behind him, Alfredo could see he had something clutched to his chest. He froze, staring at the object. Then he pointed.

"That's it?"

Holmes grinned, and drew the object out into the dim light. It was a box of pale wood, the surface old and splintered at the corners. There were two light concentric rings on the top—stains left by hot coffee mugs, Alfredo realized. The edge of the lid actually ran down diagonally from the top to almost the opposite bottom corner, so that the whole box would practically split in half when opened. There were two tiny brass hinges at the top of the lid, which was secured shut at the front by a tiny brass escutcheon and a hook slotted firmly through the latch.

Holmes turned it in his hands, clearly pleased with his discovery. Alfredo whistled. "Okay, I hope this has all been worth it. Looks a little... small?"

"This," said Holmes, regarding the box, his voice a low, reverential whisper, "is worth the life of a dear friend. It is our ultimate weapon, as it were. The means to an end."

Holmes continued to stare at the box for a moment. Alfredo's eyes darted between it and his friend several times. The suspense was killing him.

"So, you gonna open it?"

Holmes snapped out of his reverie and slid the box under one arm. "Not yet. We have precious little time remaining. Let's go."

"The tunnels?"

Holmes nodded.

Alfredo flicked his headlamp on. "Follow me, chief."

Back in the sewer tunnels, the steady roar of running water close by but out of sight was disconcerting after the mausoleum-like silence of the museum. The pair descended the ladder and emerged into the large chamber. Alfredo made for the break in the wall, ducked through it, then stopped and turned back when he realized Holmes wasn't with him.

"Something wrong?"

Holmes held out the wooden box. "Here. Hold this."

Alfredo walked back to his friend and took the box gingerly. It was light—much lighter than he had expected—and although a nice little piece of work, it had clearly seen better days, the wood rough and dry under his fingertips. Not to mention the coffee rings.

What the hell is inside it? Alfredo thought as his fingers brushed the little brass catch. How valuable could it be if someone had been using it as a coaster?

Holmes pulled his UV marker pen from one pocket and the boxy UV lamp from the other. Casting his eye around, he then stepped up onto some brick rubble piled against one wall. He reached up and wiped the dust from a metal reinforcing plate with the cuff of his jacket.

Then he stopped. He nodded at Alfredo, motioning for his friend to come closer, then handed him the UV lamp.

Alfredo knew the drill. He juggled the wooden box under one arm, then flicked the light on, holding it up high for Holmes. Holmes, meanwhile, pulled his phone from his pocket and peered at the screen.

"Don't think you'll get much of a signal down here," said Alfredo.

"Lucky I am not in urgent need of a pizza delivery then," said Holmes. He thumbed through several images, then, flexing his other arm like he was about to conduct an orchestra, he began to write, his eyes flicking back to the phone repeatedly.

As he wrote, fluorescent blue letters appeared and glowed under the lamp.

Alfredo frowned as he watched. The characters Holmes was copying were the regular alphabet, but Alfredo couldn't read any of it.

"What language is *that*?" he asked.

Holmes continued to write. "I must admit, I'm not entirely sure myself."

He wrote five lines in the strange language, and then he wrote something Alfredo could read and understand all too well.

An address, in English.

Brooklyn.

The brownstone.

Then Holmes capped the UV pen and hopped off the pile of bricks. He looked at the floor, scuffing at the pile, then he bent down and began selecting pieces, moving them into some kind of shape.

Alfredo flicked the UV lamp off. "Hey," he said, "I don't know what you're doing, and I know better than to ask. But whatever is going down, I really *hope* this is a good idea."

Holmes moved some more bricks, then he stopped and stood back, surveying his work. He looked at Alfredo.

"Do you trust me?"

"You know it."

Holmes reached for the box with both hands. Alfredo handed it back.

Holmes nodded. "Then let's hope my deductions are correct." He turned and glanced up at the metal plating. Without the UV light, it was just black iron. "And that my message finds its intended recipient in good time. Come on."

Holmes left through the break in the wall. As he sloshed through the shallow stream of water beyond, Alfredo glanced down at the floor of the chamber, to where Holmes had arranged the bricks into a big arrow, pointing toward the wall and the iron plate.

Yes, he trusted Holmes. Trusted him till the end.

He only hoped that end was a long, long way off yet.

40

WWSHD?

Watson found herself once again pacing the small storeroom in the disused subway station. She'd been locked in there for a couple of hours now, only this time she wasn't alone. Lisa sat on the floor, knees drawn up, arms wrapped around her legs, head buried in her chest. It was like she was trying to make herself as small as possible, squeezing herself into the corner of the small room like she could just disappear. She hadn't spoken. Watson had given up trying. The woman was in shock, her mind retreating from the pain and the horror of her situation.

Paul Black's body lay on the other side of the room. Face-up, which Watson counted as a small blessing, given that the back of his head was missing. A small pool of blood had spread out beneath his body, but with just the light from the door's frosted, wired windows, he could have been sleeping. She had seen enough of death herself not to be troubled by a cadaver, but it was Lisa she was worried about.

Watson dry-swallowed and moved back to the door, leaning against it with her shoulder as she stared at the glass. There had been no sound from beyond for a while now. As far as she knew, they were alone in the station. The heist was going down, right now, and there was absolutely nothing they could do about it. The storeroom door was solid, unbreakable, Watson suspected—even if she could get Lisa to help her. And there was no lock on the inside of the door to pick.

Watson paced some more, sighed some more. While she had no doubt Holmes was looking for her, Captain Gregson and Detective Bell on his coattails, her attention was now on the heist. She was safe and well. Lisa too. They were out of the way. They could wait. The heist was the main issue now. It had to be stopped.

Watson bristled. She shook her head. They might be out of the way, but she couldn't just sit here and wait to be rescued like some damsel in distress. She took a breath and leaned back against the door.

WWSHD?

What would Sherlock Holmes do?

The answer came to her immediately—it was the same as what *she* would do. Because she was not just his assistant, his sounding board. She was his *partner*. She was a consulting detective, like him.

Observe. *Gather data*. Then: deduce. Whatever she could find out here, now, might be of vital importance to the case. She could help Holmes, even when locked up in a tiny storeroom with a dead body and a woman on the edge of a breakdown.

But Lisa Harley was the key. Whatever loyalty she had to Margarita's gang—whether voluntary or obligated—Watson was fairly sure it was long gone now. Lisa had seen terrible things tonight.

So had Watson.

She pushed away from the door and moved to Lisa's corner. The curator had cried for a long time after they had been thrown in the improvised cell, but now her breathing was slow, deep, steady. Watson wondered if she was asleep. She wouldn't be surprised. It would probably do her good— her whole world had been turned upside down. Coerced somehow into cooperating with Margarita and the cartel, into breaking not just federal but *international* law. Betraying her friends and colleagues at the museum.

And then there was the murder of her own brother.

But while the pre-Colombian gold exhibition she had helped organize was a front, a way for the gang to access the museum, Lisa's position as curator—and the qualifications Watson supposed that required—was anything but. Whatever the gang had on her, it was enough for Lisa to throw away *decades* of her life.

Watson lowered herself to the floor and sat cross-legged in front of the curator.

"Lisa?"

Lisa's pattern of breathing changed. She wasn't asleep. She was just silent. Brooding.

"Lisa, you want to tell me what's going on?"

"No," came the muffled reply.

Watson glanced at the door, at Black's body. "We can still stop this." She turned back to face Lisa. "It doesn't have to go this way."

Lisa didn't move, but she took a ragged deep breath. "What the hell do you know about it?"

Watson licked her lips. "I know what it's like to feel out of control. I know what it's like to make a decision—to make a *mistake*—that you know will change everything."

Lisa stirred, lifting her head, regarding Watson with red swollen eyes.

"I know what it's like when you realize that in that split second, that one single moment, your whole life will never be the same again. Ever."

They locked eyes and didn't speak for five seconds. Ten.

And then—

"My brother is *dead*," said Lisa. "I killed him."

Watson shook her head. "No, you didn't."

Lisa scowled at Watson, her mouth twisted in anger. "Yes I *did*! He's dead because of *me*. I may as well have pulled the trigger myself. It's over. It's all over."

Her voice cracked, her eyes growing wet again. Watson reached forward with both hands, and held Lisa's. Lisa jumped, as though she'd been given an electric shock. She stared at Watson, the anger fading from her face, replaced by something else.

Could it be hope? Watson wondered.

"It is *not* over, Lisa," she said. "Two nights ago, when we were outside the museum, I gave you my number. I told you I was here to talk. If you needed it. And if you were in trouble, I said I would be able to help." A pause, a beat. "I've said it before and I keep saying it, but you can trust me, Lisa. It's time you started believing that. We can get out of this."

Lisa laughed, bleakly. She looked up at the ceiling. "I hate to tell you, but it doesn't look like we're going anywhere." She lowered her head, closed her eyes. "We're not going to get out of this. We can't."

Watson sighed. She had to change tack, drag Lisa away from the circular arguments over trust and what was going to happen to them.

"We're locked up for now, yes," she said. "But we're not beaten yet."

Lisa hissed in disbelief and rolled her eyes.

"How did you get involved with the gang?"

Lisa licked her lips and stared at her knees, like she was unlocking memories best left forgotten. She sniffed and wiped the back of her hand across her nose, then she looked at the floor.

"Does it really matter?"

"It might not," said Watson, "but I still want to know. Will you tell me?"

Lisa sighed, shrugged, sniffed again.

Then she began to talk.

41

ECUADOR, 1996

"I met them years ago. In ninety-six. I was eighteen, ready for college, but I wanted to take a gap year. My parents had died the year before, both of them—they'd had me when they were pretty old, and I knew it was coming, but it was still a shock. I needed to clear my head, get out there, see things, experience things.

"From New York I went to South America. Peru. I started at the Nazca Lines, then up to Machu Picchu, then on to Colombia. The plan was to hike back into the States, visiting as many ancient sites as possible, heading through the Maya ruins of Central America, Tenochtitlan, and Aztec sites in Mexico, then finish up in Texas and fly back home."

Lisa laughed, dropped her head. "Archeology and history. That was all I was interested in. That was my *whole* life. And here was the chance to see it all with my own eyes, to say I had been to those places."

Watson tilted her head as she pieced the puzzle together. "So you met Margarita in South America?"

Lisa sniffed and nodded. "I was travelling alone the whole trip. Which was stupid, I know now. But I was eighteen and I thought I owned the world.

"I was in southern Colombia, a couple of hundred kilometers north of the border with Ecuador, moving from town to town, trying to improve my Spanish. Hey, it was an adventure, right? Then one place I was staying got torched—apparently the town was owned practically outright by a drug cartel, who were at war with their rivals. I lost everything except the clothes I was wearing and my passport, which I always kept on me. I was alone, in the middle of nowhere. I didn't know what to do. I was sitting in the back of this bar, just a shack by the road, really. It was raining—I remember that. It was like the sky had opened, dumping more rain than I had ever seen in my whole life. The roof of this place was corrugated iron. You could hardly hear yourself think in the place, with all the rain.

"But what was I going to do? I was eighteen. Alone. My Spanish wasn't good enough, just a phrase here and there. I wasn't prepared. But I was *eighteen*. I thought I knew it all."

Watson sat quietly and listened. The picture Lisa was painting was leading to an inevitable conclusion that Watson almost didn't want to hear.

"They made you an offer, didn't they?" she asked.

Lisa nodded. "I met Margarita there. She was young—younger than me. She said she was a traveler too, down from Mexico. She said she was in the same boat. She had nothing, nobody. She'd been trying to figure out what to do when she saw me. Said she'd been watching me all day. She said she'd found a way out, did I want in? She'd met some people, she said. They would give us money and a ride up to Bogotá. They'd arrange everything so we could get to Mexico, and then up to the States.

"And all we had to do was carry a package for them."

Watson sighed. "Drugs?"

Lisa laughed again and rolled her eyes. More tears flowed. "What do you think? But I didn't ask. We met them the next day. They gave us a thousand US dollars each, in cash, and then they taped heavy plastic bags around our bodies. They said we wouldn't be caught. They said it was an easy job, they did it all the time. And I just wanted to go home.

"Then they separated us. Margarita said she would see me in Bogotá. They gave me a car—a pile of junk, more rust than anything else. They told me to drive to a place called Popayan. Someone would meet me and drive me the rest of the way to Bogotá.

"Only I got caught."

Lisa stifled a sob and wiped her eyes.

Watson squeezed her arm. "What happened?"

"I was driving. It was just dirt roads, and a pick-up came up behind, sirens on. The back was filled with men in uniforms, all wearing sunglasses. They had guns. Big guns. They made me pull over and get out of the car. They held me at gunpoint while they searched it. I knew they wouldn't find anything, but then I knew they would then search me. I didn't know who they were—police, or drug agents. I didn't understand what they were saying, but they just kept shouting at me. Then one of them pushed me against the truck and lifted my shirt. He found the packages."

Lisa took a breath and looked Watson in the eye.

"They shot them. All of them. They came in another truck. Another pick-up. They just started firing. I think the police got one of them, but they were caught by surprise. Didn't stand a chance.

"I hid. I thought I was going to die. And then someone called me by my name and helped me up. Margarita. She had a gun too—a machine gun. It was so big and she was so small, I nearly laughed. She told me that they weren't police. The truck, the uniforms—all stolen. They were from another group—another cartel, fighting for the territory.

"Margarita put me back in the car. Told me to keep

going. Told me everything was going to be okay, that they had handled the situation. She told me I had kept my head and that was good. I had done well. Then she turned to the other men—there must have been ten of them—and she started shouting orders. This small girl with a big gun, bossing around these men. But they didn't argue. They just did what she said.

"And then I started the car and Margarita leaned in again and said that I owed them my life. She said she'd be watching me, always."

Lisa rolled her neck and took a deep breath. "Anyway, it worked. I got back into the States. Delivered the packages. Got paid, too—more money than I had ever seen in my life. I mean, fifty thousand dollars? Of course, I knew what a drug mule was, I wasn't stupid, but I thought that surely that was more money than most would make in a lifetime, right? At first I wanted to burn it, but then I realized I could use it, undo some of what I'd done, maybe. So I changed my name. Went back to Ireland for a while. Even tried to forget about archeology and history. I went to university like I had planned but took computer science instead. Got through two years before I decided I couldn't fight anymore, that I had to go back."

Watson nodded in understanding. "To archeology?"

Lisa smiled sadly. "How can you give up what you love? What's the point of life without a purpose? So I transferred, social anthropology and archeology. Finished my degree, then got into a post-grad program back in the US. Got a PhD. Got a great job too." Lisa laughed. "I was back in New York, living just a few miles from the brother I hadn't seen in fifteen years."

Watson frowned, shaking her head. "Why didn't you see him?"

"What was I supposed to do? The gang... Margarita said she was watching me. She had people all over the US, including New York City. *Dangerous* people. I'd done my best to hide, to put the past behind me. If they found me, found my family, I didn't know what they would do. So I stayed away. Tried to get on with life."

Lisa sighed heavily, ran her hands through her hair.

"But they found you anyway?" asked Watson.

Lisa nodded, sighed again. "They knew about it all. About my new name. Where I had been. That I'd come back. They knew about my job at the museum, of course.

"And then one day she was there. Margarita, waiting in my apartment. She had men with her. They tied me up. Beat me. She said it was time I repaid the debt owed. That fifty thousand? Payment for a lifetime of service—she even called it her *investment*. That's why they'd given me so much."

Lisa looked Watson in the eye. "It was the Miranda Collection. She knew that it was coming to the museum. She wanted me to help them steal it."

Watson frowned. "The Miranda Collection?"

Lisa nodded.

"I don't get it," said Watson. *Holmes was right*, she thought, *it* was *all to do with narcotics*. But something didn't add up. "Surely the primary income of a drug cartel is drugs? What would they want with diamonds?"

Lisa shrugged. "I don't know. I managed to piece a bit together. There'd been a change in the hierarchy, somewhere at the top. When I'd met Margarita in Colombia she'd just been a small cog, a ground-level captain. But even then there had been something about her, about the way she had commanded those men. As far as I can tell, she's in charge now. She got rid of the competition and installed herself as the big boss."

"So there's been some kind of power struggle?" asked Watson. She leaned back and stared at the wall, running Lisa's story through her head. "The cartel is damaged, somehow?"

"That's what it seems like. She said it had been difficult;

'the transition,' she called it. Before she took over there had been some sabotage or something, problems with their supply chain of raw materials, and she said the war had been costly, losing them both money and manpower. We organized the gold exhibition as the cover to give her access to the museum. She posed as the main sponsor, using a shell corporation run by the cartel. The work she was putting into it all. It was so elaborate."

"So the jewels," said Watson, "they're a cash injection."

Lisa nodded. "A big one. Once the gems are re-cut and sold on the black market they'll be untraceable."

"And Margarita will have enough money to rebuild her organization from the ground up."

"I think so."

"But that's good," said Watson. Lisa looked confused, so she continued. "Don't you see? If their organization is in such a bad shape, then this is it for them—the last throw of the dice. She will have put *everything* they have left into the heist. It's all or nothing. If they don't pull it off, they'll be finished. The cartel will fall."

Lisa's eyes widened at Watson's deduction.

Watson stood to stretch her legs. She paced the storeroom, then stopped and glanced down at Paul Black's body. There were still parts of the mystery yet to be solved.

She turned back to Lisa. "When did you go to your brother for help?"

Lisa jerked her head up, her expression confused for a moment. Then she nodded, as though she had just latched onto Watson's train of thought.

"Margarita said I had to come up with a way of stealing the collection. If I didn't, she'd consider my own life repayment for the debt I owed."

Watson nodded. "So you went to Liam."

"Yes," said Lisa, tears welling in her eyes. "He was so

pleased to see me. I told him I was in trouble but he said he would help, he was just glad to have me back.

"He was the one who actually came up with the plan. He knew about the disused parts of the subway network and how some of the tunnels connected up with the sewers. The MTA had been chasing urban explorers out of there for years. He devised the route, figured it all out. He even moved apartments—he found one that he said could get him into the tunnels, so he could work it all out."

Watson nodded, thinking back to the water-pumping station in the basement of Liam Macnamara's brownstone.

"It looked easy, I guess," said Lisa, frowning to herself. "We just had to turn the security systems off at the museum so Margarita's men could lift the Miranda Collection and take it out through the sewer to a subway train. Then Liam would drive it down to a rail yard in Brooklyn, near some piers that the cartel often use to smuggle cocaine into the city. Margarita's men would unload everything and take it back to South America by boat, using the route they already had in place. They'd be in international waters before anyone even knew the museum had been hit."

Watson looked down again at Black's body. "But your brother couldn't do it alone, could he?" she said. "He needed help, from someone else in the MTA. Someone with authority. Not just to drive the train down to the rail yard, but to steal it in the first place."

Lisa nodded. "He went to Paul. We had no choice, otherwise it wouldn't have worked. But they were old friends. Liam trusted him. Paul explained how the signals and traffic on the subway were controlled from a secure MTA center somewhere. He used to work there before becoming a station supervisor, so he knew the system."

Watson turned on her heel. The laptop in Paul Black's office. The same one he showed to Margarita before she had killed him.

"And you had the computer expertise, right?" she asked.

Lisa smiled. "I had two jobs: deactivate the security at the museum and hack into the MTA control center so Paul could control the signals from anywhere with an Internet connection." Her face dropped. "We arranged a meeting between him and Margarita. Margarita paid him to help—I guess he thought she was paying us too. We never said anything."

Watson folded herself down onto the floor in front of Lisa again.

"So he murdered your brother, thinking he could take a bigger cut." Watson shook her head. That decision, that misreading of the situation, had been Paul Black's biggest mistake.

One that had cost not just his own life, but Liam's, and Victor's.

And, before the night was out, quite possibly hers and Lisa's too.

42

PAUL BLACK'S GREATEST MISTAKE

Paul Black laughs with the other men, even if he doesn't understand what they're saying to him. It doesn't cross his mind that they might be laughing *at* him, not with him, but they jostle and rib and Paul Black thinks he has hit the big time. One simple job and he can retire. One simple job and he can leave this godforsaken city and its godforsaken people. The people that rush and yell and are always in a hurry and who don't care and who follow each other like ants into the tunnels. You know what some people do on the subway? It's disgusting. People are pigs.

And Liam is a sap. He's stupid, old, weak. He likes his job, likes people, thinks he's doing the world a service. He's a stupid, old, weak potato-eater. He should go back to the old country he so often talks about.

There's only one thing that matters in this life, and Paul Black knows what it is: money. Money fixes everything. They say that money can't buy you happiness but he thinks people who say that are stupid too. Money can't buy you happiness? *Puh-lease*. Money can get him out of here. Pay off his debts. Let him shrug the city off his shoulders like the heavy black coat the damn place feels like.

Paul Black is clever, too. You don't get one past Paul Black. Oh no. Because the plan Liam has come up with is good but doesn't need two to work it, not with Lisa's hack through to the MTA control center. She's good. Pretty, too. Shame she'll have to be next on the list. But, hey, what can you do?

What can you freakin' do?

Time to cut out the competition. That woman, Margarita, she'll like that. She's good. Smart. She knows a fellow businessman when she sees one. She's a player, like him. And he's seen the way she smiles at him, the way her eyes light up when he goes to see her. She tells him he needs to be careful, to stay away, to not bother her, to get on with the job, to play his role and not get involved or there will be trouble for everyone. She's fiery, that one. Got a way with words, all that Spanish. Hot stuff.

And she likes him around. He can see that. That temper, that's cover. She likes him like he likes her.

And as for trouble, well, he has a notion he can save them all a whole heap.

They keep everything in that room under the museum. It'll need to be scrubbed clean when the time comes, but right now they're using it as their base. Everything is there. Crates of it. Uniforms, ski masks.

Guns.

Guns and *ammo*.

So Paul Black picks his time and he enters the tunnels when he knows there is nobody there and he takes one of the uniforms, a black one-piece coverall with a zip-up front, and he takes one of the Uzis out and he looks at it in the beam of his flashlight. It's black, small, but damn, the thing is heavy. Its surface shines—it looks oily but it's dry to the touch. It's also simple. So very, very simple. Clip goes there. Pull the trigger. Bullets come out the end.

Bingo.

He takes a clip and he hefts it in his hand and then he feels like a goddamn hero so he takes another clip. He slams one home and it goes clunk and it feels good, and the gun feels good, the balance a little better with the ammo in place. The other clip is in the pocket of his coveralls. Just in case.

And Liam. That schmuck. There's a way into his place—the tiny apartment he just moved into. Chosen for a reason, the rent through the roof despite the lack of square footage —just like every other apartment in the city. But unlike every other apartment in the city, this one has a little secret in the basement: a pumping station, one which not only provides access to the wastewater, but to the main tunnels. Which is exactly what Liam needed. Easy in, easy out.

Paul Black laughs. Yeah, that. Easy in, easy out.

Liam is going to get a hell of a shock.

He hefts the gun and he holds it up, aiming it at nothing. He squints along the top and then he clicks his tongue and puffs out his cheeks as he goes *chooff-chooff-chooff-chooff-chooff-chooff-chooff-chooff*. And then he raises the barrel and it's all he can damn well do to stop himself blowing across the top of it.

He heads out. He knows the way. Knows the tunnels.

Knows it all.

The apartment is dark. He kicks the rug back into place, looks around. The apartment is dark and small, a real dump. Liam lives alone. Probably always would have.

That isn't going to be a problem for him real soon.

The armchair under the window is comfortable but it creaks when he sits in it and it creaks when he moves. It's not leather, it's vinyl, and it's peeling. It creaks again as Paul Black tries to get comfortable. He stretches his legs out, crosses his ankles, re-crosses them. Pushes against the arms, trying to get his back into the chair. Damn thing. Cheap-ass.

Like everything else in the apartment, like the apartment itself, like Liam himself.

The Uzi rests across his knees. It feels heavy. Cold. Powerful. The things you could do with an Uzi in your hands. He pictures the scene now. He pictures Liam pleading. No. *Begging*. On his knees. Paul Black tells Liam to turn around. Paul Black points his gun at the back of Liam's head and Liam is no more. Like he was ever anything to begin with.

He waits for an hour. The darkness begins to lift. Light creeping in through the blinds behind his head. Furtive. Like the light itself is unsure, uncertain. Like the light itself knows what is about to go down, here, in this room, in just a few minutes.

Just a few minutes.

Someone shuffles up the stairs, outside, the sound coming from behind Paul. It's confusing for a moment, then he takes a deep breath behind the thick wool of the ski mask. Damn thing is hot. It itches. Every breath tastes like brick dust.

The rustle of thin plastic, the key in the lock and the door opening. The door is closed with a click so as not to disturb the neighbors.

Paul Black smiles. They're going to be disturbed soon enough.

Paul Black smiles, but he feels nervous. Can he do it? Can he pull the trigger?

Can he solve the problem?

Of course he can. He has no choice now. And it's the right decision. He knows it. He's about to show Margarita what kind of a man he is. He's about to become a goddamn hero.

The door to the apartment opens before Paul Black has even paused in his thoughts, and Liam walks in. Heads to the kitchen. Keys on the counter. Plastic bag swings up next. It's full of white cardboard boxes.

It's now or never.

Now or never.

Now.

Liam Macnamara turns around and Paul Black stands up and he points the gun and soon all his problems are solved, forever.

43

THE DEDUCTIONS OF MS. JOAN WATSON

Watson stood and moved across the storeroom to Black's body. She crouched down and examined his coveralls. They were identical to the ones worn by the rest of the gang.

Black was wearing his own shoes, though. They were black too, but cheap, the kind of shoes that are fine for a nine-to-five office job—a job as, say, a low-paid MTA supervisor—but little else.

The cuffs of the coverall legs were turned up. Watson pinched the fabric and stretched it out.

It was as she suspected. The bottom of the coveralls were dirty, a thin layer of beige dirt rubbed well into the fabric. Watson unfolded one of the cuffs with a finger and thumb. There was more of the dirt, loose, in the cuff. Beige, light, dusty. The same residue that Holmes had spotted in Macnamara's apartment, and had—correctly, it now seemed—identified as being from South America. The coveralls had been boxed up by the gang and shipped with the rest of their gear. Black had shed some of the material onto the floor of the apartment while he waited for Liam to show up.

Lisa called out from the other side of the room, "What are you doing?"

Watson stood up, brushing her hands off on her pants. "Testing a theory," she said. She walked back over to Lisa, deliberately drawing the curator's eyeline away from the body. "What about the money in Liam's kitchen? We found about fifty thousand dollars hidden in the bread bin. Black hadn't touched it, so he couldn't have known it was there."

Lisa laughed and lifted her head. "That was going to be our escape route. Eighteen thousand from Liam's 401k, about twenty thousand I had left over from the smuggling and another twenty I had saved. Everything we had, pooled together."

"Escape route?"

Lisa closed her eyes. "You're right about the gang, aren't you? About Margarita. About what she'll do with us when the job is done. They're not going to leave anyone behind, are they?"

Watson paused, and then she said: "No."

Lisa shook her head. "Maybe I knew that. Maybe I was just kidding myself. But it was Liam's idea. The money. Said we needed a way out. I tried to argue but I went along with it anyway. I guess I knew too, really. The money isn't enough to completely start over, but it would have been enough to get away. Out of the country, anyway. Somewhere away from *her*. Out of her reach. And then I found something else out, maybe a way to keep the money." Lisa sighed. "Well, I *thought* I had. Maybe I was just fooling myself with that one too—"

Lisa stopped, her head snapping around as a key was jammed into the lock of the door. Watson pulled back against the far wall, reaching down, motioning for Lisa to stand too, all the while cursing at the interruption.

The door opened; one of the ski mask-clad men stepped in and looked around, then he waved at the two women with his Uzi.

"Time to go," muttered Watson. She walked through the door ahead of Lisa, and was met in the foot tunnel by another man. He waved at her to keep going, then he followed behind. Watson led them to the station's tiled atrium, then, her guard waving her on, down to the station platform. As she walked in, she noticed the station's name, written in a curved arch of tiles opposite the stairs that she hadn't paid any heed to when she had been following Lisa earlier: City Hall.

The stolen subway car was at the platform, running now, the door of the cab open and Margarita at the controls. She glanced up through the front windows at her two hostages, then returned her attention to the panel in front of her. Paul Black's laptop was open and balanced next to the dead man's switch.

Watson exchanged a look with Lisa, then glanced around. Their two guards were the only members of Margarita's gang there. The rest, she supposed, were at the museum.

Margarita moved to the cab's doorway and called out to one of the men. They had a conversation in Spanish, one that seemed to increase in heat in just a few seconds. Watson caught Angelino's name, but little else. Eventually, Margarita clearly furious, her associate shrugged and turned, heading back for the station entrance, while his colleague stayed with their boss.

What was going on? Neither of the two men had been Angelino—they may have been masked again, but Watson thought she'd be able to recognize the whole group now, ski masks or not. Margarita's temper was short but she'd snapped even quicker than before.

Watson frowned. If she didn't know any better, she would have guessed that Margarita's right-hand man, Angelino, had gone AWOL.

Interesting.

Watson glanced sideways at Lisa, but the curator's

expression was blank as she seemed to stare into the middle distance. She was starting to shut down again. Watson felt like she was about ready to collapse herself, but instead she rolled her neck and lifted her feet, bending her legs at the knee to flex her muscles.

She wanted to be ready—*had* to be. Any opportunity, any opportunity at all, and she was going to take it.

Margarita cast an eye over Watson and Lisa, but quickly looked away and stepped back into the cab.

Watson bit her lip.

Time was nearly up.

And that was when Margarita's phone rang.

44

THE MEETING AT THE BROWNSTONE

Alfredo did another circuit of the front room, shoulders hunched, hands hidden in the voluminous pockets of his hoodie. He passed the bay window, glanced at it, trying to get a peek of the world outside through the closed blinds. Then he circled back to the fireplace. He stopped, turned to look at Holmes sitting in the armchair. Then he sighed and began another turn.

Alfredo wasn't a pacer. He liked to keep it cool, calm. It was something he'd learned during his recovery. Anxiety was the enemy, that prickling restlessness, that feeling you'd forgotten something important, that you should be doing something productive. As he came out of his addiction, he'd learned to recognize that feeling, to plough it back into his work. It was something his own sponsor had once told him, something that had changed the way Alfredo looked at the world.

Energy can be neither created nor destroyed, but it can change form. It was just up to him, Alfredo Llamosa, to choose that form. To use that energy.

But here, in the large brownstone that Holmes shared with Watson, the interior feeling somehow bigger on the inside than the outside, Alfredo was stuck for options. He was charged with energy and there was nothing to do but wait.

And so Alfredo paced. He made another circuit, then he looked at Holmes again.

Pacing might have been bad, but sitting still had to be worse, surely. He didn't know how Holmes did it. How he had sat there, in the art deco chair with no arms next to the fire for... well, ever since they'd got back. He was still, entirely motionless, his eyes fixed on a point somewhere in the middle distance.

The box from the museum was on his lap. He had one hand resting on the top, the other hung straight down to the floor. Every now and again, Holmes would curl that hand into a fist.

He was thinking. Alfredo could see that. But about what, Alfredo didn't like to guess. He had enough on his own mind. Like those men with guns. Like whatever the hell it was that Holmes had in the box. The ultimate weapon, he'd said. Like he would flip it open and there would be a big red button inside—one big red button to unleash Armageddon. Maybe the box was like the "football" the President's staff kept with them at all times, a briefcase so named because the many documents it held—nuclear launch codes, the commands that could end the world—made it so fat the sides bulged.

And Alfredo thought about Watson. She was still somewhere out there, in the city. She was alive—she had to be, because she was being held hostage and being held hostage meant that you were alive, right? Alfredo had half-expected to bring her back with them, but it was the box Holmes needed. His ultimate weapon.

Alfredo took a breath, tried to calm himself. He made another circuit of the room, but he made an effort to slow himself down. He stopped at the fireplace and leaned on the mantel. He glanced back across the room. He took in the bookcases, the furniture. The table with the red top had been pulled in from the other room and there was something big on it, covered in a black cloth. Next to the fireplace, on the other side, a black metal frame stood against the wall, two pairs of silver handcuffs hanging from the top bar.

Alfredo frowned. His fingers found his phone in his pocket but he resisted the temptation to pull it out and check the time. He'd given up on that after the twentieth time. All it seemed to do was make time go slower, make the wait longer.

So he shook his head instead and tapped his fingernails on the mantelpiece. "What if they don't get it?" he asked.

Holmes said nothing, but he curled his dangling hand into a fist again.

Alfredo pushed himself away from the fireplace and stepped into Holmes's line of sight. "What if they don't get the *message*, Holmes? What then?"

Holmes glanced up at him. There, a flicker of life, an acknowledgement at least.

And then it was gone. Holmes's eyes moved back down, his attention returned to nothing at all.

Alfredo sighed and walked to the stairs and then back.

"We need to call the police," he said. Then he turned around. "Your friends at the NYPD. Gregson and Bell. They must be doing something, right?"

No response.

Alfredo sighed. He waved a hand in frustration. "We need to call the *FBI*, man. We gotta do something." He walked back to the fireplace. "We gotta do *something*."

Then he turned on Holmes, and pointed at the box.

"What's in the box?"

Fingers splayed, fist curled. A sigh from Alfredo.

"I want to know what's in the box, Holmes!"

And then a knock on the door. It was polite, casual, just three raps in quick succession.

Alfredo froze. He looked at Holmes. Then Holmes met his gaze, and he nodded.

"You are about to find out," he said, then he nodded toward the hallway. "Would you be so kind as to let our guests in?"

Alfredo swept his baseball cap off, curling the brim between his hands. He drew breath to speak, but what the hell was he going to say? Holmes had this under control. He had to have.

Just a little faith, right?

Alfredo replaced his cap, then he turned on his heel and strode into the hallway. He opened the glass porch doors and peered through the peephole in the brownstone's front door. He couldn't see anyone.

He opened the door a crack.

"Hello?"

The door was flung back into his face, smacking him in the forehead and knocking his cap off. Alfredo cried out in surprise and toppled backward, jarring his elbows painfully against the wooden floor.

Shapes came at him—big black shapes in uniforms, in ski masks, carrying guns. Uzis. A big gloved hand grabbed a handful of clothing and lifted Alfredo up, then turned him around. Another hand shoved him in the back, sending him careening into the front room. Alfredo hit the deck on his knees, then was immediately yanked up by hands under his armpits. He cried out, then he felt his throat close as he found the short barrel of an Uzi in his face.

Alfredo looked at Holmes, eyes wide, breaths short, fast. The detective was still sitting in the armchair. Unmoving. Box on his lap.

Two more men sidestepped Alfredo—*how many were there?*—and moved to stand either side of the armchair. Holmes ignored them and ignored their guns, which were lifted and pointed at his head.

Footsteps, from the hallway. *Slow* footsteps, measured. Confident.

Holmes's eyes flicked up to the newcomer. Alfredo craned his neck around to see. He looked the same as the others— big guy, wide. Powerful. Black coveralls, black ski mask, black everything. Except instead of carrying an Uzi, he had a pistol. An automatic, compact, matte finish. *Glock or something*, thought Alfredo.

The man stepped up to Holmes and pulled his ski mask off, revealing a bald head and a chinstrap beard. The curving tendrils of a complex tattoo curled up out of the neck of his coveralls.

Holmes smiled. "Mr. Angelino," he said quietly. "I see you received my message."

The big bald man smiled, and raised his gun, and aimed it squarely at Holmes's forehead.

He thumbed the safety off.

45

THE CITY HALL LOOP

Sherlock Holmes walked down the steps and onto the platform of the City Hall subway station. His hands were in the pockets of his pea coat. He stopped at the bottom of the stairs and looked across the tracks at the name of the station emblazoned on the wall opposite. Beneath the name, filling the entire arch of the roof vault, was a plaque commemorating the station's opening. A relic, like the building itself, of another time, another age. The tiles glowed in the bright light cast by the iron chandeliers. Above, the leaded windows were dull black mirrors. The air was still, the tang of dust and damp ever-present.

He looked to the right, to the left, each side curving away in a tight semicircle.

He turned, headed left, his footsteps echoing in the cavernous, empty station.

Somewhere, somewhere near, a train rumbled by, but Sherlock Holmes was alone.

Around the curve of the platform, the train tunnel itself became visible. There was another archway and stairs leading off into another atrium at this end too. Holmes walked slowly past the arch, then he stopped at the sound of footsteps behind him.

He smiled, not turning around, not just yet. He knew what he would see when he did: big men, men dressed in black, men holding ugly, angry guns. Men with their faces hidden behind thick black wool.

Then he heard clicking, the creak of leather. Holmes's smile dropped and he turned. The six men who had come down the stairs each had their Uzi pointed at him. They moved forward in a coordinated phalanx, evidence of their training in the jungles of Colombia, Ecuador, Peru. They moved around Holmes in a tight semicircle.

Holmes kept his hands in his pockets.

Somewhere a train rumbled.

And then she walked down the steps and came through the arch. Holmes watched Margarita Caballero, unarmed save for her cruel, knowing smile, and her escort of two more black-clad foot soldiers as they approached. With them, Watson and Lisa, their arms behind their backs, their faces and clothing smeared with dust and dirt. Holmes looked Watson in the eye, but he didn't speak. Watson gave him a tiny nod in greeting, her lips flickering into a faint smile but it was gone almost in an instant. She glanced around, searching. Then she locked eyes with Holmes again, her own held a fraction wider than before. Holmes was alone, with a lot of guns pointed at him. Watson was anxious. Afraid. Perhaps more now than she had been just a few minutes ago.

Holmes turned his gaze on Margarita. He knew the smile—knew the *mechanism* behind it. It was not a warm expression, borne of good humor. When Margarita smiled, it meant that things were going her way. That she was in control. And in the kind of business she was in—particularly in her position at the top of the cartel—being in control meant everything. Being in control meant staying alive. And right now the balance of control appeared to be firmly in her favor.

Margarita took a few careful steps forward, planting one booted foot in front of the other and swaying her hips like a fashion model, the men covering Holmes shuffling aside to let their leader come closer.

Holmes didn't move, his eyes never leaving hers.

Margarita cocked her head, her eyebrows dipping together in confusion, but the air of arrogant amusement never left her.

"Is this some trick, Mr. Holmes?"

Holmes shook his head. "I have come as agreed."

The cartel boss glanced over her shoulder, as if to confirm that her men were still there, that Watson and Lisa were still in her power. There was something there, a tiny sliver of uncertainty. Then she turned back to Holmes.

"Sherlock Holmes," she said. "I think you are famous here, huh? I am told you are a very clever man."

Holmes dipped his chin, regarded Margarita from under his eyebrows. "There are some who hold that opinion, yes. Myself included."

Margarita laughed. "I think I like you, Mr. Sherlock Holmes. Maybe if we had met under different circumstances, there would have been much we could have done for each other, huh?"

"Alas."

Margarita's expression hardened. "You are a clever man and yet you are here to play games with me."

Holmes pulled his hands from his pockets. The two men behind Margarita twitched their guns, almost instinctively, but none of the others moved. Holmes glanced around the circle of men, then he turned back to face their leader.

"No games, I assure you. Not now. As I indicated to you earlier, I have come to make an exchange for the lives of Ms. Watson and Dr. Harley."

Margarita shook her head. "And yet you bring nothing?

What do you think is going to happen here, underneath your fine city, Mr. Holmes? How does a clever man think this will end, huh?"

And then Sherlock Holmes smiled. He held Margarita's gaze. Just for a moment, the cold grin on her face faltered.

"No tricks," said Holmes. "No games. Nor do I come empty-handed."

Footsteps from the archway. Margarita and her two guards turned to watch as Angelino descended the stairs and stepped onto the platform.

Watson and Lisa craned their necks to see, then Watson turned back and shot a look at Holmes. Holmes clenched his teeth, the muscles at the back of his jaw bunching.

Angelino, like Margarita, was unarmed, but not empty-handed. As he walked toward the group, he held a wooden box in front of him. It was a perfect cube, the wood rough, the brass catch on the front glinting. He held the box away from his body, like it was hot, or would explode.

Or was holy.

Angelino stopped in front of Margarita, who stared at the box. Then she looked up at her assistant, her expression curling into an angry snarl.

"Angelino! *Qué está pasando?*" She waved at the box. "What is this *mierda*?"

Angelino looked at Holmes. Holmes gave a single, short nod.

Angelino reached around the front of the box, slipped the brass ring from its latch, and pulled back the lid.

Nestled inside, on a bed of green cloth, was a skull, its surface mottled brown, chalky, delicate. The jawbone was missing, while the upper row of teeth was partially intact, those missing replaced with gold replicas. Inset into the eye sockets were two dull, unshaped red stones.

Margarita stared at the skull, then turned to Holmes.

"I think you will find, Ms. Caballero," he said, "that I have kept my part of the bargain to the letter."

The semi-circle of foot soldiers surrounding Holmes moved as a single unit, turning their guns away from him.

Turning them on Margarita.

46

THE TURNING OF TABLES

Margarita looked at Holmes. There was fire in her eyes.

Watson took a deep breath, her heart racing. She glanced over her shoulder, and saw that one of the two men guarding her, the pair that had stuck by Margarita while the others were out on the job, had turned his gun to cover the other.

Margarita snarled. "*Malparido*, what have you done?"

Holmes smiled. He returned his hands to the high pockets of his pea coat, and he stuck his elbows out, like he was giving a shrug, like the answer was blindingly obvious.

"I have given Angelino and his men exactly what they came to New York for, Ms. Caballero," said Holmes. He walked past her, past the guns, exchanged a look with Angelino. Then he pulled one hand out of his coat and gestured with an open palm to the skull, nestled snugly in the open wooden box. "The mortal remains of an ancient tribal leader and holy man of the Awa-Kwaiker people." He glanced up at Angelino. "Known to some as Ambu Pã, the Sun Man." Angelino gave a tiny nod, then Holmes turned back to Margarita and cocked his head. "The Awa-Kwaiker, Ms. Caballero? You might have heard of them, seeing as your organization has them under its jackboot."

Margarita's eyes widened. She drew breath to speak. Holmes smirked, and returned his attention to the skull, bouncing on his heels as he clasped his hands behind his back.

"This is not just a skull. It is a *relic*, and a very important one at that, stolen by Spanish conquistadors in the late fifteenth century from a shrine deep in the Chocoanos forest in what would later become northern Ecuador. In the last five hundred years or so it has travelled the world, the once sacred artifact rendered to mere 'savage' curio. It ended up in New York sometime in the late nineteenth century, and then it vanished. *Poof!*"

Holmes mimed a puff of smoke with his hands. He glanced at Angelino, who was watching him with a small, confident smile. Holmes nodded sharply.

"Until I found it. It wasn't lost, merely misplaced, vanished into the inaccuracies and vagaries of the American Museum of Natural History's catalogue." Holmes looked at Margarita and shrugged again. "Well, can't blame them really. They've got forty million objects stored away up there. I mean, what's a skull in a box when it's at home, eh?"

Margarita looked back at the skull, her lips parted like she couldn't quite take in what Holmes was talking about. Angelino remained silent and unmoving, but now his eyes had moved from Holmes to his boss. His ex-boss.

Margarita looked up at him.

"Angelino! *Qué está pasando*, huh? How is this thing so important that you would ruin everything, huh? This… this *thing*, it is worth nothing."

Holmes shook his head. Angelino spoke, finally, his voice a deep bass growl.

"You are wrong, Caballero. This is worth the whole world to me, and to my people."

Margarita looked at her assistant—her *former* assistant—then back at Holmes. Holmes turned to Angelino.

"Actually, on that point, your former employer is quite correct," he said. He turned around, glanced at Margarita, at Lisa, at Watson.

Watson shook her head. "Sherlock, what does he mean, that it's worth the whole world?"

Holmes stepped closer to his partner, then he turned to face Angelino. "Excuse me, could we, erm…?" he asked, pointing at Watson.

Angelino nodded, and gave an order to his men that wasn't in Spanish. Within moments, Watson and Lisa's bindings were cut and they were released. Watson rubbed her wrists as she looked at Lisa. Lisa stood, staring at her hands, as though she was having difficulty processing the situation.

Watson didn't blame her.

She moved closer to the skull. "Sherlock? How much is the skull worth?"

He joined her. "In commercial terms, little to nothing. There is a small quantity of gold, some minor value in the eye stones perhaps, but other than that it is, I'm afraid, an archeological item of only moderate historic interest. Certainly it is nothing compared to the quite frankly dizzying value of the Miranda Collection." He turned to face Margarita, still held at the steady gunpoint of her men. "The theft and removal of which you had so very carefully arranged. *But*, not carefully enough, it seems." The corner of his mouth went up in a smile. "If you want to get ahead in business, you really should pay more attention to the kind of people you hire as your henchmen."

Lisa stepped forward, rubbing her raw wrists as she looked at the skull. "That's what I've been looking for for weeks," she said. She turned to Watson. "I was searching for it when you caught me at the gala."

Watson gasped. "This was the other escape route, the one you mentioned you thought you'd found? But how did you know about the skull?" She turned to Holmes. "And how did you find it?"

"The difficult part," said Holmes, "was identifying the language that Mr. Angelino and his compatriots were speaking." He looked back at Angelino, then gave a small bow. "If you will forgive the profiling, it was clear they were not descended from the conquering Spaniards, but from the native population of Colombia. More specifically, Angelino and his *brothers* are members of the indigenous Awa-Kwaiker people, who have lived in northern Ecuador and southern Colombia for centuries. As such, they are some of the last fluent speakers of Awa pit, or *Cuaiquer*, a language in very great risk of dying out completely."

Lisa nodded. "I learned about the Awa-Kwaiker while I was working with Angelino to organize the museum job," she said. She glanced at Margarita, who was looking very sour. "She left him to do most of the work while she handled the public front of the gold exhibition."

"We spent much time together," said Angelino, bowing his head. "Dr. Harley was interested in our people and our problems. Our homelands have been taken over by the cartels and their men. They treat us no better than slaves, forcing us to clear our land to grow their crop, the coca plant."

Holmes nodded. "Indeed. The source of much conflict. Angelino's people are forced to work alongside the cartel's gangs simply to survive, but they've been fighting against the yoke of oppression where they can. I dare say there was a recent glimmer of hope, wasn't there, Angelino?"

"We heard there had been a change, somewhere in the cartel," he said. "Someone new had taken over."

"Which would have disrupted the organization, even at the ground level," said Watson. She looked at Angelino. "Right?

There was an opportunity to fight."

Angelino nodded. "We are fighting a war on the ground," he said, "but my people are fragmented and leaderless while the cartel, they are organized, less like a gang, more like a... a *corporation*."

"A corporation with its own private army," said Holmes. "And while the efforts of Angelino and others like him have been a headache to the cartel, they have until now been somewhat ineffectual. But it's sort of poetic, really," he said, drawing a circle in the air with his finger as he turned to Margarita. "The rebellion of the Awa-Kwaiker was just destabilizing enough for you to make your move and take over the organization, while it was that very takeover and the disruption that gave Angelino his chance to group the various factions of his people together."

Margarita hissed. Whether in anger or disbelief, or both, Watson wasn't sure. She turned back to the box in Angelino's hands. "And the skull?"

Angelino looked down at the precious object in his care. "I have tried to organize the fight, but we have too much conflict of our own to deal with. We need a figurehead to unite behind, a true leader."

Holmes pursed his lips as he regarded the skull. "The Sun Man," he said, his voice barely a whisper.

Watson frowned, but Holmes didn't appear to notice. He looked at Angelino, his face suddenly animated again.

"Which is why you volunteered for the cartel's little New York excursion," he said. "While your boss arranged for the theft of the Miranda Collection as one last desperate attempt to shore up enough funds to re-establish the cartel properly, you searched for the relic of the Sun Man. There was a thousand-to-one chance of actually finding it, of course, but you knew it had to be in the museum, somewhere. That was the last place it was recorded."

Angelino nodded at Lisa. "At least I had help, but time was running out."

Watson looked at the skull. "So who's the Sun Man?"

Holmes nodded at Angelino, who spoke. "There is a legend of the Awa-Kwaiker, that a great warrior captured the light of the day, and used that light to show us the way through the darkness. He is Ambu Pã, Sun Man."

Watson felt one eyebrow go up. Margarita, still silent, shifted the weight on her feet.

Holmes cleared his throat. "The legend goes on to state that the Sun Man will one day return to help the Awa-Kwaiker in their time of need." He rolled his hands in the air. "Lighting the path, figuratively speaking."

Now Watson understood. Such folklore, she knew, was remarkably common across many disparate cultures. She nodded at Angelino. "So with the relic returned, you think you'll be able to go back home and unite your people?"

"I don't know," he said, "but I believe I have a chance. The relic of Ambu Pã has sacred value to the Awa-Kwaiker. The return of such a symbol to its rightful home may be all the motivation we need to unite and fight the cartel on our home soil." He smiled. "Even if nobody actually thinks the legend is true."

Holmes nodded, glanced at Watson. "Cut off the supply of raw material," he said, clicking his fingers, "and the cartel crumbles. Particularly now that it has been decapitated yet again, its new boss in US custody and its ready funds completely exhausted organizing an all-or-nothing museum heist."

Watson looked around the group. She could understand Angelino's plight, understand the need to fight against oppression, against vast criminal organizations like the one headed by Margarita.

But... the men were still dangerous, weren't they? They were killers. *Murderers*. Surely Holmes didn't think they could all just be sent back home to help organize the fight against the cartels?

In an empty subway station, in the company of big men with lots of guns, Watson didn't exactly think she could just come out and say that, either.

"Sherlock," she said, trying to find the right way to put it. "What about *Victor*?"

Holmes turned, jutting his chin out at Margarita's only loyalist, the man being held at gunpoint by his former colleague. "Not all of the group are in with the Awa-Kwaiker. Some still follow Margarita's orders. *Followed*, anyway." He turned back to his partner. "Angelino told me what happened to Mr. Black."

Angelino snapped the box holding the relic shut, then he turned to his men and began giving orders in his native tongue. Watson drew Lisa close to her, putting an arm around her shoulders. Lisa had stood up well, but she slumped a little in Watson's grip, her head hanging down. Meanwhile, one of the men guarding Margarita stepped up to his old boss, motioning for her to move with his Uzi.

"Sherlock—"

Margarita screamed, shouldering the man who approached her and yanking the gun from his hand in two smooth, fast movements. The other men turned, raised their own weapons, but it was too late.

Holmes held up his hands, gesturing for everyone to stop.

Margarita stood just behind Watson; Lisa had dropped to the floor in front of them. Margarita had one hand around Watson's elbow.

She lifted the Uzi in her other hand to Watson's temple. "Get back!"

Angelino's men adjusted their aim, looking for a shot. Holmes quickly ducked in front of the group, so he was between them and Margarita.

"Stop," he said to them, then he turned around to face Margarita. "Let Watson go. There is no way out of this station."

He took a step forward. Margarita took a step back, pulling at Watson. She released her hostage's elbow, but then locked her forearm around Watson's throat.

"*I said get back!*" Margarita pointed the gun at Holmes, then back at Watson. Holmes stopped moving.

"Let her go," said Holmes.

Margarita stepped back again, dragging Watson with her toward the edge of the platform.

47

THE END OF THE LINE

Watson tried to relax her body, enough to make it easy for Margarita to pull her backward, making sure her legs didn't get tangled in her captor's. There was an Uzi an inch away from her right temple. The slightest mistake, the smallest slip, and it could all be over so very, very quickly.

Holmes got farther away, his arms out, palms facing backward, as he motioned for Margarita's former employees to keep back. They all had their guns aimed at their old boss, but Watson thought the chances of a clean, safe shot were about a million to one.

Not that that was what she wanted, anyway. There had been too much death already—and while Watson knew Margarita would have the bloodiest hands of all, not just in New York and Colombia but everywhere the cartel had its claws, what she deserved was justice, a fair trial. Not a summary execution in an abandoned subway station.

But Watson also knew just how much danger she was in. As a woman who had battled her way to the top of a major criminal organization, Watson knew just how ruthless, how determined, Margarita was.

Which meant this wasn't over, not by a long way.

Margarita would be prepared to fight to the last. And fight *hard*.

Which meant Watson had to do the same.

Holmes drew himself up. "I can understand that this whole enterprise represents the culmination of your rise to power," he said, circling his hands in the air now. "One single, *gigantic* operation, meticulously organized, planned to the very last. One final, audacious, all-or-nothing investment of time and resources and what little money you have left squirreled away in a tax haven. A plan that would not just re-establish the cartel but re-affirm your absolute control. The injection of millions of dollars would put paid to any critics and buy not just power but *loyalty*. And those doubters who remained, those who dared to continue their defiance, wouldn't last long."

Margarita said nothing, but she stopped moving. She adjusted her grip around Watson's throat.

"Of course," said Holmes, "I imagine the conditions in the penal system of Colombia would be quite harsh. Then again, that's not to say it's exactly a cakewalk here in the United States. But I'm fairly sure Colombia would be rather keen to get you extradited from US custody. Quite a coup, for both sides, really. A chance to foster a new spirit of cooperation between the federal law enforcement agencies of both countries." Holmes nodded, clearly pleased with his logic. He clasped his hands in front of him. "So I can understand your reluctance to come quietly, as it were." He fixed her with a dark look. "But release my colleague, and we will ensure you are treated fairly."

Margarita turned the gun from Watson's temple to point it at Holmes. She reached out with it, dipping the barrel as if she wanted to tap Holmes on the forehead with the weapon.

"Stay where you are!"

Holmes unlocked his hands and held them up. Not in surrender, but to indicate he wasn't going to try anything.

A moment of distraction. The gun away from her head.

Watson took her cue.

With one hand she pulled at the arm around her neck. The other arm she rammed backward, her elbow connecting with her captor's ribs at full force. Margarita doubled over, the hot breath forced out of her lungs blowing through Watson's hair.

Released, Watson pushed herself to the left, reaching for Margarita's gun arm as the gang boss staggered backward. She managed to push Margarita's arm to the side, but even partially winded, Margarita began to fight back.

She was strong.

"Get down!" Watson yelled as she was pushed away.

Margarita toppled backward; her finger slipped on the trigger of the Uzi, sending a wild line of bullets up the wall of City Hall station. The cream and green tiles exploded, showering the platform with ceramic shards and dust, and then shattered glass as the leadlight windows over their heads were shot out before Margarita managed to regain her footing and control. Gasping for breath, she took two stumbling steps backward and lifted her gun.

Her new target: Watson, lying on the platform in front of her.

Watson slid herself forward on the floor and kicked out and up. The move was awkward, the range slightly too far, but she managed to knock the end of the Uzi, enough for Margarita to surrender her grip on the weapon. Now the gang leader was unarmed, and Watson was out of the way.

From behind Watson came the sound of the men raising their guns again. Watson could hear Holmes shout "No!", but he sounded like he was a million miles away.

Blood rushing in her ears, Watson pushed herself up off the floor, lunging at Margarita.

"Watson, take care!" yelled Holmes, but her focus was on Margarita. They were nose to nose, and Margarita snarled as she pushed back against Watson. Margarita might have been stronger, more muscular, but Watson had the laws of physics on her side. Heavier, travelling with momentum, they slid backward.

Then the floor vanished and Watson felt herself topple forward, Margarita in front of her. They fell off the edge of the platform, down onto the tracks. The impact jarred badly, knocking the air out of Watson's lungs. Margarita pushed her off easily; Watson rolled, hands clutching her stomach.

"Watson! The third rail!"

She blinked and coughed and as her ears cleared she could hear a faint electric buzz. She rolled her head. There, just a few inches from her face, was the shiny silver surface of the subway's electrified third rail.

She looked up. Holmes was lying on his stomach over the platform edge, his arms reaching out for her. Watson coughed, her eyes raw with brake dust, but she extended her arms. Holmes locked his hand below her elbow and pulled.

Upright, she leaned against the platform and coughed again. She shrugged Holmes off, and waved down toward the tunnel.

"Get after Margarita," she said. "Don't let them shoot her."

"All in hand, Watson."

She looked up, squinting. Margarita was running down the middle of the tracks, four of her former employees in pursuit. She had almost reached the black nothingness of the tunnel entrance.

A horn sounded. Two bursts echoed around the station, then the tunnel entrance seemed to explode in a nova of white light.

Margarita stopped running, tripped, and fell to her knees between the tracks, silhouetted by the brilliant headlights of a subway train as it emerged from the tunnel. Watson drew her forearm up to her face to try and block the glare; when she did, she saw into the cab. There was an older man at the controls, thick, collar-length silver hair swept back from a pockmarked face bordered with heavy, old-fashioned sideburns. Standing beside him, dressed in NYPD windbreakers, were Captain Gregson and Detective Bell.

And then: footsteps. Lots of them; booted feet pounding the hard floor. Holmes turned on his hands to sit on the platform edge, legs outstretched, Watson standing in the track beside him, as armed men flooded into the station, two squads coming out of each of the two arched entrances, a third running in from around the curve of the tracks from the opposite end. Like Margarita's men, they were dressed in black, but these men wore flak jackets and helmets, and instead of Uzis they carried larger, longer automatic rifles. Across their chests, their backs, were emblazoned three large letters in bright yellow.

DEA.

The SWAT teams spread out across the platform. They shouted, they motioned with their weapons. Still sitting, Holmes raised his arms. Watson did the same. She looked around the station as Margarita's men were forced to their knees by the federal agents. Even Angelino complied, making a show of putting the wooden relic box down on the floor next to him before he lowered himself.

Down the platform, the subway train had pulled up just by the tunnel. Gregson and Bell disembarked from the cab, while from the passenger compartment came another SWAT team, followed by DEA agents wearing vests over their regular shirts.

Margarita was sitting on her haunches, in front of the train, still spotted by its lights. She didn't resist, did not even move as she was surrounded.

Captain Gregson stood on the platform edge by her, hands in his pockets.

"Margarita Caballero," he said. "You are under arrest for the murder of Victor Judd, and as an accessory to the murder of Liam Macnamara, not to mention criminal conspiracy, criminal trespass, and attempted grand larceny. You have the right to remain silent. Anything you say can and will be used against you in a court of law. You have a right to an attorney. If you cannot afford an attorney, one will be appointed for you. If you are not a United States citizen, you may contact your country's consulate prior to any questioning."

Gregson paused, and tilted his head as he looked down at Margarita. As she was handcuffed by the agents on the track, she turned her head and stared up at the Captain.

"And believe me," he said, "they can't *wait* for you to give them a call."

48

A SAFER CITY

"Good work, you two."

Watson, Holmes, and Captain Gregson stood on the platform. Watson pulled the silver survival blanket around her shoulders tightly. She didn't think she needed it, she felt fine, really, but she'd accepted it anyway. She knew that any moment now, as her system eliminated the huge boost of adrenaline she'd just received, she would start to feel the effects of her ordeal.

Well, the physical effects, anyway. Psychologically, she knew it would take longer. But getting home would help. Home, a bath, her bed. She was shaken up, but she knew that normality would be just a little bit closer after a few hours'—*days'*—sleep.

She glanced over at Lisa. The curator was sitting against the wall of the station as a medical team fussed over her. Watson at least had some experience. For Lisa, this was going to be far more traumatic.

The station was still full of DEA agents, keeping Margarita's men under armed guard while Angelino had a deep discussion with three officers, his hands cuffed in front of him, the wooden relic box on the floor by his feet.

Holmes nodded at the Captain. "Thank you. How goes the operation at the museum?"

"It's under control," he said. "Thanks to your information, a joint task force of the NYPD, DEA and FBI raided the museum an hour ago. The Miranda Collection had been lifted from display, but they hadn't moved the boxes out of the museum yet."

"And the security staff?"

Gregson smiled. "Released. All safe, no casualties."

Watson glanced back over to Lisa. The medics seemed to have finished with her, and had given her a survival blanket too. Watson watched as a medic and DEA agent spoke to her; Lisa nodded, and the pair walked away, leaving Lisa on her own for a moment.

Watson nudged Holmes, nodding toward Lisa. Holmes glanced over, then looked at the Captain. Gregson waved them away, and the pair went over to the curator.

Lisa looked up as they approached. Watson squatted down, and gave her a smile.

"Hey," she said. "How are you doing?"

Lisa returned the smile. It was weak, but there was something there: a little relief, a little hope.

"I'm alive," she said. "Right now that seems to be what matters. Thanks."

Holmes closed his eyes and gave a little bow. "Actually, it is you we should thank."

Lisa's face creased into a confused frown. She glanced at Watson, but Watson just shook her head and looked up at Holmes as he stood over them, his hands buried in his pockets.

"Your plan, Dr. Harley. It was as inventive as it was risky, but it worked out to the letter. You have my congratulations."

"I don't—you mean the relic?"

"I do. The perfect symbol to gain Angelino's trust. With the skull I was able to convince him whose side we were on, and he in turn was able to convince his brothers." He bowed again to the curator. "Well done."

Watson shook her head. "But how did you find the skull when Lisa couldn't?"

"Ah," said Holmes, dropping on his haunches. "It took a little digging, but we are fortunate to have the remarkable resource of the New York Public Library so close at hand. Once I had identified the ethnic roots of Angelino and his men, I was able to translate a few key words from the subterranean conversation he had with his friends—difficult from an audio recording, but enough to pick out references to the Sun Man. With that information all I had to do was go to the library to compare an original catalogue of material plundered from southern Colombia by the Spanish conquistadors with a later catalogue compiled by one of your predecessors at the museum, Dr. Harley, one Professor Quinn. Included in the catalogue was a set of photographic plates which allowed me to confirm the existence of the skull in the museum in the late nineteenth century, at least. By comparing the museum's current online catalogue with historical versions, I discovered a transposition of catalogue numbers, resulting in the artifact being mislabeled and stored in the wrong collection. A simpler task there could not have been."

Watson raised an eyebrow.

"None of which," said Holmes, "would have been remotely possible without your help, Dr. Harley, whether consciously or unconsciously given."

"Okay," said Lisa, the smile growing on her face. "Thanks, then."

Detective Bell came in through the nearby archway, speaking into his phone. Watson and Holmes glanced up as he approached. He nodded a silent greeting, then quickly finished his call and joined them as Watson and Holmes stood.

"This is going to be big," said the detective. "That was the

Department of Justice liaison. There's been an international warrant out for Margarita Caballero's arrest for *eight years* now. Taking her in is pretty huge. Because she was going to use one of her major drug-import routes to export the gemstones, they're hoping they can trace the whole network and shut it down. New York City might just be a little bit cleaner after tonight."

"More than just New York, I hope," said Holmes. He turned to look over at Angelino. The big man was still talking to the DEA agents. He caught Holmes looking at him, and gave him a nod, and, lifting his cuffed hands together, a thumbs-up.

Gregson, watching, joined Watson and the others. He nodded at Angelino.

"There are a lot of negotiations to do," he said, "but I think they'll be able to reach a bargain. They're already talking about backing Angelino up, taking him back to Colombia with the full cooperation of narcotic task forces from both countries to help shut down the cartel's production at the source."

"Somewhat ironic," said Holmes, "that while my original supposition that they were a Colombian cartel has proved to be correct, the crime they had planned had no direct connection to the drugs trade at all."

Gregson pursed his lips as he looked at his consultant. "Speaking of which, there is just a little matter of theft from the museum to account for."

Holmes rolled his hands in front of the Captain. "A necessary transgression. I had no choice but to liberate the artifact to demonstrate my trustworthiness to Angelino. Besides which, the object was *stolen* from his people in the first place."

"There's more, too," said Lisa. The group looked down at her. "The skull was part of a single collection of hundreds of objects from the Awa-Kwaiker." She shrugged. "Now that we've located the catalogue error, we should be able to find the rest."

Holmes turned to Gregson. "Such items would have immense cultural significance to them. The official repatriation of the collection would help Angelino's task even more."

Gregson nodded. "Agreed." He looked down at Lisa. "The DEA and ICE are going to need to talk to you," he said. "Angelino too, I'm afraid. But first you should get checked out at the hospital."

Lisa nodded, drawing the silver survival blanket tightly around her. Watson could see the woman was shivering again. As was she. Shock was setting in, the events of the last few hours finally starting to catch up.

"Okay, I think I need to get out of here and go home," said Watson. She looked at Holmes, who nodded.

The pair said their goodbyes to Lisa, and walked through the arch and up into the station atrium.

"Very good work indeed, Watson," Holmes said quietly as he walked by her side. "I understand the danger and the difficulties, but I want you to know how much I admire your courage and tenacity." He stopped walking; Watson took another step and turned around.

Holmes looked at her, his lips pulled into a tight smile. He gave a nod.

Approval.

Watson allowed herself a laugh. She shook her head, and turned back around, just as one of the SWAT teams appeared from a nearby passage, led by a DEA agent. In the middle of the armed group was Margarita, cuffed, two heavy, gloved hands on her shoulders guiding her forward.

As the group walked past, the gang boss looked at Watson. Her expression was flat, but not emotionless. Watson could almost feel the hate and anger radiating off her in waves, like heat.

The group headed up the stairs leading to the surface. Watson watched them leave.

Holmes bounced on his heels, his hands curled into fists by his sides.

"Everything all right?" he asked.

Watson nodded. "It will be."

Holmes laid his hand on her shoulder.

"Let's go home," he said.

49

JUST A HINT OF THE ANDES

Watson dumped the shoebox onto the kitchen table in front of Holmes with a heavy *thunk*, carefully calculating the height of its fall to create maximum irritation. The spice jars inside rattled together.

Then she stood, hands on hips, next to his chair as he continued to read something on his tablet. She stared down at him. He remained unperturbed. Next to him on the table, Clyde sat eating a lettuce leaf.

Watson sighed—*loudly*—shook her head, thought about making some more tea. Following Holmes's revelation that the spice rack had in fact been filled with soil samples, she'd decided to do an impromptu stock take. If nothing else, it took her mind off the fact she'd been held hostage, at gunpoint. That she'd seen a man shot in the head right in front of her. Three days later, she still wasn't sleeping well.

So Holmes read his tablet in silence, and Watson put the kettle on, then stood back and regarded the upper row of cupboards over the bench.

"If you insist on having a clear-out," said Holmes, apparently still reading but now waggling a finger vaguely at her over one shoulder, "then I should avoid the fourth cupboard on the right for the moment."

Watson's eyes moved to the door in question. "Am I going to regret asking what it is you've put in there?"

"Let us call it an experiment, and leave it at that, shall we?"

"Oh boy," Watson muttered under her breath. She decided to focus solely on the preparation of tea.

"Ah, here it is!" Holmes turned on his chair, tablet in hand.

Watson glanced up. "Here what is?"

Holmes dragged his finger along the tablet's screen. "In the *New York Mail.* 'Preparations are underway for the repatriation of a number of historic and cultural artifacts from the American Museum of Natural History to representatives of the Awa Federation of Ecuador, the New York institution has announced. The objects, believed to have been acquired by the museum in the mid-nineteenth century, are part of a pre-Colombian collection that was miscatalogued and presumed lost until a curator, undertaking research, identified one object, a jeweled skull, as part of the historic cache.'"

Watson nodded as she poured boiling water into two mugs.

"That's great," she said. "I'm so glad they're actually going through with it."

Holmes lowered his tablet. "Acting on my advice, of course."

Watson rolled her eyes. *Whatever,* she thought. "Okay, sure," she said. She turned from the counter. "Lisa is back at work then? Seems a little soon."

"She isn't, as yet," said Holmes. "I spoke to Gregson earlier. She is under arrest, as are Angelino and his men. They are apparently cooperating fully with the authorities as some kind of plea bargain—she is helping the museum identify the lost artifacts of the Awa-Kwaiker while Angelino prepares to return with them and his own taskforce."

"Okay, so, they'll let her go? Angelino too?"

Holmes nodded. "Sounds like they have come to some kind of arrangement."

"Maybe then Lisa can focus on her life again. Like dealing with the loss of her brother." Watson folded her arms, leaning back against the counter. "She's been through a hell of a lot."

"Yes, indeed."

"Hey, have you spoken to Alfredo yet?"

Holmes nodded. "By electronic means, yes."

"And is *he* okay?"

"Alfredo is *always* okay."

"Sherlock!"

Holmes shrugged. "I am merely quoting the man directly. But we have agreed to go to a support meeting tonight." He rolled his neck and turned back to the table. "Should do us both good."

Watson turned back to the tea, laughing.

"The mighty Sherlock Holmes admitting that a support group will do him good? I'm going to tell Alfredo you said that."

Holmes lowered his tablet. "On no account, Watson. Alfredo and I have established a certain kind of relationship. Such a revelation is liable to disturb that balance. I fear the consequences."

He looked over his shoulder at Watson, his eyebrows raised, like he was expecting an answer.

Watson gave Holmes a look, then went to the fridge for the milk. Inside, nearly all of the shelves were stacked with plastic food containers.

Watson slapped her arm against her side.

"Sherlock, what is this?" She pulled one box out and peeled back the lid. Whatever was inside was red and sticky.

Holmes waved at the fridge. "I hope you like Mongolian barbecue. We do have rather a lot to get through."

Watson thought about it. Thought about it some more.

"Wait, is this…?"

"Chekhov, yes," said Holmes, with a grin. "Got a good deal from that place down the street. They *processed* him for me, shall we say."

Watson slid the box back and grabbed the milk. A few moments later, she handed her partner a steaming mug.

"I see," she said. "Now I'm going to have a bath. After a day and a night locked in an old subway station I don't think I'll ever feel clean again."

She had reached the stair bannister when Holmes called out from the kitchen. At the same time, there was a faint chime from somewhere upstairs.

"If you are going to luxuriate in a bath," he said, out of sight, "you may as well use the time wisely. There are gaps in your knowledge, Watson!"

Watson felt her shoulders slump. What was he talking about now?

"I've just sent my monograph on the soils and clays of northern South America to your tablet."

Oy.

"Well," she said, "I hope that's as good as it sounds."

"There will be a pop quiz later."

Watson sighed, rolled her eyes, and headed upstairs.

ACKNOWLEDGEMENTS

Let's get one thing out of the way: I love *Elementary*. *Love* it. I'm a fan, and a devoted one at that, and I have to extend my grateful and sincere thanks to series creator Rob Doherty and his team for letting me play in their sandbox. That also goes out to the stars, Jonny Lee Miller and Lucy Liu, and Aidan Quinn and Jon Michael Hill for creating a cast of memorable characters that were a real joy to work with. I hope I've done everyone the justice they deserve!

My thanks to my editor, Miranda Jewess, and the whole team at Titan who made this happen, and to my agent, Stacia J. N. Decker of the Donald Maass Literary Agency, who helped a dream come true.

Special thanks to Vivi Trujillo and Hernán Ortiz for their expert assistance with cursing in Colombian Spanish, and to Daryl Gregory for bringing us all together. I also have to thank Greg Young and Tom Meyers of the Bowery Boys New York City History podcast, who over the last few years have helped feed my obsession with that great city. If you want to check out their work—and I recommend you do—you can find them at *boweryboyspodcast.com*. Thanks as well to

Paul Cornell, Kim Curran, Lee Harris, Emma Newman and Victoria Schwab for their unfailing support.

Finally, to my wife Sandra, who puts up with… well, quite a bit really. She's as much of an *Elementary* fan as I am, so I hope this new adventure brings you as much enjoyment in the reading as it did for me in the writing.

ABOUT THE AUTHOR

Adam Christopher is a novelist, comic writer, and award-winning editor. Adam is the author of *The Burning Dark* and the forthcoming *LA Trilogy*, as well as co-writer of *The Shield* for Dark Circle Comics. His debut novel, *Empire State*, was *SciFiNow*'s Book of the Year and a *Financial Times* Book of the Year for 2012. Born in New Zealand, he has lived in Great Britain since 2006.

For news and information about books and events, sign up to his author newsletter at www. adamchristopher.ac and follow him on Twitter @ghostfinder.

For more fantastic fiction, author events, exclusive excerpts, competitions, limited editions and more

VISIT OUR WEBSITE
titanbooks.com

LIKE US ON FACEBOOK
facebook.com/titanbooks

FOLLOW US ON TWITTER
@TitanBooks

EMAIL US
readerfeedback@titanemail.com